The Prey

by Tim Heath

Book 1 in *The Hunt* series

Copyright © 2017 Tim Heath
All rights reserved.
ISBN-13: 978-1545200162
ISBN-10: 1545200165

*****

Also by Tim Heath
Cherry Picking
The Last Prophet
The Tablet
The Shadow Man

Short Story Collection
Those Geese, They Lied; He's Dead

Dedication:

For my wife, Rachel—standing with you always as you battle on.

1

January 1ˢᵗ

A car screeched to a halt, horn blaring at the man just standing on the crossing. The driver of the car shouted words that the man at the crossing could not register, nor would he have understood. He spoke no Russian.

Five minutes earlier he'd left his hotel, which rose five storeys high and a whole block back from St Petersburg's main thoroughfare, Nevski Prospekt. The street was named after someone he knew very little about and was always busy, though its three lanes meant rarely did it get as blocked as some of the roads it intersected. Light snow was falling as Richard had exited his five star dwelling, the standard of hotel in keeping with its location, and his usual choice of resting place.

Richard was thirty-six, single and travelled extensively, for work mostly. He was financially stable without being rich. Enough to do most of what he pleased, but still having to work all hours to keep up his lifestyle. The pavements around him were full of people. It was nearly Orthodox Christmas, and the tourist season for that limited time of year was very much in motion. However, he wasn't there to shop. As he walked, before he was even one hundred metres from his hotel, two men were following his every step. They'd been watching him for a long time. Not only as he left the airport two days before, nor even just as he boarded the plane in London. They'd been outside his house as he left for the airport, they'd dropped in on his office a week before that too, though not to see him. They were just observing, seeing if the Spotters had done their job. The next two minutes were about to answer that very question.

Richard noticed the white piece of paper straight away. He'd been looking for it, anyway. When a note had been passed under his door half an hour before, he'd assumed it was a joke, some hoax. No one had been in the corridor as he'd opened the door to check. He'd read the words carefully. Something had caught his attention about it all, the photo attached helping him to summon up the courage to finally grab his coat and wrap his scarf around his head.

He'd been expecting something to happen since landing in Russia's second city. Now it appeared to have taken place.

The white piece of paper was stuck to one of the many drain pipes that ran down the front of the elegant buildings he'd been passing, pouring streams of water across the pavements when it rained. They were frozen solid right now, huge chunks of ice sticking out of them like cotton wool from a bloody nose. Adverts of all sorts were plastered to the metal pipes, but he wasn't interested in what they had to say. Grabbing the piece of paper, he found exactly what he'd been told he'd find attached to the back with a staple. A lottery ticket.

His heart raced, every fibre of his being awakened as if by some new reality. Suddenly feeling conspicuous, he started walking again, stuffing the ticket into the pocket of his jeans, continuing to walk down Nevski as if just another tourist who'd taken an advert off the pipe, heading for some strip club, restaurant or any number of places the illegally placed flyers were trying to get him to visit.

Ahead of him was an underpass that helped pedestrians traverse the road that crossed Nevski at that point. He entered into it. Richard paused underneath, a number of market style stalls occupying the walls of the pavements beside him, sellers and pedestrians mingling as people do in large, crowded cities. The two men following him paused, too, before one man continued on ahead, the other hanging around at the entrance the Englishman had just used.

Richard pulled out his phone, needing to check for sure that what he was holding was really worth what the note had told him. It was the first day of January, most people outside having been up all night celebrating the New Year, fireworks rocketing through the night as only a major city could do. The ticket he held between his gloved fingers had the date showing as Wednesday 8th July from the previous summer. His mobile shook in his hands as he held it, before he took a breath, knowing he had to steady himself. There was no signal standing where he was anyway, so he started to walk again, climbing the other sloping pavement, which took him back up to Nevski, now across the junction. His phone indicated it had a signal, and opening up a new browser window, he searched for the lottery results from that day in July. Moments later, on the third result listed, he had them confirmed. The six numbers that had been drawn were the same six he held in front of him at that moment. He read the text on his screen; *Wednesday's triple rollover jackpot for £10,550,987 was won by one lucky ticket. The claimant has until January 2nd 2016 to claim their winnings.*

It was exactly what the note under his door had said. He looked up, swore under his breath, and stepped into the road, a car braking sharply, window open and the driver shouting something at him.

The two men watching him had seen what they needed to see. Speaking into their bluetooth headsets, which never left their ears, the first of the men simply said; "Game on."

∞∞∞∞

Racing back to his hotel room, he didn't wait for the lift, striding the stairs two at a time, his long legs racing the three flights to his front facing suite. He'd slept well the second night, despite the fireworks that only really slowed around three in the morning. His first night, he'd hardly slept at all, the noise of the city, the life so busy around him, just too much to give rest to his eyes.

He called his travel agent but their offices were closed with it being a bank holiday in the UK. He swore again. Grabbing his bag, he threw whatever he had into the case and dropped in his limited toiletries, which he needn't have bothered to bring due to the hotel's vast offerings, and zipped it shut. His return ticket was valid for Monday's flight. Today was Friday. He left his room.

In the hotel's foyer, he handed his key in, the room already paid for in advance for the rest of the weekend.

"You are leaving already, sir?" said the lady behind the desk, her English accented but very good.

"Yes, something has come up. I need to fly back to London immediately. Could you please order me a taxi straight away?"

"Of course, sir," she said, phone already in hand, putting into action his request.

Just five minutes later a taxi pulled up outside, the driver coming to take his case as Richard got into the back seat.

"Polkovo airport please, the international terminal," he said to the driver, not knowing if he spoke English, but the car pulled away suggesting that he'd at least understood, if the lady at the hotel had not already made mention of the destination.

Behind the taxi, three vehicles were now trailing the Contestant. Cameras watched from every main junction, drones flying the skies constantly mapping Richard's position.

It was vital they had him tracked the whole time. If they lost sight of him, they might lose the money, and a whole lot more besides. That wouldn't be allowed to happen on this Games day, the shame of defeat far costlier than the measly millions that was a drop in the ocean to those pulling the strings.

Traffic was slow, even on a day that most people had off. As Russia's biggest holiday, there were plenty of people travelling between family engagements, not to mention those starting their own winter sunshine holidays now that the ten day break was upon them. That meant there were queues at the airport before Richard even got in, having paid the driver with a bundle of rubles, more than he needed to, but it had still cost less than when he'd first arrived and taken a taxi in the opposite direction.

There was no one at the British Airways desk, nor was there a flight again that day, anyway. Richard cursed himself, not for the first time that day. He scanned the boards high above him, the destinations in English, a small mercy he was at least grateful for. Nothing suggested a flight to England was happening anytime soon. He looked at his watch. Panic was starting to set in.

∞∞∞∞

Elsewhere, the image of Richard glancing at his watch for what must have been the sixth time in the last half hour was greeted with ironic laughter. They were going to win again with this one. The odds on the screen in front of them all were lengthening considerably. The man with most of the money riding on this one—for it was his Hunt this turn—busy on multiple telephones, constantly in contact with his Trackers, speaking with immigration personnel at the airports, lining up his people to make it as impossible as he could for this latest Contestant to ever leave Russian soil, let alone land in England with enough time to be able to claim his prize.

∞∞∞

Richard could see international flights were a dead end. He had a little over twenty-four hours, in his reckoning, to get back to London and make the claim, and there were no flights going to London, or anywhere of interest, for at least the next six hours. Flights for later that night were not yet showing, but when he'd made the call to organise flights originally, there had never been any nighttime options listed, he was certain of that. He'd have to find another option, but with the potential of over ten million pounds now so close and within his reach, he'd be as resourceful as he could to get that money. He already felt it was his—to allow something to take that from him now was madness.

Next to the main terminal was a small private terminal where, it was assumed, the rich and famous would fly in and out from. Banging loudly on the door, it took two minutes before the security guard was annoyed enough to open it, staring at the tall but not very threatening man in front of him.

"I need to hire a jet," Richard said, fast and loud. He repeated himself, this time slower.

"No English," was all the guard replied, before pointing to a lady walking towards them. She was dressed in Russian border control uniform, and carried a pleasant but obviously suspicious smile on her attractive face.

"Please, can you help me?"

"And what is it you need, sir?" she said, Richard pleased she at least spoke his language.

"I need to hire a jet. I have to get back to London urgently and there are no flights leaving that are any use to me from the main terminal."

"You have money?" she said, her fingers rubbing across her thumb as if to emphasise the point.

"I have a credit card."

"Has to be cash, I'm afraid sir, and besides…" she said, glancing across at the two men watching her, fully aware of who they were and why they were there, "all the pilots are off today. It's New Year. They finished yesterday."

Richard put a hand to his forehead, trying to smooth away the tension, suppressing a scream that he wanted to let out at that moment. With nothing more to say, he left. He was fast running out of options and the panic that this brought on was bordering on being crippling, hopeless, pitiful even. He wasn't yet going to give up. He jumped into another waiting taxi.

"Where to, sir?" the driver said, turning to him as Richard got into the front passenger seat, clutching his bag on his lap.

"The main railway station, please, and as quickly as you can. I'm in a hurry."

"I'll do my best for you, sir. So, what brings you to my great country?"

"Business really, but please, just drive. I have a hurting head and just need to get onto a train to Moscow."

"Very well sir, you just sit back and enjoy the journey. I'll get you to the station before you know it."

It took them an hour, in fact, sixty agonising minutes mainly sitting in lanes of traffic, people crossing the roads between the sitting cars like ants on a forest floor. Richard paid the driver, pulling his bag behind him and walked towards the main entrance.

Inside the Moskovski railway station, there were banks of window booths, only about a third of them staffed, each of these with long lines of people in front of them. Richard went over and stood in what he deemed the shortest, though there was little in it. They were all much longer than he needed right now. Scanning the boards, he tried to make out what he could, the lettering and titles all in Russian Cyrillic, but at least *Moscow* was still basically recognisable. There were several trains listed, the fastest of which was due to leave in thirty minutes.

Fifteen minutes further on, the queue had reduced by about a third, but was clearly not going to be quick enough. Frustratingly, he'd seen people jumping between queues, sometimes whole families coming to join a single person in front of him, adding size and therefore time to each booking. Then there were the people who were obviously just pushing in. Queuing, especially for an Englishman in a hurry, clearly was not working.

Walking forward, Richard too jumped straight to the front of the next window, a couple just leaving, an older lady who was next in line not seeing him as she was picking her bags up slowly. There were a few shouts of obvious complaint from behind, but no one there to cause any trouble.

"I need a ticket to Moscow on the express leaving in just over ten minutes, please."

"Passport," the lady said, sounding more like a robot than an actual person, and showing as much charisma too. He handed her his documents, the migration card falling out from the passport as she flipped through it, taking note of his visa too that was attached to one of the pages of his passport. She tapped away, deliberately slowly it seemed to Richard, before tapping into a calculator an amount that Richard understood to be the price of the ticket. He opened his wallet and dropped three one thousand ruble notes through the hole at the bottom of the window, the lady checking the notes against an infra red device, before returning to him his change and then after another minute his tickets. She pointed in the general direction of the platforms, but Richard was already moving, having noted the platform number and its location as he'd been queueing.

The train must have been at least twenty carriages long, though he opted to board on about the sixth one and work his way through to his compartment. It was another five minutes before the train started rolling away, Richard comfortably in his seat by that point.

Around him, the Trackers were keeping him in their sights. The train option had done nothing to his odds. The longer it all took, the less chance there was of actual victory. The odds would continue to lengthen that night.

∞∞∞

In the secure location, the ten oligarchs stood around the screens, the Hunt's Host in deep conversation with someone on his mobile, concern showing on the edges of his forehead.

"Twelve, you worried?" a man in an expensive tailored suit smirked at him. The man known only as Twelve, in this setting, ignored the comment, instead turning so that the others couldn't see his conversation.

"So between the train arriving and the flight from Moscow to London you confirm there is a three hour gap?" he said, anger coursing through him though he did his best to keep his composure. He wasn't going to give the others the pleasure of thinking he was afraid he might lose this one.

"Yes, that's confirmed," came the reply on the phone, one of Twelve's many people working behind the scenes. They all used such people when it was their turn to Host.

"That's too much time. We need to arrange a welcome party for him in Moscow."

"Is that in the rules?" the voice said.

"I don't care. It's my Hunt, my rules. Not a word to anyone. Now get on with it," and the call ended.

2

The train rolled into its destination in central Moscow at the precise time it was meant to arrive, the platform first appearing a full five minutes before the train eventually came to rest. Richard was the first one off the train, and was already pushing his way along the platform as people passed uniformed officers who were standing at the front of the platform, a human presence between the train and the station itself. They spotted Richard and a group of border police walked quickly and blocked his exit.

"You must come with us, Mr Taylor," is all they said, the use of his surname, and therefore sudden realisation that they knew who he was, only just sinking in.

"What is this about?" Richard said as soon as he was seated in a room they'd led him to on the side of the station.

A man was looking through his passport that had been demanded from him as they entered the room. After a few moments, the Russian officer replied.

"You arrived in St Petersburg two days ago, and your migration card and flight tickets confirm that you are expecting to leave on Monday, 4th and yet here you are, in Moscow, heading to the airport." He hadn't mentioned anything about the airport, the thought taking root as the Russian continued. "You were at Pulkovo 2 earlier today, trying to charter a flight from there, also." The Russian information net was clearly working overtime. They were good.

"Tell me, sir. Why are you suddenly leaving? Your actions have made you stand out. We don't like guests in our country suddenly changing their plans, as you have today. It makes us nervous."

"Look, something has come up and I needed to leave early, that was all. I tried to contact my airline but they are closed because of the holiday. I've come to Moscow because there are some more flights from here."

"What has come up that you would leave so suddenly?"

Richard knew it was not their place to ask such a question, his suspicion raised. He couldn't tell them about the ticket, they'd most certainly take it from him and maybe claim the money themselves. He didn't trust any one of them, and that mistrust was growing the longer the day was passing.

"That's none of your business!"

"It is if I choose to make it my business. You need to tell me what you are thinking of doing otherwise I will be forced to arrest you."

"Arrest me? For what? I'm just trying to get an earlier flight home than I have booked. Is that a crime in this bloody dictatorship?"

"There is no need to be so rude, Mr Taylor. We are only doing our job."

"And what job would that be? Detaining innocent foreigners?"

"If you tell us what you are doing, we can determine if you are in fact an innocent foreigner, can't we?"

"Look, my father has been taken ill suddenly, I've only just been told. I must get back to him immediately or it might be too late."

"You are lying, Mr Taylor. Now that does make me suspicious. They were right to flag you up for our attention."

"Who was right? Who has made up these lies about me?" Richard was glancing around the room, increasingly more afraid. He glanced at his watch once more.

"Need to be somewhere, sir?"

"Like I've told you, time is running out and I need to be on that flight to London. It's vital that I am."

"But you are still not telling the truth. Maybe you did something in St Petersburg? Maybe you hurt someone there? Is that it? Shall I check with the authorities up there and see what they say?"

"What? I've done nothing wrong, you stupid people! I'm just a man who needs to change his flight to an earlier one. This is ridiculous! I demand to speak to the Embassy!"

"They'll be on holiday too, Mr Taylor."

"It doesn't matter. Someone will be around. I'm a British citizen and I demand that you let me speak with the British embassy here in Moscow."

"Very well," the man said, knowing the law governing that right.

Ten minutes later, the conversation was over. Richard had been told what they could and couldn't do, and there had been a brief conversation between the embassy representative and those holding him before the call was ended. The Russians opted to take the most frustrating option open to them regarding Richard.

"Very well," they said to him, handing his passport back to him and slowly moving towards the door. "You are free to go. But under the terms of your visa that you applied for to enter our country, we will return you to the only city you have permission to visit and allow you to take your prearranged flight home from there. Your train leaves in five minutes and we can't have you miss this one."

The door was opened, Richard led by the arm to another train, shorter than the one he'd come down on, and was ushered into a carriage that was mainly empty. The uniformed officers remained on the platform until minutes later when the train started to pull away from the station.

He was heading back to St Petersburg. There was now no option, no time to make it to England. He sank deep into his seat, and knew enough was enough. It had been all too good to be true, after all.

Three days later he boarded his return flight to London. The weekend had been a write-off, the thought of losing so much money eating at every fibre within him. Sleep was impossible. He'd ventured mainly to strip clubs since getting back, drinking for thirty hours solid.

∞∞∞

In the secure location, the Games day had finished with another success. The winning lottery ticket had been claimed in the end, by another anonymous person, just in time. More importantly, Twelve had come out of the day with his honour intact. The oligarchs would go their separate ways, continuing their lives of wealth and influence, never making reference to the things they were a part of, until once more they'd come back together, the odds would be set, and another Contestant selected for their entertainment.

∞∞∞

Alex Tolbert had been told about the report by a technician working with him at MI6. Both could have lost their job instantly if it was known what they'd shared. It made the seriousness of what they had learned all the more real.

Alex had been part of the British secret service for nine years and had built up a reputation of being one of the best.

The report that he'd been passed was confirmation from Russia from an undercover source named Andre Philip. He'd been giving MI6 specific information on a new situation for the past year and had got himself deeply involved within the Russian political and business elite, where the real money and power was. Andre was not part of MI6 himself, and being Russian, neither really could be, but his skills and natural ability helped him to just blend into the scene, and made him a reliable connection over the years. With a good track record, it made what he had been sharing with them for the previous twelve months all the more intriguing.

"Anissa," Alex called to his colleague of six years once he found her, she having not been in her office when he'd last checked. Anissa Edison was thirty-nine, though she didn't look a day over twenty-five. She'd taken up a position in Military Intelligence after serving for over a decade in the army, involved in combat situations in a number of places around the world. She'd been wounded twice, the last time enough to cut short her army days and the offices of Vauxhall House came calling soon after. She'd connected well with Alex almost immediately, on a purely professional level. Married with two children herself, she was a fine example of someone mixing a busy career with a growing family.

"I've just heard something you need to know about," is all he said, taking her by the arm. They went outside the building for a walk, a common practice when their conversation was of a delicate nature, not sure who might otherwise be listening in, in a building full of spies.

"It's real. Everything we've heard about, we've had a report back from Andre."

Anissa was processing everything she was hearing as they walked in the relative quiet of the park not far from their offices. She was usually a frantic note taker—a pen was never far from her hand—though being outside, didn't have the opportunity at present.

She'd known about the workings of Andre Philip, his mission to dig deep into the Russian oligarchs, the billionaires who held so much wealth and power in modern day Russia. She'd heard the whispers, as had Alex, about an organisation of these very men, who would gather together to trade power, connections and political muscle. Men who'd take part in the *Igrii* which means *games* in English. All very secretive, all very hidden. Men of wealth who wanted nothing more than privacy most of the time, besides their obvious displays of what money could buy.

"What did it say, again?" Anissa asked, wanting to store every detail in her mind at the outset.

"The report was logged three days ago, from Andre himself. He simply said that it was real, he had proof, the

Games existed. He listed some names, clearly non Russians, and there were some dates. The only other name mentioned was Dmitry, no surname."

"It's not like there aren't a million Dmitry's in the world."

"True," Alex said, "but maybe not so many that happen to be multi-billionaires with political influence in Russia."

"You said this was received three days ago. Why the delay?"

"That's just the point. I haven't been told this officially, despite it being our operation. Someone who owed me a favour, the person who'd received the message and passed it on, was alarmed when nothing was done about it. He let me know today, checking I hadn't been told."

"So why are MI6 holding this from us?"

"I've no idea. What's more, since he left this message, Andre has apparently vanished. He's not reported in at any of his arranged times."

"Do they have him?"

"It's hard to tell, but I'd doubt that. Best bet is that he's gone to ground, maybe wary of his position in light of them finding out what he has done. Remember, this was all just a rumour until we could confirm otherwise. These men have extreme power in Russia, and they'll use it to shut out any knowledge of what is happening. If word got out, their Games would be over."

"So it's really taking place? I mean, there are really people who find these tickets in Russia and all that?"

"That's what I want to find out. Right now, I don't know what to believe. We have to tread carefully. The fact that our own bosses haven't thought to let us know tells me something stinks about it all and that it might even have connections here in London."

"What, in MI6?"

"I don't know, right now, but think about it. We went out on a limb, were granted some funding, found a mole that we insisted on keeping between the two of us. They were never happy about that set up from the beginning. Now that mole reports that he's been successful, that he's proved the existence of this ring and yet three days later we have not been told about it."

"Who's seen the report?"

"I don't know, but it certainly went to those higher up than us. It was read the day it got reported, but we couldn't tell by whom."

"So what are we going to do about it?"

"Right now, we need to tread a little more carefully, but carry on as if we know nothing. We can ask questions about Andre; as far as they know we are still awaiting confirmation from him. Let's see if we can track down where he is. Under no circumstance must we give up his real identity." All transmissions up to that point with MI6 had been carried out via a codename Alex had given to Andre. "That would now appear to be fatal."

"I don't like it. If someone within MI6 is covering for them, it means we're rotten to the very highest level. It's not what I joined up to be a part of."

"Me neither, Anissa, but we can't just leave Andre to his fate. He's risked everything to get this information out to us, and whilst someone doesn't want us to know about it, we do. So we have something to go on. We have these names and some dates. I'm assuming they are dates of previous events. So we'll start with these. We'll work out who these people are that he's listed the names for, and what these dates have to do with any of them. We also have the name Dmitry. Let's cross check that with the richest men in Russia and see how many options that leaves us with. And be careful. Until we know exactly what we are up against, I think we have to keep this between us. We don't know where exactly the Service is compromised."

"Okay, let's get to work. I'll take the names, you look at the dates and the Russian connections. We'll chat here tomorrow, same time. I'll work from home."

They each parted company, Alex heading back to the office, though he'd spend most of the afternoon in a nearby café searching information on Google, and Anissa went straight to her car which was parked underground beneath Vauxhall House, home of MI6.

3

Two months later

Annabel Herbertson wasn't to know anything was amiss as she handed her passport to border control at London's Heathrow airport. Ever since they'd been given her name by Andre Philip two months before, Anissa had been tracking her, and a number of others.

Eight weeks later Anissa still had little understanding of why these names meant anything. None of them had any connections to Russia, only one of the four names given had ever even been there. Annabel was a single mum who was holding down two part time jobs, managed mainly when her son was at school, though she had help on two evenings as well. Living in a small flat in Hackney, London, there was little about her that suggested anything more than your average working class family. Forty years old, born and still living in London, Annabel had no criminal record and didn't even have a driving licence. She rented the flat she lived in, as did most of the high rise block's many residents, the building an eyesore thrown up in the late 70s to ease London's growing housing issues. It made no sense to Anissa to even be watching

Annabel, until today, when she boarded a plane to St Petersburg.

"Alex, we have movement," she said, catching her colleague as he was driving on what was meant to be the start of a one week holiday.

"Go on."

"Annabel Herbertson, forty years old from Hackney. She was one of the four names Andre mentioned. She's just cleared her passport through security at Heathrow, due to board a flight to St Petersburg in one hour."

"Christ! It's happening—I'll be right with you."

∞∞∞

At that same moment, in the small seaside city of Tarragona, on the west coast of Spain, Teo Vela was holding his bag as he waited for a taxi to arrive. When it did he made the short journey to the city's airport, and once there, checked in through security before waiting at his gate. With one stop in Madrid, he was then due to board an evening flight to St Petersburg. A Spanish national, his had been the one name that made little sense once it had been handed to Alex. When he had Googled the name there had been no real leads in the UK, the few results coming up either too young, or too old to have any relevance.

∞∞∞∞

One time zone east of Spain, in Dublin, Ireland, Dubhán Maguire was boarding a flight from the airport of the city where he had been born, though he now lived a sixty minute drive south. A builder by trade, he'd developed a local reputation and had a steady flow of regular work to tide him over, but not enough to keep up with rental costs in the capital. He'd downsized, twice, before setting up a permanent workshop in his new adopted village, his skills going down well with the locals, and he did as much free work as he did paid, though he didn't mind too much.

His name had also been on the list, and though he was Irish, Anissa had been able to track him and keep somewhat of a close eye on him, though she had no access to the Irish border police and therefore was unaware that he was also about to board a plane that would eventually drop him in St Petersburg, via a short stopover in Amsterdam. At thirty-five, he was the youngest of the four. Divorced twice, despite his age, he lived alone, though because of his work he was always around people, especially the other tradesmen he had set up a small business with. He sat looking out of the plane's window, wondering why he was actually doing this. Maybe it was all true, maybe this would be his big break, he kept reminding himself.

∞∞∞∞

The last of the four was a second generation British lady of Jamaican origin named Twila Dalton, who lived in the city of Leeds in the north of England. She was forty-seven and worked as a fitness instructor in one of the city's many sports centres. She was getting to the point where she knew she couldn't keep up with the demands of training, her body showing the signs of the harsh punishment she'd often put it through over the years, not to mention at times the drugs she'd pumped into her veins to help build muscle. She was a fading beauty, desperate to put the clock back but unable to do anything to stop it. This trip offered her a new start, as she set out in her car, driving the hour or so it would take to get to Manchester airport, and a flight to Russia that offered her everything she needed to start over again. Her passport also flashed up on Anissa's screen as Alex joined her later that morning, the second confirmation that same day that anything on these four people was worth the time they had spent investigating them.

It had been a frustrating two months. Nothing more had yet been heard from Andre Philips, this informant's silence having been reported to their bosses at MI6, whilst enquiring at the same time if anything had been heard from him. The answer that followed, which was that they'd not heard anything from Alex's mysterious informant, had made it clear it was a cover-up. Anissa had found little on the names listed, all seemed to be normal people doing very normal jobs. None of them travelled very far, there was nothing to stand out at all that would make anyone take a second look, besides the fact that in his seemingly last message to his MI6 handlers, Andre had taken the time to list them in his report.

Alex had looked at dates too, but with so much potential conflict, it was hard to really track what exactly they meant. They were all dates in the past. There seemed no pattern as to when they took place—two were on a weekend, the other four on each weekday except Friday. They were in different months, on different days of the month. It made little sense. There was no pattern.

In relation to Dmitry, he'd had a little more success, though still nothing concrete. A common Russian first name, there were at least half a dozen men sharing that name that might be counted as a Russian oligarch. He'd written down the six names on a clean piece of paper, certain that one of those men was part of these secret Games. It was a start at least. He spent many hours reading up on these men, writing down what he thought was important, mapping out as much as he could the connections and influence each man had, not knowing who or what he and Anissa were up against, and therefore recording as much as possible so as to be useful later, if and when they were ever to place a surname to his first name.

Now, though, they suddenly had movement. Without any obvious warning, and almost beyond their expectations that anything would happen, two of these people, the two based in England that they knew of, suddenly decided to leave the country, on journeys that would take them to Russia's second city.

"What do you think?"

"Right now, Anissa, I'm not sure. But it's my hunch that Andre knew these folks were being watched right back when he made that report. We have to assume the other two are on the move as well, though we probably won't hear from the Irish and you could never trace that fourth name, anyway."

"It makes no sense. These names, these people, we've both looked at them closely. They aren't anyone."

"I know, but maybe that's the point. Let's start by how they obtained a Russian visa in the first place. These things take time and therefore need planning. You can't just wake up and decide to fly to Russia. They each had to have known when to fly and must therefore had made plans of some sort. Annabel is a single mum with a son who's only just a teenager. I doubt she'll have just left him on his own. We need to find out what they each knew about today."

"Can we track flights to Russia? Maybe we'll pick up these other two people as well, assuming they are also involved in all this today."

"It'll be hard. We can say there is a security risk, but even then we might not get access to what we are looking for. The Russians aren't going to give us open access to passenger manifests, either."

"There must be something we can do?"

"We could just board a flight and see for ourselves what is happening."

"Fly to Russia, Alex? Are you mad?"

"I am meant to be on holiday, after all. You can make some excuse about something, I'm sure. We can use diplomatic channels to clear our need for a visa. It would enable us to have a look around."

"The FSB would be watching us closely. Ever since what happened with Charlie Boon they've been very cool towards us."

"I know, but I have a contact I think will be willing to help within the FSB." He was talking about an agent named Sasha, an agent who'd made himself known to MI6 the previous year after one of his colleagues had been killed in a bomb attack in Zurich which had been aimed at another MI6 agent. "He's probably our best bet."

"Okay, Alex, let's do this. I'll clear it with home and meet you at the airport."

"Don't say where you are going, Anissa."

"Alex, he's my husband. I've already told him everything we've been up to these last two months. He thinks we're crazy, but he won't say a word."

"He'd better not!" but there was a smile as Alex said that, though Anissa still gave him a look that told him not to even go there.

"Russia it is then," she said, grabbing her bag and leaving the office.

4

In a busy part of the heart of the city, the oligarchs started to arrive. Although they had begun in Moscow, the capital and power base of the nation, they'd made the shift to host their Hunts in St Petersburg five years previously. Most of those who were based in Russia lived near their capital, where their business and political connections were mostly located. St Petersburg, once the capital itself and still very much the cultural centre of their nation, offered them something different. A break from their day to day life, a place of indulgence. And as the first of the men pulled up to the five storey residence not five minutes' walk from the Hermitage, Peter the Great's stunning Winter Palace, few could guess at what was about to take place.

The car pulled away, though three security men joined him, security personnel that all of Russia's richest men now had around them in constant supply. The door was opened automatically for them, an electronic lock released as the tall Russian had approached it, his eyes, posture, and movement scanned and recognised. The building was otherwise off limits and totally impenetrable for the average citizen.

Outside the building, at the expense of the property's owner, sat three teams of four, each aware of the others but operating independently, all highly paid to keep the building's integrity, and the lives of those fortunate enough to be admitted, secure.

As the tall man entered the building, he was greeted warmly, "It's wonderful to see you again, Fifteen." First names were strictly off limits, even in a building thought to be so safe. Instead, within this group of ten men that were soon to be gathered together once more, they were simply referred to by their number, which corresponded to their position within the league, based on their wealth.

"As always a pleasure," he replied, taking the grand staircase which would lead him up to the second floor, the heart of the whole operation. Banks of monitors covered one wall, with a team of dedicated people keeping the technology side of things running in real time and keeping the network as extensive as they could make it. Very few sporting events had as much coverage as they used to keep track of every Contestant. And the next Games day, which was due to start the following morning, had four Contestants.

Drinks were readily available, people helping themselves as they pleased. Besides each man's own security personnel, who mostly remained on the first floor anyway, there were very few people around, which was part of the plan. The Chair person who put on the event was there for sure and sat independently of the other oligarchs, an impartial viewpoint, if that were possible in such circles. Rich as well, so as to hold a similar position with the other oligarchs, the *Chair* which was the usual term in Russian, ran the show. You didn't cross the Chair and remain in the Games. It was a select group of people that played. The only other person in the room, besides the ten oligarchs, the Chair and the technicians who were needed to operate all the graphics, was the *Odds Maker* who set the odds as well as controlled the bets. Rarely was money actually traded. With men of such wealth, it mattered little, though when it was traded, it became extreme. Lives had been shattered when things had turned into personal conflict in the past. Rules now forbade any one oligarch directly interfering with another oligarch's Contestant. That didn't stop it happening, of course. Mostly, however, it was power, or connections, that were traded. Sometimes promises were used too, like withdrawing from a certain region if the bet was lost. This was especially common when business interests overlapped with another oligarch you were coming up against.

As with all in Russia, though, honour and shame became the biggest factors for most men. To lose a Hunt in front of their peers brought shame upon that person. The money they might have lost meant nothing, a loss of face before the others meant everything. Honour would be restored only by getting back everything they had lost, and there were strict rules around this too, but few oligarchs adhered to them. Honour was honour. If someone happened to take their money, they'd break them until they had bled them dry of every last cent, penny or kopeck. They took no prisoners. Bets were not set on simply who would win or lose—Contestants had very little chance of winning, anyway. Instead, being a real time event, it was often based on what ways they might try, or how quickly they'd fail. Any number of things would be used to make a bet between other oligarchs, besides the simple joy of watching poor and helpless folks scrambling for something they had no right to have.

Still, oligarchs were encouraged to make bets along the way—it wasn't to be a spectator sport, nor did the men let it become one, as entertaining as it all might have been for them. Each oligarch took turns to Host a Hunt. A Hunt consisted of a Contestant—their Contestant—being handed a ticket which the oligarch had sourced. They were effectively daring this unwitting Contestant to now try and take the money from them, even if the innocent foreigner had no idea they were being involved in some big game.

That meant each oligarch also had their own teams of people constantly moving around Europe. Some were there to source lottery tickets. If an oligarch knew it was their turn to Host a Hunt in six months' time, his *Buyers* would monitor the appropriate country for options. Starting with countries like the UK and Switzerland, where claimants had one-hundred and eighty days to collect the money, they'd move onto Belgium, one-hundred and forty, then Ireland, Portugal and Spain, ninety days before trying France or Luxembourg which only allowed sixty days—though that just added something to the mix. They looked at both the national lottery systems, as well as the Euro Loto, which was sold across many countries—claimant time for both depending solely on where the winning ticket was purchased. These teams had often suddenly had to travel to another country the day after a successful ticket was discovered, in the hope of being able to get to the claimant before they contacted the lottery or, often just as vital, before another team of Buyers got to them.

Especially with large wins, the mainly less well off people that played the lottery were often concerned about the publicity that came with such a large pay out. People they only knew a little suddenly made out they were life long friends, always slipping in the need for some extra cash for this or that. By offering to give the winners an instant cash equivalent, a surprisingly large amount of people took them up on the offer, too blown away with the sight of so much cash to think anything further about it. Usually the Buyers pretended to be from the lottery itself, which made sense. How else would they know where the winning ticket was won, arriving on the doorstep with cash to the exact amount won, offering to make a switch there and then—the money for the ticket? Simple, anonymous and instant.

The bigger the winning ticket, the greater the interest in the Hunt. Billionaires liked nothing more than flashing their wealth before the other oligarchs. Whilst a million pound lottery ticket still made for a good prize for any Contestant, there was always something extra special when a Buyer got their hands on one of the really big wins—€30 million, €45 million and even right up to over €100 million at times. Those Games days certainly had an edge to them, when so much was on the table. The bets were always a little more juicy, too.

So teams of Buyers worked constantly throughout the various nations the most popular lotteries were run, always selecting Europe, for two reasons. Firstly, it had to be near enough to give the Contestant an idea that they might be able to make it, in such a short time. Usually they only gave the Contestant one day to make it back to claim. Secondly, other regions, especially North America where there were plenty of large lottery wins, demanded claimant's details be made known. Whilst there was still a legal case going through where someone was trying to challenge that, it was unlikely to change the rules too much. Most victorious oligarchs found a way of then claiming their ticket, usually through a number of other people, recouping the money they might have paid out months before. Pocket change to be used in future Games, no doubt. Occasionally the oligarch would leave the money unclaimed, framing the ticket in a show of obvious defiance, as if to say;

here's a winning lottery ticket for over £10 million that I can afford not to claim.

The other team of people that each billionaire employed, besides their Buyers, were their *Spotters*. Important as it was to have a high value lottery ticket to put into a Hunt, it was nothing without a worthy Contestant. The Spotters were the people that dug deep into people's lives, tracking them for months, looking for the right types of characteristics that were deemed necessary to make someone interested enough to become a viable Contestant. Each team of Spotters and their respective oligarch no doubt had separate requirements, but common across the group were things like greed, a person's willingness to take a short cut, a person's ability to think on their feet and determination not to give up. The better the Contestant, the greater the Hunt. The odds reflected these well, too. Whoever provided a really good Contestant for a Hunt they were responsible for, made the odds that bit more exciting. After all, if the person who found the ticket just did nothing with it, there was no Hunt, no chase, no fun. They'd perfected their processes over the years, realising that people who were already in St Petersburg for another purpose, were actually less likely to do much about it all. But people who they'd managed to get to the city for that very purpose, were more likely to make a decent go of it.

Of course, between the various Hosts, who varied from Hunt to Hunt depending on who was selected for any particular event, when you had influence over such things as the border guards and the transport networks, it made it much easier to frustrate the plans of the Contestants. Without knowing anyone was actively working against them being successful, nearly all would fail. Some got lucky, for a while, though that never lasted for long, the new found wealth vanishing as quickly as it arrived as the oligarch moved in, closing down their businesses, affecting their family members so much that in the end the winners had nothing left and no fight to offer.

This was why they kept it all so secret. They were having too much fun to allow anyone to expose what they were doing and risk making more people aware of their Games, or worse still, shut them down for good.

The final group of people involved, and these were provided by the organisation, and therefore run by the Chair, were the *Trackers*. These were the teams of people that followed each Contestant during Hunt time, relaying real time updates on progress and positioning, going places maybe the drones couldn't access or where there were no CCTV cameras. They were not allowed to interfere with the Contestant, just relay the information in real time to the Games Room. The Trackers, like the Buyers and the Spotters, had no access to the actual league of oligarchs, unaware of who they all were, sometimes even unaware of what was actually going on. Most of the people in these teams were now freelance, though some still held positions within Russia's security departments, which made getting access to certain information a little easier at times.

"Gentlemen," the Chair said, otherwise referred to by the nickname *the Wolf*. This was a person you didn't cross who held a lot of power within the room. "It's great to see you all again. Tomorrow we have a very exciting day ahead of us, with four Contestants primed to perform in front of our eyes. Eleven, Fourteen, Fifteen and Nineteen, we are at your bidding tomorrow as you announce your particular Contestant and the prize that might await them." There was a slight murmur around the room, but it soon settled back down. "Enjoy the drinks, everyone, and sleep well. I look forward to seeing you all tomorrow."

The Wolf left the staging area that sat near the centre of the room, the bank of screens directly behind, and exited the room. A few of the men stood around in groups, men sticking to their own circles and wealth even in a group of such financially fat men.

The building, all five floors making the same house, had enough rooms on the top three floors to house all of the guests, which had become the practice from day one, everyone contained within the same four walls.

At that moment, as evening fell, the last of the four unwitting Contestants had arrived in St Petersburg, travelling to their hotel to rest for the night. Little did each really know what tomorrow had in store for them.

5

Alex sat down in the business lounge at Heathrow airport later that day, Anissa parking her car, as per a conversation they'd just had moments before. The direct flight had already left for the day, but a flight connecting through Zurich then on to St Petersburg would still just about get them in before the day was out, though there wouldn't be much time to spare.

He sipped a can of Coke he'd grabbed from the bar, around half a dozen other people, mainly men, scattered around the well furnished lounge. From where he was sitting he could see the tarmac outside, planes of all sizes moving around or sitting at the various gates, presumably waiting for passengers to come, or go, before they would soon be flying out again, Heathrow being one of the busiest airports in the world. He could also see the entrance from where he was sitting and he put down his tablet which he had been scanning for news as Anissa walked in through the door and then over to his position. A few heads had turned in the lounge, some male subconscious instinct acknowledging the presence of a younger woman, but they soon lost interest as she walked over and joined her colleague, who rose to greet her.

"Have any problem clearing things with home?" Alex said as they sat down again, passing her a can of drink that he'd bought for her earlier.

"Thanks for this. No, you know how he is, always concerned for my safety, but he actually warmed to the idea that you were going with me, clearly feeling I was safer with you, so there you go."

"A good man, your husband, clearly," Alex said, not really knowing him at all. She understood the joke. Truth was, there had been a little friction at home in the early days, especially with how well they'd so obviously clicked, not helped by the fact Alex was a single guy. As the years had gone by, things had calmed down a lot on the home front, as her husband and children understood mum had a demanding job that required she travel a lot, though the last few years had been largely based in the UK, much to their delight. It made the need to travel at such short notice a little easier. Her mother was coming to stay that weekend, to help out with the children and allow her husband to play football on Sunday morning, though the kids would go and watch him do that, as they always did. Anissa was a little sad to miss it this week, unsure exactly how long they'd be away but making arrangements regardless should the inevitable happen and she not be around for the family's usual Sunday ritual. She opened her can of drink just as their flight was being called for the first time.

"Looks like I'd better down this one quickly," she said, taking a big gulp, which nearly made her choke, the fizz catching her nose, taking her a few seconds to regain her composure.

"Careful there," Alex said, pushing her on the shoulder.

"Get over yourself," she said as they stood up, collecting their bags together and heading for the door.

The flight was smooth the whole way, the transfer in Zurich just thirty-five minutes but easily enough time to make the connection, and they were touching down in St Petersburg just before eleven that evening, local time, having lost two hours with the journey east.

Whilst in Switzerland, Alex had received confirmation via a text message that Sasha would be meeting them when they landed, and sure enough, this dark-haired Russian man was the first to spot them as they exited the aircraft, his eyes able to pick out other security service personnel as only a fellow agent could. They'd never formally met one another, though over the previous twelve months the Brits, especially Alex, had been made more aware of him, some of his colleagues meeting with Sasha in Stockholm the previous year.

"Come this way," he said, having been introduced to Anissa and shaking their hands. He led them through a side door, away from the crowds who were working their way through the lines of immigration that, even given the late hour, were already starting to build up. They passed no other personnel as

Sasha opened and closed doors, taking them through a series of four inter-connected rooms before emerging, just three minutes later, out through a final door that lay between the arrivals and departure halls of the terminal's main buildings. His car, a black Mercedes with tinted windows, sat not more than twenty metres from the door. They were in the car in less than ten seconds, Sasha opening the rear door for Anissa, both British agents getting into the back seat before Sasha ran around to the driver's side and pulled away.

Given the hour, traffic was a lot lighter than it might have been. Sasha drove fast along mostly three lane roads until he reached the edges of the city, vast tower blocks appearing to crowd in from every side, as many still being built it seemed as were standing. Now the traffic slowed a little as the roads became two lane and then one in places. Anissa looked from the back seat, little being said as the car sped along the tarmac, an alien world to her English eyes racing past her. Neither agent had ever been to Russia before, and they didn't speak a word of Russian either.

"This must be quite urgent," Sasha said, his English good and clear, even if it had a distinctive accent to it, "if you've come at such short notice and need me to sneak you into the city. What's up?" he asked, eyes darting between the rear view mirror where he had been mainly addressing Alex, though he eyed them both, uncertain of who was leading the investigation, whilst also keeping an eye on the road in front of him.

"It's complicated," Alex started, giving him a run down over a few minutes on what the last three months had entailed, finishing with him saying that they would give him more details when they got settled in the hotel.

"Man, that's got to be the craziest thing I've heard all year. Mind you, what I've come to find in this line of work is that you never know what level of madness is around the next corner, so I'll hear you both out for sure. You must know, this is highly irregular, and I'd be finished if my bosses knew what I was doing. Even talking to you like this is dangerous."

"We know. We appreciate everything you've done for us so far, especially last year in Sweden." Sasha couldn't help get the feeling that the British felt like they owned him now, and it bothered him greatly. If they were to reveal to the FSB that he'd leaked them information as he had in the past, he'd be finished. Dead, most likely. So it worried him that once again MI6 had come calling, wanting another favour, expecting him to just drop everything. There had been no threat, and it had been his nature to go and help them, a very rare breed in his circles. But he couldn't escape the sense that the threat was there, bubbling under the surface, ready to pounce any moment he refused to do what they asked.

The fact he didn't know either of these two agents also concerned him a little, his interactions with Charlie Boon and his female colleague Zoe last year a frosty one to start but something that had served both their purposes well. Why he was now dealing with two new agents, he wasn't sure. A sense of wanting to do the right thing prevailed once again, given the little information he'd been told about their purpose for dropping into his city that night.

Just under forty-five minutes after leaving the airport, Sasha pulled up alongside an expensive looking hotel in the centre of the city, named after the October revolution. The main railway station, which connected the city with Moscow and then beyond, faced the south side of the hotel. Sasha helped them into the foyer of the hotel.

"You'll be okay from here. They speak your language and the last thing you need is me hanging around you, making you stand out more than you need to. I've booked you into a double room suite, in keeping with the cover story, but the beds come apart and there is plenty of space to have some privacy, so don't worry about it. Here's my card with my details on it," he said, handing them a small business card that he used for such times as this. He certainly didn't want calls coming for him at the office.

"Thanks," Anissa said, taking the card and shaking his hand, which he returned, a strong but gentle grip.

"I'll come for you tomorrow morning, out front at the same spot. Be ready for ten and I'll just pull over and you can jump in. I doubt there'll be the space to park as there is at the moment." Despite the time, there had been only two free spaces outside on the crowded street, and given the impression they had received of St Petersburg being a busy city, they understood tomorrow the roads would most likely be crawling with cars.

Sasha left them, returning to his car and driving the twenty minutes north of the river, that it took him to get home. Thankfully the bridges were not yet opening overnight, something reserved for the summer months which effectively cut the city in two, with no way across until the giant bridges closed again, allowing what waiting traffic there was to pass once more.

Alex grabbed the room key, returning with it as they both walked towards the one lift they spotted, which was fully glass, apart from the base. They went up to the fourth floor. Clean green carpets welcomed them as they found their suite, which once inside proved bigger than Anissa expected. It opened up on two sides, being a corner room with views across a nearby park from one of the windows.

"This is a nice room," Alex commented, already getting to work on moving the beds apart, having placed the one small travel bag he'd brought with him on a small sofa that sat against one wall. Each half of the bed had its own duvet and sheets, as was common practice in such hotels, and he dragged the bed with ease around the L-shaped corner into what was some sort of lounge area, though they could easily rearrange the sofas later.

Ten minutes later, the beds were at either end of the room, leaving each occupant out of sight of the other. A lavish bathroom led off from the main door, a free standing bath and stand alone shower just some of the features. It was already gone midnight as Anissa started to unpack the few items she had with her, which included enough changes of clothing for about four days, a little more underwear too, in case the stay got prolonged. They had the suite for three nights, including that night, and beyond that, she didn't know what was needed.

Alex turned the TV on as Anissa went to freshen up a little in the bathroom and prepare for some sleep. An ice hockey game was playing on the channel as the set came to life with the match deep into the third period already, though the score between the two teams, which he presumed were Russian, was showing as level. He sat down, only half interested in the match, but happy for the background noise, and connected his tablet to the hotel's Wifi network once he got it all working. Several emails downloaded and he took the next twenty minutes scanning through them, replying to a few. There were very few work emails—they thought he was on holiday, anyway, so that certainly helped. Anissa had emerged from the bathroom, and whilst saying she would read for a bit, had now switched off her lamp. Alex said good night and he too started to prepare for some sleep. It was just before one.

∞∞∞

Across the city, Annabel Herbertson and Twila Dalton were both already sound asleep. Annabel had landed in the afternoon, so had been able to explore a little, the tiredness and sheer differentness of the city and country she was suddenly in, catching up with her fast and she'd lain down just after eleven.

Teo Vela had only just landed, his flight a little delayed on the way in, and he went to his room as soon as he had the key, working his way through the mini bar whilst watching some Spanish football which he was happy to find on one of the many channels he seemed to have available. Sleep would come, as the alcohol overcame him, at around three in the morning.

Dubhán Maguire was sitting in an Irish bar as the clock struck two, a pint of what appeared to be genuine Guinness but at a highly inflated price in front of him. By the fifth pint, his maths never too good, he'd almost forgotten how much the rubles were worth against the Euro and therefore just how expensive each one actually was. He'd end up staying all night, a lad about town on his own time whilst being abroad, getting back around dawn to his hotel in which he had spent less than five minutes on arrival. As morning came round he was fast asleep, breakfast long past being served by the time he finally awoke from his slumber.

Regardless of what time they woke, each of them found a piece of paper under their door in the morning, each with a photo attached and some directions leading them to what the photo displayed—in each photo, there was simply the image of a lottery ticket.

6

Annabel was the first one up the following day. She'd come across the piece of paper under her door as she left for breakfast. Her hotel was in the east of the city, halfway between the metro station Narvskaya and the Baltic railway station, which linked that part of Russia with the three Baltic states. The photo that was attached to the note didn't show the actual numbers that were on the ticket, just the date. It was nearly six months ago, and as she sat down for breakfast, confused as to what it all meant, she was looking through her phone. It was a Euro Loto ticket and a quick search from that date confirmed that there was one winning ticket worth €15 million, the minimum amount available with that particular draw. She sat up, a tremor running through her body.

Three tables down from her, monitoring everything she was now doing, two women sat quietly, their plates empty in front of them, though a glass of half finished juice was still before them. Each had an ear piece in, hidden from view by their hair. They had noticed the sudden change in their subject, as she had studied the photo and then spent a few minutes on her phone. She'd obviously found what she was now looking for. All this was reported back to the Games Room, every change, every reaction reflecting new odds, new bets being made by the oligarchs funding the whole operation. It was less than thirty minutes later, Annabel having abruptly left the breakfast hall and then the hotel, that the two Trackers were able to confirm what they were all waiting for back to the others.

"Game on," they reported, and the Hunt had started.

∞∞∞

Twila was thirty minutes further north of Annabel on the Petrogradsky island, just north of the river Neva. She too was up for breakfast as she came across the note, assuming it to be something to do with the hotel, leaving it in her room whilst she had a leisurely but healthy breakfast of mostly fruit and a little salad and sliced meat. In the breakfast hall, it was a team of one man, one woman that were closest at hand and watching her. The news that she didn't have the sheet of paper with her went down a treat in the Games Room, the Host behind her choice taking a hit in front of his peers. It wasn't uncommon for that to happen, sometimes multiple notes and messages were needed to get their Contestant to understand what was happening.

She was followed back to the room, where she took a shower after doing a series of exercises on the floor next to her bed, a long established habit that she did without much effort, her body the better for it even if it did nothing to ultimately reduce her gradual decline. Once dressed and out of the shower, she came across the note again, realising there was hand writing on it and a photo, not what she'd noticed before. She sat on the edge of her bed taking it in, looking for anything else it said before re-reading it and just holding the photo in front of her face for a minute, gazing at what she could see, which wasn't a lot. It appeared to be taped to some sort of silver metal piping, though she couldn't make out what or where it was, though the attached note seemed to imply where to go. She was immediately cautious, wary of getting led into a situation that might be anything but safe. She picked up her coat and bag, and left the room. The camera on the hotel's system had been tapped into by the technicians so her exit from the room was noted and it was reported in real time that she was on the move. Three people waited in the lobby of the hotel, with others already on the streets, guarding the location they were hoping she was heading for.

"We have visual," one of the Trackers said, as Twila emerged from the stairwell into the reception area, heading for the desk, in fact, which was the other way from the doors. She spoke briefly to someone at the desk and was then handed a map, which she took to a table and chair to one side and opened out in front of her. She spent three minutes studying it before leaving.

"I think we have a nibble," the Tracker reported, before they all followed her out, one after the other, two going the opposite way, not to make it obvious that they were keeping track of her, but there were plenty of people on the streets already, and besides, Twila was oblivious to anyone watching her at that moment.

∞∞∞

Teo Vela had slept well and was awake before nine, but sat up reading in bed for a little before turning on the TV. He skipped breakfast altogether, which wasn't provided in his budget hotel, and went out to find a coffee shop, completely missing the note that had been slid underneath his door. This had been noticed quickly by the observers and arrangements were being put in place to get this information to Teo in another form before too long. Still, it meant inside the Games Room, his odds lengthened, making him an interesting bet for some. Just how far he'd go was yet to be seen. He was the outsider of the four, little really known about him in relation to what they knew of the other three Contestants.

∞∞∞

By midday, Dubhán had yet to emerge from his room, much to the mocking jeers of some of the oligarchs watching on in the Games Room. It made his Host work the phones eagerly, calling into action those that were part of his background team, seeing what they could do to rouse this lazy Irishman. He'd been a gamble from the start, which was also what made him such an interesting character to want to choose. It had certainly won the Host some kudos with his peers when he had announced this Contestant but now looked to be backfiring. If they couldn't get him to enter the Hunt soon, there'd be no real contest as far as he was concerned.

Men acting on the instructions of Fifteen were seen entering the hotel shortly after twelve, the Trackers noticing the event but failing to report it in. It was obvious that the Host would do something—they always did. The Trackers had a very clear job description, and getting on the wrong side of an oligarch for no obvious reason was certainly not one of them.

7

Alex had risen first the following morning, getting out of bed quietly, not wanting to wake Anissa who he couldn't see, unaware if she was yet awake or not. He pulled on a pair of jogging bottoms and a t-shirt and left the room just before eight. Anissa had been reading but knew he liked to go jogging in the morning so left him to it. It would give her time to get showered and dressed before he arrived back anyway.

By ten they'd finished breakfast and were standing in front of the hotel, where Sasha had dropped them the night before, as agreed. After just a few minutes' waiting, both agents starting to get a little cold as neither had a hat or gloves with them, making them stand out as obvious tourists, Sasha pulled over and they jumped in the back seat once more. He pulled away as the road cleared a little in front of him, taking an immediate right and working what looked like the side roads, which were clearer and where progress was a little more rewarding.

"Where are we heading to?" Alex said, his tone calm.

"There is a wonderful place not too far from here that has some great views of the city, plus they do a delicious lunch, if we need it later."

Nothing much more was said, besides a little small talk about their night's sleep, though Sasha was not one for such talk. Twenty minutes later they pulled up into a space, the front wheels of his car mounting the kerb in front, though from the look of the other cars around, it didn't seem to matter one bit, as long as you weren't totally blocking the small street. A canal ran alongside the road, an ornately decorated church prominent in the distance. Both British agents admired it as they climbed out of the back seat.

"It's the Church on Spilled Blood," Sasha pointed up, hand gesturing in the direction they were both looking. "Its architect had his eyes gouged out after he completed it, so that he wouldn't be able to create anything more spectacular."

Anissa looked at Sasha to see if he was kidding but turned back when it was clear this straight faced Russian was just giving them some history.

"The building was used as a storage area during Soviet times, which nearly destroyed the interior, which is wall to ceiling in mosaics. Quite spectacular," and he turned, heading back up the road. "Follow me," is all he then said, both Alex's and Anissa's eyes taken from the church as they finally turned and headed after Sasha.

The end of the road intersected with Nevski Prospekt, the city's main road that linked the two sides of the centre. On the corner was an extremely ornate building, which appeared to be a book store and Sasha led them inside, much to Alex's initial surprise. As if guessing the confusion, Sasha commented; "Upstairs there is a great café, with huge windows looking out across to the Cathedral."

They hadn't noticed that, across from the bookstore, opposite in fact, stood a giant cathedral, gardens visible in front though it was not yet the season for any plant life. The café, at the front of the building on the second floor and overlooking Nevski, was busy. Sasha found a table, moving another spare chair so that the three of them could sit down. Alex couldn't help but feel it was too public and crowded to really allow them to talk much about anything. Sasha clearly thought otherwise. Around the various tables it was now obvious there were a large number of tourists, the occasional English voice heard, but Spanish, German and French too, plus a few others they couldn't pick out, as well as Russian, but it wasn't really the place locals came to that often. The prices for one thing clearly showing the café was aimed mainly at the tourist market.

The views were impressive and the five tables by the windows were by far the most popular. They were a little further away but the view was still dramatic. The windows were floor to ceiling, most probably twenty feet at least, and light poured into the area, though it wasn't a particularly sunny day. A waitress came over and Sasha ordered something for himself, before turning to his two guests and seeing what they wanted. Once the order was placed, the waitress left them, stating she'd be back with their drinks in a little over five minutes.

"So what's all this about then, Alex?" Sasha said, looking at this stranger across the table from him. Alex involuntarily looked around, Sasha continuing as if reading his mind; "It's okay to speak freely here, no one is bothered by us, no one can hear us. These are just tourists taking in the sights. They'll come and go. If anyone is obviously listening, we'll soon know."

"Okay, I believe you. Look, Sasha, we're going to need some help on this one." Alex passed across a piece of paper, prepared that morning for such a moment as this, which contained the four names they'd been given two months ago. "We believe all four of these people might have entered your city within the last twenty-four hours. Two we know for sure left the UK yesterday, before we did. Of the other two, we aren't sure. One is Irish and we never traced where the fourth guy came into things. His name would suggest he's Spanish or Portuguese, most probably living there, too. Nothing checked out for anyone using that name as being currently resident in the UK, anyway."

"And what do you want me to look for? Are they a threat to security here?"

"I don't believe so, no. Certainly nothing in their past would suggest they were capable of anything, mind you until yesterday, we'd been looking into them for two months already and nothing about them suggested they were anyone of interest, until both the women suddenly cleared security through British airports, destination Russia."

"Where did you get the names from again?" Sasha had been told this clearly already, and they all knew this.

"From our contact, that's all I can say at this moment. He clearly knew even then that this was going to happen."

"And last night you said it involves a number of very rich people."

"Yes."

Sasha sat back in his chair, moments later the drinks coming which gave them a little more time in silence.

"What's the crime?"

It was a good question, Anissa picking up the workings of this younger man in front of her. He seemed to be straight up with them, which was refreshing, given the stereotype often used for the FSB.

"That's what we want to find out. We have nothing on this organisation, if it even exists. For months, years, it was just a whisper in the background. Nothing of substance. Then we were put in touch with someone who would go deep, off the radar."

"You have some form of informant, here in Russia?"

"Something like that, yes. It was a long shot really, and only a few at Six were happy about us looking into it. He isn't an MI6 agent, not even directly on the payroll. We'd heard very little, but two months back he reports in, only a little information, and very obscure. He listed these four people," Alex said, tapping the piece of paper he'd placed in front of Sasha as if to clarify the point, "a number of dates that have passed, and a first name of presumably a Russian male, who we must assume is somehow part of this whole thing."

"The name?" Sasha said, taking a sip from his tea, Anissa watching him closely from behind her own glass of juice, but only out of curiosity.

"Dmitry."

"Dmitry? Just a first name?"

"Yes, that's all the report said. And this is the last we've heard from him."

Sasha put his tea back onto the table in front of them.

"That's not a lot to go on, and you still don't know what the crime is."

"True," Anissa said for the first time in the conversation, "but these four people, if they are in this city today, will give us a good idea as to what the hell is going on. This is the first time we've got something to go on. We find these four people, we find some answers."

"And you've come to me because MI6 haven't given you the go ahead?"

"Something like that," Alex said, looking to Anissa but continuing himself. "Though I was the main contact for the mole, his report never reached me. Officially, I've never been told that he gave us these names, these dates or the name Dmitry. They've not reported to me that we've lost contact with our man since this report was sent."

"So somebody, presumably high up in your service, is keeping a lid on this whole situation?"

"Yes," they both said in unison.

"What a marvel—you Brits think it's only my employers that are full of crooks!" Sasha laughed, his point well made.

"Can you help us?" Anissa said, warming to him the more she got to know him.

"It won't be easy, and believe me, if certain people from Moscow are involved in this, rich people with power, we could be walking into a nightmare. But I said I'd help you, and that is what I intend to do. We'll take a look for these four people if, as you say, they have all just arrived in the city. I'll make contact with migration services, get a list of everyone's names that landed at the airport yesterday. We'll start there and see what it shows us. Most major hotels will also require that guests register their arrival, so if that is done in a timely manner, it might show where they are staying. That said, I wouldn't expect to know that information for a few days. The hotels have seventy-two hours to report these details."

"They might be gone before then."

"Yes, well, assuming they arrived in Russia as you say, their migration card which they would have completed on arrival will tell us what we need to know. It'll prove if in fact they have arrived, and will also tell us the day they are due to leave. Anything more than three days and the hotels will report their whereabouts before they've returned home."

"I don't think we'll have that luxury. Something tells me it'll be today or tomorrow that whatever they came for at such short notice, they'll do."

"Then we haven't any time to lose," Sasha said, standing up and putting on his coat. "I'll call in at the office and get the information on the migration cards. You can wait here, enjoy the ambiance, or go for a walk. I'll come back in two hours."

They agreed to his plan, scanning the menu as he left them, though they weren't yet ready for lunch. They finished their drinks, deciding a walk was called for, and left the café, keeping an eye on the time for when Sasha was due to head back.

8

Annabel Herbertson had located the ticket easily, the directions she'd found pushed under her hotel room that morning leading her directly to what turned out to be a drain pipe attached to a building just a short walk from the hotel. The Trackers recorded the fact she'd found the ticket. History told them that a Contestant would always try to make a run for it if they got to this stage.

She returned to the main road, people walking past her, going about their every day life. An old woman carried two bags of shopping, a young woman carried her designer dog in a little bag hanging from her shoulder, easily navigating the icy pavement in high heels. Life seemed so normal, and yet for Annabel, she'd just come across a ticket worth more money than she'd ever hope to make in her life. World changing money, for her and her young son.

She decided then and there not to return to the hotel. She had her bag, and therefore her documents, with her. The clothes that were left behind were nothing compared to the mission she had before her. Get out of that place and back to London that day, and she'd be rich beyond her wildest dreams.

She didn't know if it was the closeness of riches, or just the fact she now had something she dreaded losing, but suddenly it was as if she didn't feel safe anymore, as if every old woman carrying shopping was a threat to her, every young Russian beauty out to get her. She needed to move.

Recalling the railway station was nearby, she started to walk towards that. Whoever had posted the note through the door clearly knew where she was. They'd focussed this thing on her. Now she felt vulnerable. Were they watching her that very minute? She located the station and an array of buses and coaches were spread out on a horse-shoe shaped road in front of the building.

She entered the main concourse, the Trackers behind her at every turn. Going for a train was a smart move as most Contestants headed for the airport, unwittingly playing into the hands of the Hosts who could pull in favours with migration police. Her odds had dropped, as another Contestant offered the rare possibility of actually getting out of Russia, clearly the first, and easily hardest hurdle, to overcome.

Annabel, not understanding anything around her, saw what she thought she was looking for, confirmation that trains were heading out of Russia from where she was departing. Tallinn, the capital of Estonia and due west of her position, was showing. She'd flown to Tallinn once before, many years back before she was even a mother, and knew it offered cheap direct flights to the UK. Finding a man who was queuing who spoke

English, she quickly explained to him what ticket she wanted to buy and he went with her, happy to help, speaking Russian with the lady behind the counter, and once her passport had been checked, nothing more was said. She thanked the man, passed over the rubles that had been indicated and was handed her ticket. The whole process from entering the station to obtaining her ticket took less than three minutes. The gods were smiling on her, she mused. She jogged to where she needed to be, feeling every minute counted, though she had ten minutes to board the waiting train, which was ample.

Three of the Trackers also boarded the train, Annabel spotting them walking past the window, ignoring them as best she could, but there was something about them she didn't trust. She'd also seen one of them at her hotel. Two other men, who were part of the Host's party, also boarded the train. As the whistles were sounding, and the train started to pull away, she made her move, low so that no one could see her, and back to the door, easing it open as the train slowly picked up speed. Being sure she was out of sight, she leapt off, landing back onto the platform less than fifteen metres before it ended. The train continued to pick up speed, moving away from the station, its passengers unaware of what had just happened.

She doubled back to the front of the platform once more, using a different cashier's window this time, and motioned as best she could for a ticket for the next train, due to leave within the hour and also going to Tallinn. It had helped, despite not knowing any Russian, that she'd just seen the kind of information needed, and she even passed her documents across as the instruction was given, paying the ticket price, a little more than the previous one had been, but it was a faster train with fewer stops. It was due to arrive in Tallinn thirty minutes before the previous train, which is why she'd done what she did. Looking around, no one was obviously following her. She found a quiet café to hide in, paid for a drink and sat down, waiting for the hour to tick by before she'd reappear, check her surroundings and make for her new seat on the express train.

It was thirty minutes before the concern was raised within the Games Room that they didn't have a visual on the Contestant. The Host, a little anxious by this point already, was in constant contact with his two men that he'd sent to board the train. Their instructions had been very clear—under no circumstance was Annabel to be allowed to enter Estonia. They walked the length of the train, expecting to pass her at any moment, but getting to the last carriage, there was no obvious sign of her. The Trackers had now reported this information too, a frenzy of noise coming from the other oligarchs, as once more the possibility of a Contestant actually getting away was made clear to them all. The Hunt had suddenly become very interesting.

∞∞∞∞

A little north of where Annabel had picked up her ticket, Twila too had been on the Hunt for her own ticket, and once she'd come across it, discovering it to be an unclaimed £1 million from the UK Millionaire Maker game, she too had felt that burst of power and fear that hit every Contestant. Panic set in almost immediately, which is really what ultimately stopped most Contestants. Twila, however, managed to control that initial high, and started to focus. She ran back to the hotel she'd been staying at, the Trackers needing to work hard to stay in touch with her, losing her briefly before she was spotted entering the hotel, taking the stairs and ascending three at a time, wasting as little time as possible. She grabbed everything she had, most of which she hadn't bothered to unpack anyway, and zipped up her bag. She'd paid for the room up front and for the next few days, so it didn't matter if she was heading out without telling them. Checking she had everything, her passport in her handbag, she dropped the room card on the floor before closing the door behind her, heading back to the stairs and descending back out onto the street. She'd been not even five minutes.

In the Games Room, since she had been picked because of her athletic prowess, there was a rumble of admiration. What she did next would indicate whether she really had a chance or not, but as she avoided all the waiting taxi cabs, again a roar went up in the room. Bets were doubled, declarations made that put some of the other oligarchs, especially Twila's Host, in a difficult position should she also become successful in this particular Hunt. The Trackers following Twila had the use of a car at this point, which enabled them to keep a watch on her. Avoiding the taxis meant she had opted not to head towards the airport, a trip south through the city at that time of the day sure to delay her for hours.

"She's heading for the station," one of the oligarchs said, the Host already seeing that possibility and putting men in place within the main concourse as well as on the platform. The thought that two Contestants were taking trains made this an unprecedented Games day already.

Twila, indeed, was heading west, across a bridge over one of the many canals, heading in the direction of the Finland Railway station, which connected the north side of the city by rail with their Finnish neighbours to the west. However, she opted not to enter the station, instead approaching a small white transit van with a board in the front windscreen indicating it was heading to Helsinki. The bus was already nearly full, and as she got on board, paying her rubles to the driver, the doors closed and the bus pulled away.

The team of Trackers followed the vehicle. The men that the Host had sent were only able to watch from a distance as they came running from the station, unable to see where she'd gone or which bus she was in. The Games Room erupted, two of the four, and the only active Hunts at present, seemingly going against their billionaire Hosts, shaming them for being outwitted by such common people—and two women, at that.

∞∞∞

Sasha had now rejoined Alex and Anissa and they'd driven some distance before stopping for some food. While they had been waiting for him, the two British agents had spent their time exploring a little of the cathedral. A number of people were begging outside the entrance to the building, clearly hoping to stir the consciences of those leaving the church. They'd then wandered along the canal, circling the domed Church on Spilled Blood, various market stalls visible a little further beyond, though there was not a lot of foot traffic. They both purchased a hat from the market, the cold starting to get to them, even though it seemed the worst of the winter had long passed. The canal was still mainly frozen, though the centre was clear, the ice littered with cans and champagne bottles, the odd remains of fireworks also visible.

When the two hours had been up and it was time for Sasha to return, they walked back to where he'd parked before but as no spaces were obvious, they continued to the main Nevski Prospekt. Sasha pulled over, blocking a bus lane that was thankfully empty at that point, and they got into the back seat as they had in on each of the previous occasions.

Now sitting down around a large wooden table, three bowls of warm Russian soup in front of each of them, a red metal teapot to one side, Sasha started to explain what he'd found out.

"All four of these names appear on migration cards received at Pulkova airport yesterday," he stated, both Alex and Anissa lowering their spoons as the confirmation hit them. "None of them are staying more than three days." That meant the chances of hearing from a hotel before they'd left again were remote.

"Can we stake out the airport on the day they are due to leave?" Anissa said.

"Yes, that's possible. To what purpose?" Sasha said.

"Besides, it would tell us very little," Alex added.

"I put a flag on these names. It's common practice, and just informs my office if and when an attempt to cross the border is made. The border guards will not see the warning. I only used the basic level, which just informs me. If I'd done anything else, it might alert others to our interference in the situation."

"Yes, very good. So, we will at least know if and when they decide to leave the country, assuming it isn't on the very day they stated on their migration card."

"Exactly."

"And we won't find out from their hotels where they are staying?"

"It's unlikely, Alex, no. The law requires them to inform the authorities within seventy-two hours, five days as a maximum. Very rarely do the hotels get around to doing it before that time. These people would therefore most likely have left before we are told."

"If they are still in the country by then," Alex added.

"You think they'll do whatever they are here for before that time, then?"

"Look, if we are to believe all that the rumours say, and they have been just rumours up until now, then these four people have been brought here for a very specific purpose. It could even be today, maybe tomorrow. We need to find these people as quickly as we can."

"My city is five million people. We don't know where they are. There are well over two thousand six hundred hotels in St Petersburg. Even if we narrowed down the search to a particular area, or price bracket, we don't have the time or personnel to make such a search in the hours we have. I'm sorry."

"So what can we do?" Alex didn't like the idea that he was just idle, waiting for something to happen that would give him the next piece of the puzzle, always behind the events, always chasing something, never ahead.

"We wait, and in the meantime, let's look into the other information that you have and see where we get to. You mentioned some dates…"

9

Almería, south coast of Spain

The flight from Gatwick had been easy, as the two person team of Buyers working with Thirteen touched down on the daily easyJet shuttle that was working that route. All around them on the approach, they'd seen fields of white, the polytunnels covering acre upon acre and growing all sorts of produce to be shipped globally, especially to the UK. The sea lined one side of the runway as the plane taxied to its position on the tarmac.

The pair, both of Ukrainian origin, like their boss, were in Spain's hottest region because someone was waking up potentially €33 million richer following the previous day's Euro Loto result. The Buyers had been in London hunting down another potential option, but the claimant had beaten them to it, already notifying the UK Lottery that they had the winning ticket. In those cases, procedure was just to walk away, because once the big guys knew about it, the risk of exposing their presence wasn't worth the hassle.

The airport was small, flights in and out limited. It made getting through security very easy, and they were walking out from the front of the terminal twenty minutes later, keys for their rental collected and car waiting out front for them in the car park. The heat was hitting them already, though they weren't too bothered by that. Pine trees with cones the size of tennis balls greeted them as they walked up a ramp that took them into the parking area. They located their car without any trouble, got in, air conditioning working away, and were off before ten o'clock. They had a lot of work to do if they were to be successful on this one, and it was very possible that there could be other Buyers in the market for the ticket, though Thirteen had reassured them that was unlikely. He was the only Host of the Hunt in just under three months time without a ticket, so he figured he'd get this one without much of a problem, if they were willing to sell. A ticket of this value, whilst not overly rare, did make for a good prize.

First stop was the main bank in the region, a multi national that had branches not only across the whole of Spain, but right across Europe, too. They had called ahead to the bank—it wasn't everyday that such a cash withdrawal was required, but the funds had cleared the day before and the money made ready in €500 notes as requested, each bundle of one hundred notes worth a cool €50,000. With six hundred and sixty bundles to collect, it required several large boxes to store it all. They hoped the back seat of the car would have enough space to house all the boxes. The boot was small and already cramped with their flight luggage.

By eleven, the money was safely collected and stored in the car, the staff at the bank curious to see quite who the mystery clients were, though normal client protocol meant they'd been as discreet as one would expect from such a large bank.

The Buyers called their tech guy next.

"Anything?" they said, the phone on speaker as they drove back out of the city, mountains clearly visible ahead of them. They'd spoken English to their contact person who was of Romanian nationality. He was the vital third piece to any Buyers' team, as he constantly monitored, and often hacked into, systems, listening for what he could. Usually, after such a big win, someone said something. He had tracers put on most luxury websites selling anything from yachts to Caribbean getaways. It was a known fact, that before a claimant ever contacted the lottery organiser, which usually had to wait until the morning after, they were already virtually spending the money they had yet to collect, searching anything their mind could come up with. It had proved the fastest way to track a lottery winner, and was now widely used by all the Buyers working for the various oligarchs.

"I'm still looking. Possibly something here, just sending you GPS now," and a text message came through to a hand held tracking system they were using. If a claimant only checked one website, it was nearly impossible to trace, unless you knew almost exactly what region to search in. But multiple searches made from the same IP address and they had their target. "Two searches made from those coordinates late last night. It appears to be a small village in the mountains. The Ferrari they were looking at is hardly practical for tight mountain roads, neither are the ocean going yachts they were looking at just after. Not very easy to store a vessel like that in such a remote place. I'd say we have our winner."

"Thanks, keep watch and we'll let you know how it goes."

There had been the odd occasion when the Buyers made a run for it. Millions in cash can do that to any individual, making them feel they were invincible and so far away from those that might miss it. Those people always ended up dead, and very publicly, too. The killings had been a sign and a warning not to mess with an oligarch. Their network was just too far reaching, there was no hiding ultimately, unless they never used the money. But what was the fun in that? Most Buyers knew their place, part of a much bigger team, paid well and given generous budgets to travel widely. It was a good life if you could make it work.

The female of the pair now driving the roads of Almería typed in the coordinates that had been sent through, the map taking just moments to configure before displaying a route, time and distance in front of them. They were fifty minutes away, and the morning was pressing on. It was critical they got there in time.

"Roma," the driver said, reconnected to their computer expert once more, "we aren't going to be there for another hour or so. You'll need to take out the telephone signal from that area."

"Already onto it. I figured the same a few minutes back. I've taken out the internet too, for good measure. It should ground them, and if not that, at least stop them calling it in. Mind you, a win of this size usually takes them a little while to get around to actually claiming the money. It's funny, you'd think playing the actual thing they'd be more prepared for winning, but they never are."

"True, anyway, I don't want to keep you, and clearly you are ahead of the game on us anyway," he said, glancing to his partner. The computer whizzes always thought they were one step ahead of everyone else. "If there is anything more to come from the area, let us know."

"With the internet and phone lines out, I'm not sure what you expect me to do from here. I'm only so good."

"Good point. Keep safe," and he hung up, laughing. "So he's not all powerful, after all."

∞∞∞∞

Travelling at some speed, they were approaching the village forty-five minutes later, taking the turns carefully. The map led them just beyond the centre of what was only a small mountainside community, and brought them to a free standing house that was probably part of the farm next to it, no other buildings visible. The house itself was small and compact, built of stone. The roof seemed in need of a little attention. There was one car, a small Fiat, parked next to the house, in front of a single garage. Goats moved around in an adjoining field. There was an orchard of some sort at the end of the garden. As they were deciding what to do, whether to park up behind the Fiat on the drive or leave the car on the road, a man was seen looking through the front window. They pulled up behind the Fiat and got out. Moments later the front door opened.

"Are you from the internet company?" the old man asked in Spanish, the female of the pair the only one fluent enough to understand him.

"No, sir, but we know the whole area is down, phone lines too. We've been trying to call you all morning. We've been sent from Euro Loto HQ. Congratulations on last night's win."

The man froze on the spot, as if shocked that his secret was out despite not having told anyone, but then relaxed—of course they knew, they were the ones selling the tickets.

"Please, come inside," he said, ushering them towards the door.

"Thank you, my colleague will just bring some boxes in from the car so will join us in a moment," she said, walking towards the door, her partner already starting to manhandle the four large cardboard boxes from the back seat.

Inside, the house was messy. A photo stood above a small dressing table of a younger woman, the photo itself in black and white.

"That was my wife," he said, noticing the lady looking at the photo. "Died many years ago, now. Before we'd had the chance to start a family of our own. I've basically been on my own for a long time."

"Well, that's about to change, I'm sure."

"Yes, that's what I'm afraid of."

"You have nothing to be afraid of, sir," she said. The many times she had been through this situation helped her to come across as motherly, caring, like a nurse speaks to her patient. "We know it can be very difficult for people like yourself following such a big win. That's why we've come to you today with a cash payout. There doesn't, then, need to be any publicity. It'll be totally up to you who, if anyone, you choose to tell." She smiled and let that last phrase sink in as her partner brought the last of the four boxes into the room.

"This is all the money, you mean? Here?"

"Yes, sir. We can transport you to a bank of your choice, if you'd prefer. But yes, from our experience, when it comes to people in your situation, they prefer to take a cash prize and stay out of the papers. You see, those that didn't do it that way end up getting run out of town. First, the neighbours start calling around all the time, pretending to be friendly, but really they all want a piece of your good fortune. Then it's a relative that had not been heard from for years suddenly showing up on the scene. Letters come pouring in from every hopeless case under the sun asking for just a few thousand here, a few thousand there. It drives most people crazy." Her partner had opened the top box as she'd been speaking, the old man's eyes taking in the sight of more cash than he ever thought he'd see in his life. His defensiveness changed as soon as he saw the money, going over to touch some, being handed a bundle of notes as he got to the boxes. Once they'd seen the money, they were always as good as sold on the idea.

"Of course, we will need to see that you have the actual ticket. You see, it's just regulations. We can't do anything with you until we've confirmed that you are in fact in possession of the ticket."

Now, it became necessary to check that he did actually have a ticket. Winners always made a move at this point to prove the fact, and the old man was no different.

"Here you go," he said, the ticket having been sitting on the lounge table all along, though under a book he must have been reading, probably to help him sleep the night before. She scanned the numbers and there was no doubt, it was what they expected.

"Very good. So, what would you like to do with the cash?" They always worded it like that, making up the mind of the claimant for them, just assuming they were taking the option presented. Of course, the claimants themselves just assumed this was how it always happened, being the first time for them, but reasoning that those standing before them must do this all the time.

"I think I'd like to take you up on the offer of taking me to my bank. I don't think I could manage these boxes by myself in that old Fiat, after all. Nor does the idea of leaving such amounts around the house fill me with anything but dread."

"Of course, sir. We'll take you right away," and her partner started loading the boxes back into the car. "One more thing, sir. I will have to take the ticket from you."

"Yes, of course," and he handed over the ticket, not a moment's hesitation, the cash prize already in front of him. He had no need for it anymore, after all.

10

The momentary silence of the Games Room in the five storey mansion in central St Petersburg was broken as a roar of delight went up. Annabel had finally popped up on their grid again, her passport cleared at the Ivangorod border station in western Russia, meaning she'd crossed the river into the EU, arriving in the eastern city of Narva, Estonia. Whilst there were a few bets that might have a pay out, the real power came from seeing fellow oligarchs falling. A Contestant who managed to escape Russia was humiliating for the hosting oligarch, and the other oligarchs loved to make that fact known. Reputations were made or broken in that room, based on how far someone would go, what stops they'd pull out, in order to come out on top. Whenever a Contestant had made it out of Russia, their odds of then claiming the reward jumped dramatically, just under twenty per cent of people getting that far had gone on to claim their prize. Only one man had attempted to claim without even leaving St Petersburg, by sending the ticket via Fed-Ex to his wife, who happened to be sleeping at her lover's house the day the courier arrived, and therefore failed to receive it in time. Since then, with no fun to be had chasing a package across Europe, the delivery companies had all been seen to. Most were now owned by the very oligarchs in that room, as they all looked to increase their grip on situations that might otherwise befall them.

The Trackers, who had been on the first train and were still clearing the border when the call was put through to them, would continue on to Tallinn, the destination Annabel was heading for. The two men who had boarded the train on the instructions of the Host would get off before the border. There was a high chance their names would flag up on the western side of the border and they'd then most likely be detained. They weren't any help to their boss locked up somewhere. He'd have to pull in other favours, instead.

∞∞∞∞

Twila had been followed all the way to the border by the car that her team of Trackers were using. She'd been trying to pick up any form of internet signal so that she could book a flight to the UK, but nothing had been showing in that barren and wild part of Russia. She hoped that across the border and into Finland, she would pick up something. Certainly once she got nearer to the capital.

She wouldn't get that far, however, as the Host of her Hunt was a man with huge connections within the migration services, and he had put a flag out with the border guard at the crossing she was heading to. She was to be taken from the bus and held for questioning. A six hour delay was all it would take to end her chances of ever getting across to the UK in time to claim. He'd make her sit it out, the holding cell no doubt feeding back CCTV footage of a woman pacing around, angry and agitated, annoyed that the money was slipping through her fingers. Sometimes they'd try and pay a bribe to get moving again, and officials not within the tight control of an oligarch or two would often take the bribe. Occasionally, and strictly against the rules, an oligarch who had influence would use it to favour a particular Contestant whom they might otherwise have bet on to succeed a little longer. It was certainly a two way street. This time, she would be out of options. The other oligarchs had worked out what the Host would do, knowing his connections within the region, owning at least half the city of Vyborg, which was the last major stop off before you hit Finland, very popular with Russian aristocracy down through the ages.

∞∞∞

Teo Vela had eventually been made aware of the ticket, though it was already afternoon. He headed straight to the airport once he realised how much he stood to win. It could have been an easy victory for the Host, a man who'd spent a lot of time and money setting that particular Hunt up, but given the time of day, there were no easy flights that would get him back to Spain any time soon, so the oligarch took the bold move to make no effort to stop him boarding a plane, two Trackers also on the afternoon flight out of Pulkovo 2, meaning the Hunt took on a new edge—there was still an element of risk. If needed, he could delay the Contestant when he finally reached Spain, either getting to him in Madrid via a delay to the onward flight, or some other way once he'd landed at his small regional airport. Doing the maths, the Host thought there was no great danger of losing, and the added risk certainly brought something to the room. It meant there were three Contestants in the Hunt, and after Annabel's location had been discovered, two of these people were now out of Russia, which added a lot to the occasion.

∞∞∞

The fourth and final Contestant, who hadn't appeared from his room until after two that afternoon, was the very hungover Irishman who'd picked up the piece of paper and just laughed at what he saw as an obvious joke. The fact that he still held on his person a valid lottery ticket for just over €3 million wasn't a thought his Host wanted to dwell upon. Most losing Contestants gave up their ticket in some way, only rarely did the Buyers need to pay them for it. As Dubhán left the hotel and headed back to the one place he'd been so far in the city—the Irish pub—two teams of men followed him. One, the

Trackers, the other a group of hard and ruthless men organised by the Contestant's Host, a man already angry that all his efforts had come to nothing. He had underestimated how much of a stupid drunk the man was, assuming he'd be smart enough to understand what he was in possession of and at least make some attempt to claim the money. As he sat in the bar, another pint in front of him, spending money he couldn't really afford, he was joined by the men sent to follow him from his Host. They would wait and see what he did. If he went to the toilet, they would get him then. One way or the other, they would teach him a lesson he wouldn't see coming, and get back the ticket he had not deemed valuable enough to even try and pursue.

11

Alex, Anissa and Sasha had been working through things when Sasha's phone sounded. The Russian took the call, occasionally glancing at his British counterparts, before ending abruptly.

"News?" Anissa said.

"We've got movement, Annabel crossed the border into Estonia one hour ago. The Spaniard also flew from the airport this afternoon."

"So it's happening today, it must be. These people are actually taking part in one of these events."

"So it would seem," the Russian said, for the first time convinced that the whole thing was actually as they'd been telling him.

"And no news on the other two?"

"Nothing, but they have the details, so if anything comes up, I'll be informed."

"What's in Estonia for Annabel?" Alex asked.

"She'll be heading for the capital Tallinn, about two hours from the border. There are direct flights to England from there."

Anissa looked at her watch.

"She's cutting it mighty fine by my reckoning." She pulled open her laptop that she'd been working on but had switched it off while they waited for anything further to develop. After a quick search she found the website for Tallinn airport, the departing flights listed on the main screen. "Two flights are departing for England this afternoon, an easyJet to Gatwick at half four, and a Ryanair flight to Stansted at ten. We can discount the night flight as that would get in too late. What time did she cross the border? Can she even make that flight?"

Sasha checked his computer, the information now updated from the migration police, her details coming through as he waited. "She cleared the Russian border guard at two this afternoon. Bearing in mind she then gained an hour, it's then a two, two and a half hour journey to the main railway station in Tallinn, situated in the north of the city, but probably only twenty minutes from there to the airport by taxi. It'd be tight, but its possible."

"How long does it take to fly to the UK?"

"It's about two and a half hours."

"So she'd get in too late, then, surely? What time would she be able to claim a ticket with Lottery HQ until, anyway?"

"I think it's seven pm, and remembering that she gains two hours during the flight, she lands therefore at something like five, British time. More than enough time to get from the airport to where she needs to be."

"Bloody hell," Alex said, for the first time marvelling at the whole thing.

"How much does she stand to win?"

"That's an interesting one. Let's see which tickets have not been claimed," and Alex tapped away, several windows opening up. Two minutes later he seemed happy that he'd found the right one. "Here, this would appear to be the best fit, though it suggests there are still two days left to claim, not one. It's a Euro Loto ticket worth €15 million. There was one winning ticket nearly six months ago, and it was never claimed."

"Man, it's actually real," Anissa said, giving away her feelings a little, convinced finally that the last few months had really been worth the hassle.

"Why is it taking place today, then, if they have the chance of claiming until tomorrow, too? That would mean they all could have made it without the frantic rush."

"I don't know. But I'm sure we're going to find out."

"Look at this," Alex said, coming away from his laptop once more and turning it to them. "Nearly three months back the Spanish lottery El Gordo had one winning ticket, for €8.3 million, never claimed. It was won in Tarragona. My bet is that this is our man."

"Yes, that would make sense. We never made a connection with this name in the UK. Makes sense that they use people Europe wide."

"So what now?" Anissa said, sitting back in her chair.

"These two are too far ahead of us for it to be worth chasing them. We have to monitor them from afar. We're playing catch up, after all, but it's a vital piece of the mosaic. Once the dust settles, we can drop in on them and get their side of the story. How they heard about it all, why they flew to St Petersburg on that particular day, what happened to them in the city. Did they actually meet anyone from the Russian side? Things like that. We can start to reconstruct the picture by working backwards."

"But that means they get away with it, again."

"Anissa, we have no real choice. They are too far ahead of us for there to have been any other outcome, this time. We arrived in the city on a whisper, nothing more really. We had no real leads, besides a few names, no connections, no avenues to explore. We just turned up to see what we could find out. With Sasha's help, we've been able to begin to turn a few rocks over, and this has given us a few more clues. We've found evidence of it all taking place, right in front of us. We've seen the actions of those taking part. They now become our next link in the chain, more connected to the situation than anything we've come across so far. It all goes into the mixing pot. Whilst we'll keep digging and seeing what we can find ourselves, these people that are taking part in all this today might lead us right back to the people we are trying to find. So let's watch what happens, keep a close eye on these two that we know are heading back to what they hope will be a prosperous future, and see what more we can learn. It's all we can do."

"I see that. It just feels like we are always several steps behind. Discovering evidence of wrong doing is not the same as having direct proof of their involvement and wrong doing."

"I know that, we all do. But it's all we've got to go on. We've learnt a lot in the last twenty-four hours. Let's face it, neither of us was totally convinced this time yesterday. As I set out for what would have been a week in the Lake District, part of me wondered if it was time to put the investigation to rest. Andre had been silent for over two months, the information he last gave us seemingly irrelevant. I was beginning to assume he might not be in the land of the living any more, and that the information that was sent was in some way compromised. And then yesterday happened. It's given us a fresh start, some new information after months of scraping around for crumbs. So we track these people. If we can find out what's happening with the other two as well, that would be good. They've not yet crossed over the border, otherwise Sasha would have been told, we have to assume they are still in this vast city somewhere, trying to find a way. Maybe we'll be able to locate one of them?" He wasn't sounding too convinced but it was enough for Anissa.

"Yes, you are right. It has been a good day. It's a marathon, not a sprint, right? So I agree, it's given us some much needed hope that these last few months haven't been a complete and utter waste of our time."

"Sasha," Alex said, turning to his FSB counterpart once more, "can you draw together whatever you have on these people." He handed the Russian a list of names, known to most Russians. Alex had pulled them all from the Russian Forbes rich list chart. "I know that not all these men are involved, I'm certain of that. Unlike most, Sasha, I don't believe every Russian with a bit of power and influence is corrupt. But I do suspect a good number of these men are involved in what we are now witnessing. I've got some information on them all, anything the internet has openly available, which for a good number of these people, is very little. Maybe within the vaults of the FSB database, you might have a bit more—anything that suggests a link to the criminal underground, mafia—anything like that."

"These are powerful people, Alex, you have to understand that. To use what you alluded to earlier, with these men you don't know what we are going to find when we start turning over those stones. They have the power and influence to really sting us."

"I know that, and we appreciate anything you are able to do for us. You've already been most helpful," Alex said.

"Yes, you really have, Sasha," Anissa added for good measure.

"And I'd be hung out to dry if they knew what I'd been doing with two active British spies in this city today. I have a fair amount of freedom in my role, but I'm going to have to touch base for a while, show my face, be active in HQ once more, so that they don't come looking for me. So far, it would seem, your presence has been kept secret."

"You are sure that they aren't watching us?"

"Anissa, if they were, I'm positive you'd both be sitting inside the Kresty right now, and I'd be floating face down in the Neva." The Kresty was a prison on the banks of the River Neva in the centre of the city.

"I thought the Kresty closed down as an active prison some years back?" Alex said.

"Yes, that's what they wanted everyone to think. An inner core remains open for the most high risk prisoners we have. The whole complex is now closed, the general public kept well away. But it's more than just active, Alex."

"Okay, well let's be careful then. Sasha, you do as you just suggested. Go, show your face, make a nuisance of yourself, whatever you need to do. We'll hang around here, act like the tourists we always wanted to be, and touch base with you once more a little later. You can name the place, just send us directions via SMS and we'll do our best to find it."

"And be careful!"

"You too, Sasha. Thanks once again."

They parted company, Sasha going to fetch his car that he'd parked a few streets away, the only free space he could find at the time, and driving back to *Big House*—the towering home of the FSB in St Petersburg. Alex and Anissa packed up the things they had, putting their laptop back into its bag, and set out on foot, preferring to walk as much as possible, not really understanding or wanting to try using any form of public transport, even though it was so readily available. A little snow was falling as they made it onto the constantly busy pavements, made busier by the proximity of one of the city's many metro stations. Because of the depth of the river and the swampy ground, the St Petersburg metro was the world's deepest underground network.

∞∞∞

Dubhán Maguire had spent three hours solid at the bar, downing at least five pints of beer before he moved, finally shuffling towards the toilets at the back of the pub. His two minders, who'd been watching him the whole time, also made their way to the toilets a few seconds after the Irishman had left his seat. This particular Hunt had been called off an hour ago, as evening was drawing in. There was no way that the Contestant would be able to make a go at claiming the money by then, the oligarchs cashing out any bets they might have had, though it was promises and especially pride that was most at stake. For the Host of the Contestant, he had spent money not only procuring the ticket in the first place, but then investigating the right type of person to be a worthy opponent, arranging for his sudden trip to the city, clearing everything he might need. All for it to become worthless, as the man's drinking problem had clearly been massively underestimated. There was no fight in the pathetic drunk, and the team of Trackers had left the pub an hour back when the news came through to them that this particular Hunt was over. As they left, aware that the Host's men were also in the place watching their man, they must have known what was about to happen, despite it being against the rules—needless to say, also illegal.

Dubhán swayed as he stood in front of the middle urinal of five. The two Russians entered the toilet area, a quick scan of the space confirming there were no other people present. One of the Russians stood by the door, blocking any further people that might try and come in.

When the Irishman was finished, he turned, heading for the sink, barely acknowledging the two Russians that he had not heard enter the toilets. He turned on the tap as one of the men rushed him from behind, slamming his head against the wall above the taps, before slamming it into the edge of the sink, the Irishman already collapsing to the floor. There was a little blood showing on the edge of the sink, Dubhán's forehead giving evidence of its source, a steady stream of red flowing down his face and onto the floor, the man himself knocked out cold by the blow. The Russian leaned over his victim and pulled a syringe from the inside of his jacket pocket, a clear liquid inside, a small amount escaping the tip as a little pressure was applied. The Russian injected Dubhán in the side of the neck, the fluid taking about thirty seconds to enter the blood stream, causing the heart to fail. Counting off sixty seconds, the Russian checked for a pulse on the left wrist of the fallen man, and not finding one, reached into the Irishman's back jeans pocket, extracting the lottery ticket before he stood, careful not to touch anything else, the needle returned to his jacket pocket, for disposal somewhere else. They left the building without having been disturbed by anyone, their exit recorded on no CCTV as that had already been dealt with by their boss.

The body would be discovered just five minutes later, and reported to the bar manager, who'd come in, recognising the fallen man as a guy he'd been serving drinks to all afternoon. It was obvious he'd fallen and hit his head. An accident which they'd do their best to keep that way, the barman knowing that he'd been well aware of his clients drunken state as he continued to replace his beers, though laws such as might appear in the UK were a little more open to interpretation where they lived. Besides, the man had simply slipped and hit his head, an unfortunate accident that could have happened to anyone. An ambulance was called, the gents toilet closed off until it arrived, the body left as it was. There was no need to get the police involved in what was obviously a frightful, unfortunate, regrettable accident.

12

Twila Dalton had been sitting in a detention room of the Russian border guard at the southern most border with Finland for three hours already. She knew she'd missed the chance to catch a plane to England, the money she thought was hers for the taking long gone. She'd been told to empty her pockets on arrival, the paper ticket no doubt the last she'd see of it—mind you it had no value to anyone now, with time running out and the claim date expiring that same evening.

Twila, an unusually upbeat person, as fitness fanatics tended to be, had resisted the urge to plead her case, or let on what she was doing, instead had become resigned to her fate after the first hour passed, knowing that nothing she could do or say would speed up an otherwise standard procedure. So it hadn't worked out, never mind. She'd find another way to grow her future, another avenue to explore. She'd keep the details of the last twenty-four hours from anyone she knew. No need to let on how much she'd spent to arrange everything as she had at such short notice. She'd slip back into her old life, happy that she hadn't done anything too drastic and burnt her bridges. No one would ever know about this, she told herself. She'd put it down to an interesting life experience, would never allow herself to get tricked into something like this again, and vowed to move on. She had sensed it was all too good to be true before she agreed to venture out of her usual comfort zone, but she had needed a new challenge at the time, needed something new to get her teeth stuck into. So this one hadn't come to anything. There would be something new around the corner, she told herself, sitting in that room, left to her own thoughts as no one even bothered to ask her anything. She just assumed they were working on her paperwork somewhere, or maybe waiting for a translator to appear.

∞∞∞∞

Teo Vela had been delayed as he'd made his transfer in Vienna, his Host having been told that they would not get the people in place in enough time in Madrid to stop him later on. The delay had been enough for the irritated Spaniard to miss his connecting flight, much to the cheers within the Games Room, the Contestant's reaction captured in real time by the team of two Trackers that had followed him that far.

Images from the airport's own CCTV were also being fed into the Games Room, as Teo was taken to one side, his profile apparently randomly selected for a new high level security operation exercise now being run across the major airline carriers around Europe. His luggage was pulled from the outbound flight, meaning any chance of him being on a plane to Spain that evening were now finally over.

Teo, a flamboyant character known to friends as having a short fuse at the best of times, had vented his anger at more than one of the officials that were carrying out his search. It meant nothing that they were saying it was for his overall safety that such things were being implemented, and despite his many protests and their offers to be as quick as they could, there was little they could say to appease the man their system had flagged as the random search subject.

His name coming up, of course, was far from random. Teo's Host, referred to within the Games Room as Fourteen, was a man of intricate planning and with an extensive network of contacts and connections. He had been the one to get Teo's name put forward for the search, the delay ending that particular Hunt when he had already got so far. It had been a good showing, and Fourteen had come off well in it all, several oligarchs trading contracts he would now get to pick up. They hadn't known his connection to the infrastructure at that particular airport in Austria, one of his many companies being the firm behind the complete revamp the terminal had gone through the previous decade. Payments were still being made on that project, the construction company therefore taking out a stake in the newly formed business, giving Fourteen the connections there to be able to access, and influence, what went on within the airport. It had been the second time he'd used that particular connection to win a Hunt within the last two years, something he knew his fellow oligarchs would now become aware of.

No one missed a trick, constantly working to build an understanding of their fellow oligarchs, learning where their influences might lie, looking for ways in the future where they might be able to exploit them, holes in their connections that could leave them vulnerable to a defeat. With stakes so high, any weakness would be targeted by all the other oligarchs when it became that persons turn to Host an event.

∞∞∞

Annabel Herbertson touched down on the easyJet flight from Tallinn just before five that evening. The flight had been smooth, and she'd managed to sleep for a little over half an hour but the nearer they got to London's Gatwick airport, the more aware she became of the task before her. It should have been simple but knowing the traffic in her capital as she did, she wasn't too sure what might lie ahead.

She had her phone open and was calling a taxi before the plane had come to a stop, but no one had reprimanded her. With just hand luggage she was one of the first off the plane, having purchased herself one of the few remaining tickets for the slightly more expensive seats at the front of the aircraft. She ran most of the way to passport control, going through the e-gate where the queues were shortest, and was out through the front of the terminal just under twenty minutes after the plane doors were opened. The taxi was waiting for her as she got to the meeting point and she spotted the driver before he spotted her. She got in and closed the door and they pulled away as she searched for the address she needed, telling the driver a few moments later.

She'd given the man the address of the neighbouring building, a large office complex, stating she was in a hurry and would pay extra if he could get her there within about an hour. She didn't see the need to give him the actual address; the cab driver would be likely to put two and two together and work out what she was actually doing. No, assuming she was just a businesswoman running late for an important meeting was all he needed to believe. He would be paid well for getting her there, anyway, so that would be enough to keep him focused. She had two hours before the offices of the Euro Loto would close.

Traffic was what you might expect at that time, though the bulk of the flow was heading away from the city, only the short section of the London Orbital motorway, the M25, starting to slow a little, but after they turned off that a few junctions down, the roads were thankfully clear. He pulled up outside the office building just after six, which by anyone's reckoning, was very good going. She paid the driver, giving him an extra twenty pounds, and turned towards the building in front of her, the car pulling away. Once he'd disappeared in the taxi—no doubt happy with his last client—she headed towards the offices of the Euro Loto which was situated to the left of the office complex they'd stopped at.

Walking in through the main doors, she approached the clean and well presented reception area with confidence.

"I'd like to claim a winning ticket, please," she said quietly to the lady behind the desk, not wanting to draw any unwanted attention from the half dozen or so people that happened to be passing through the area at that moment. "It's urgent," she added, the receptionist telling her to take a seat, making a call immediately to the appropriate department, unfazed and used to that very situation. Two minutes later, a man and woman came across to greet Annabel, the woman speaking first; "I believe you have a claim to make. Please, come this way, madam."

∞∞∞∞

Alex and Anissa had spent several hours working through data, as well as through various coffee shops that occupied that part of St Petersburg. They had stayed away from the main tourist attractions, taking Sasha's warning about keeping a low profile while they were on their own. Whilst walking around a large park area they were talking through what they had come across, only speaking to each other when there was no one around them, not wanting to draw attention to the fact they were not locals, should anyone be paying them more than normal attention. Children played in a small play ground at the far side, mothers huddled around in small groups, a few dogs on leads. There was a pond in the centre of the park, ducks and various birds, as well as a large number of pigeons, making their presence felt.

A few of the benches were obviously occupied by the homeless, though these were away from all the other people, the two groups clearly knowing to avoid one another. Alex stopped talking as they passed another sleeping man, an empty vodka bottle visible and lying on the ground underneath the bench. They had been drawing up conclusions on what they'd been able to uncover that afternoon.

"These dates that Andre had left us," Alex continued, now they were out of earshot of the bench. "They almost certainly relate to previous events, similar to what we've just witnessed, happening here in St Petersburg. Only two of them had any sort of public claim happening within a day or so of the dates from the various lottery competitions I could find information on around Europe. But looking at a few more in detail, there are other undisclosed claimants all coming forward within a day or usually two of these dates, and each of these claims relates to—sometimes large—winning tickets that are about to expire."

"So that is why the dates that we had were so random, happening during the weekend or the week, and on various dates in the month, seemingly random. They were all based on when a ticket was about to expire?"

"Exactly—and here's the thing. These two tickets we know about today, the one in Spain and the one in the UK. Online it suggests that they have until tomorrow, in fact, to claim. They don't expire today, if the information is correct."

"But the events happened today and as far as we can tell, these people that we had the names for are the ones trying to claim the money—all doing so in a hurry today. That bit doesn't make sense."

"It does if you think it through this way," Alex said, now starting down another line of thought. "These oligarchs, they aren't stupid. They spend the time and money somehow getting hold of a winning lottery ticket. How they do that, we'll have to try and work out, but for now we can be safe in the knowledge that they are able to obtain genuine winning tickets. The value of the ticket depends on whatever particular lottery has a rollover. I guess the prize has to be big enough to make someone take the bait. How they get these people involved, again, remains a mystery, one I'd love to find out. But we've seen it for ourselves, somehow they get these people here and they set up an event. For the Russians—so the original rumours always went—they bet against each other in flamboyant shows of power and influence, mainly trading connections and business contracts, though money too, I expect, at times. Now, they do everything they can to stop the person, I'm sure. But even if they successfully stop them, the ticket is lost. That is unless they somehow alter the ticket, or something, or make the person believe they have one day to trade it in. Either way, there is actually a spare day, and I believe in most cases somehow these Russian men are able to claim the prize themselves, having no doubt paid out the face value of that ticket many months before. I think that's why these events happen when they do."

"So the Russians get close enough to be able to get the ticket back?"

"I assume they have these people closely watched. The fact is that after each of these ten dates Andre left us, along with the four names that now make a lot of sense, there was a significant claim made on one of the many lotteries available, most often by someone keeping their identity secret."

"Are we able to find out who the winners were?"

"It would be difficult, even if this was an official MI6 operation. We have no authority outside of the UK, anyway, and the majority of the winners are based on the continent, the Euro Loto by far the most common tickets used, as they carry a minimum €15 million prize per draw. There has been a recent prize draw of €163 million, following eleven consecutive draws without a winning combination, won by a solo ticket in Portugal. That was claimed within a few weeks, so we have to assume the Russians had nothing to do with that. The largest unclaimed amount in the UK was for £63.8 million—from just over four years ago."

"Does that date coincide with any that Andre sent us?"

"They don't go back that far. All the dates Andre mentioned happened within the last two years."

"Ten events in two years, so they are quite regular then?" Anissa said, making that connection for the first time.

"Yes, the longest gap being nearly three months. Therefore we can expect something similar to today to happen again here within a matter of weeks, maybe a couple of months. That's potentially five more times this year. We have to assume, now we are aware of it, that sooner or later, probably this year, we'll see something that gives us an entry point, a way of being on the inside, one step ahead of these men. Then we'll be in a position to know what we're up against, who is involved, and what that means for us all. We'll hopefully know any link that leads back to MI6, and therefore who we can trust."

"That's a long time for us to keep this under wraps."

They both kept silent for a little while, a few groups of parents and children now walking past them—the evening light fading fast around them—the children's playground now virtually empty. Alex's phone rang—it was Sasha.

"Yes?"

"I'm in the car on my way back from the border. I have Twila with me, will speak to you when I'm back in the city," and with that, he ended the call.

Alex told Anissa what had been said, the two a little surprised by Sasha's actions, but they assumed he knew what he was doing.

∞∞∞∞

The Games Room was now empty, the Chair following the oligarchs down the staircase, as everyone started to leave, some wanting to get back home that very night, others retiring to their guest accommodation upstairs. Usually it was those oligarchs that came out on top that stayed around for another night, the drink readily available, the mood celebratory.

Pulling the oligarch known as Fifteen to one side, the Chair had strong words to say:

"Your Contestant was found dead in an Irish pub the Trackers had followed him into. Hit his head on a sink whilst taking a piss. I sure as hell hope you had nothing to do with that?"

The oligarch, who detested being spoken to like that, following a day he'd rather forget about, remained silent, nonetheless. No one crossed the *Wolf* if they wanted to be invited back for future events.

"Make sure this doesn't come back to bite us. We can't allow any Host to overstep the mark like this. If news got out what was going on, we would all be in a difficult position. Have I made myself clear, Dmitry!" Use of an actual name was forbidden, but with no one else close enough to hear, and this coming from the Chair directly, he simply let it go.

"Agreed!" was all he replied, making his exit as quickly as he could.

The Chair also left, going to a nearby restaurant, where after having been busy for these last two days, husband and wife could be reunited. They ate dinner together that night, in one of the city's most exclusive eateries. As they were finishing, Arseni Markovic, oligarch and Host during the day's Hunt, a man known within the group as Eleven, walked out from another room in the restaurant, clearly finished for the night. He walked over to the couple, now back in the real world, where names meant a lot and being seen with the right people meant even more.

"Arseni, good to see you. This is my wife, Svetlana—I believe you've met before." Arseni took her hand, kissing it as was the right thing to do. Her husband, Sergej Volkov, was a very wealthy man, owning a number of oil wells in the centre of the country, as well as having connections into shipping and nuclear energy.

"A pleasure to see you again, Svetlana," Arseni said, leaving the two to finish their coffee, moving on and out of the restaurant.

"A useful young man, is Arseni Markovic," Sergej said to his wife.

They made a striking couple—he outspoken and a tough negotiator, she the essence of beauty and gentleness. Another example of the rich and wealthy mixing with the young and beautiful, a combination that went together surprisingly easily in the Mother Russia.

13

It was the following morning in St Petersburg, the city waking up to a little light drizzle mixed with sleet, the temperature a few degrees above zero. The two MI6 agents had enjoyed a decent breakfast eaten before most of the guests had emerged from their rooms, then packed away what items they had, returning the beds to where they had been during check-in. They didn't want the room being found as they'd changed it, in case it raised questions about the English couple travelling together but obviously sleeping separately.

Truth was, they were being overcautious, and the longer they remained in the city, the more paranoid they were becoming. They knew, out there somewhere, this machine existed, this organisation of very powerful men able to spit out anyone they chose.

They had decided late last night that the following day had better be their last in the city, though they planned to get as much time as possible with Sasha before boarding an evening flight to London. They would need the help of their FSB counterpart to make that departure safely.

Sasha had driven to meet them just after eight, picking them up from their now usual place just outside the hotel.

Expecting the traffic to be bad out front, the two British agents were surprised to see somewhat quiet streets, Sasha explaining to them once they asked him, that rush hour was around ten in the city, eight still being considered early morning. He was taking them about sixty minutes out of the city and to the east, which actually meant they were only then about a forty minute drive from the airport for their flight later.

Sasha had a dacha, a small home in the forest that many Russians had, though his was fairly new. Most people inherited the family dacha, passed on from generation to generation, often new sections being added throughout the years. The rich owned grand dachas, with five or six bedrooms, opulent second homes built in the best locations, with their own land and private lake. Most people, however, shared access to a lake, and many dachas were basically derelict, the owners too poor to do much about it.

Since most spent only the summers in the dacha, things like good insulation against the severe cold of winter was something they could do without. Only about half of the dachas in that region had their own toilet within the actual property, the others relying on an outdoor privy at the end of the garden, often attached to a banya, the Russian style sauna.

At only just over seventy kilometres from where he lived in St Petersburg, Sasha's dacha would be classed as very near, and easily accessible. He'd purchased it five years previously, tearing down what had been there, the land plentiful and with good access to a lake, which he could walk to in just five minutes.

An orphan, he had never known his parents, nor could he have inherited any family property through the generations, as they had lived in state owned communal flats. He'd made a fresh start, therefore, and had grown into a very professional person. Unmarried, there had been a few women through the last ten years but for various reasons none had ever worked out, often breaking down over work related issues in the end.

It meant that, just after nine as he pulled his Mercedes down the small dirt track, the snow basically gone and the ground still hard enough to allow easy passage, no one was around to see him or his guests. With winter not yet over, none of the other dachas would have any residents in, the ones nearest to his being quite poor, broken down dwellings.

Opening the front door to his dacha, the three walked into what was one of two medium sized rooms downstairs, with a small sleeping area up a wooden ladder above them. The smell of cut wood, coupled with the mustiness of an empty property, clung to the fabric around them, but it wasn't unpleasant. Sasha switched on the two electric heaters that were attached to the walls, before going over to prepare a fire, logs piled to one side of an open fireplace, the chimney going up through the centre of the building, allowing the fire to heat most of the dacha.

Three minutes later there was a pot of water gently boiling above the now burning fire, five large logs placed carefully by the Russian, as he then went to prepare a few clean cups for tea.

"I've got nothing in the way of food, I'm afraid, folks, just some tea," he said, it being unheard of for any Russian to drink tea without a biscuit or slice of cake. The two Brits, still full from breakfast, hadn't thought anything of it.

When the tea was ready, with three cups set before them and a pot warming gently near to the now blazing fire, they sat around the small lounge, in three chairs. Anissa took in her surroundings, loving every minute, the place reminding her of various cabins she'd holidayed in with her husband and two children down the years. That thought reminded her just how much she was missing them all right now, situated as she was in the middle of nowhere, in a country she still didn't understand. Sasha was running through everything once more regarding his time with Twila, as Alex had been asking about her ever since they had arrived.

"However they did it, there was no sign of anything on her. She denied any knowledge of anything like that, too, once I'd asked her outright about the lottery ticket—she didn't even flinch. She'd just said she was travelling to Helsinki as she wanted to see the city for a day before coming back to St Petersburg. Not that she would have been able to do that, as her visa only allowed a single entry into Russia, which she had of course already used. I didn't bother to point that out to her, nor could we actually prove that what she was suggesting regarding visiting Helsinki for just a day wasn't in fact the case. I had to let her go, what more could I do?"

"Won't it raise questions about why you went all that way to pick her up in the first place?"

"Hardly, and besides, these things happen all the time. I don't think the oligarchs involved in this thing you are investigating have any further interest in her now, anyway. What is it you say they call this event?"

"We use the words *the Games* which if I'm not mistaken is *Igrii* in Russian," Alex said.

"Correct, though I'll forgive your pronunciation," Sasha laughed.

"Well, we'll now share the little we've managed to find out while you pour us some more tea," Anissa said.

Sasha stood up to get the teapot and remarked, "Sorry that I don't have any milk to go with your tea, we don't drink tea with milk in Russia."

"So we've gathered," Alex smiled.

"Annabel Herbertson, one of the four names on the list and recent visitor to St Petersburg, yesterday claimed a winning Euro Loto ticket in London worth €15 million." Anissa let that statement sink in for a moment.

"So she made it back in time," Sasha acknowledged, tea now served to his two guests, and he went to top up the pot with some more boiling water, adding another log to the fire in the process. "What about the Spaniard?"

"We traced him to a flight changing in Vienna. A delay of some sort meant he missed any connection that would have possibly got him to Spain before last night. Last we heard he had made a flight out of there in the early hours, too late for it to be of any value to him."

"He's still worth a visit, no? Maybe he knows something the others don't?"

"It's possible, though a little outside our jurisdiction."

"Says the two people sitting in my dacha in Russia, without the knowledge of either of our nations' security services!"

"Good point," Anissa said, warming more and more to this unusual Russian they'd been getting to know these last two days.

Just then an SMS notification came through on Sasha's phone, which he picked up and read aloud in Russian, before repeating it in English, the confused looks on his guests' faces reminding him they didn't understand a word the first time around.

"It's a notification from the Mariinsky Hospital in the centre of the city. An Irishman, named Dubhán Maguire, was brought in late yesterday evening, dead. Report suggests he slipped and fell, hitting his head hard in the process." He looked down from his handset, adding; "I got this because I'd put a flash alert out for his passport at all check points. His passport must have been on him, so we can assume this wasn't a robbery."

"Can we assume it was an accident?"

"I guess we can't rule anything out, though there is no report of anyone within the police or my lot taking this up as anything but. If there would have been, I'd have found out before now."

They sat there in silence for a moment, aside the sounds of the fire next to them that had warmed up the whole place rather nicely already. Anissa nursed her cup of tea, blowing the hot liquid a little each time before taking another small sip.

"So we have four random people suddenly flying to St Petersburg to take part in something known as the Games. One gets detained at the border crossing with Finland, for no obvious reason, one delayed overnight travelling back days earlier than planned heading to Spain, and one now dead and lying in a morgue, not to mention the one that suddenly turns up in London, the winner of a Euro Loto draw made nearly six months ago, now €15 million richer for it."

"Sasha, maybe you can run through anything you've managed to find regarding FSB files held on any of the richest men in the country," Alex said, looking up now at the Russian, who'd just gone to pour the boiling water into the empty tea pot.

Sasha pulled some information from his bag, before sitting down again, dropping photocopied lists of names and various details on the table in front of them, as he started speaking.

"I started with men sharing the first name Dmitry, which is the name you said your contact mentioned. We have several rich people with that name, besides our previous president." Alex and Anissa picked up a copy of what Sasha was referring to, several names jumping out at them as Sasha read from the same sheet.

"Dmitry Petrov, probably the tenth richest Russian alive. Hugely influential in Moscow, has several people he funds in the State Duma. Made his money during the break up of the Soviet Union, mainly through oil. The next wealthiest man with that name is Sokoloff, about the twentieth richest man in Russia. Owns one of the state television companies, newspapers, online media and a bunch of similar stuff. Purchased one of the biggest internet providers last year, net worth around $2.2 billion, if you believe the hype. Next on the list is Dmitry Kaminski, worth about $2 billion and owner of most of the financial institutions in Moscow. Also has key connections with the Kremlin and is, understandably, seen as the rising star within powerful circles. He has aspirations of a life in politics in the near future, or so the rumours go. Finally, the only other Dmitry of note I found would be Pavlov, who happens to be the great grandson of the famous scientist Ivan Pavlov. His company was handed three nuclear plants that were deemed *underperforming* in the last years of Yeltsin, which Pavlov managed to turn around overnight, amassing a fortune estimated at just under $1.1 billion in the most recent Forbes rich list."

The information in front of them was further than Alex had managed himself, and for that he was pleased. Listed next to each name, as well as a few other names that were also listed in this section, was anyone linked to any criminal case that the FSB might have been involved with over the last decade or so. Only Dmitry Sokoloff, the media magnate and owner of the country's fastest broadband provider, had any dealings with the FSB, and usually on the receiving end of various law suits that had been filed over the years against his various media outlets.

"There's a shadow around Sokoloff, for sure. He has a lot of influence through the main news channel. Putin himself is a weekly guest on one of his news shows there, and therefore we've been keeping a close eye on the involvement of its owner. Nothing has been proven so far, and these questions have largely been laid to rest. Still, he remains powerful and therefore we need to show caution around him."

"So there's nothing linking these others to anything criminal?" Alex said.

"None of the other Dmitrys, no."

"And these other names?" Anissa added, digesting as best she could the information and numbers displayed in front of her.

"These are other rich and influential people that have crossed paths with my employers over the years, not always on good terms. Sergej Volkov, for example, spent five years in prison for crimes against the State before being released, all charges dropped following a presidential pardon."

"Putin?"

"No, actually, his current predecessor, Medvedev, in the four years he was President between the Putin reigns. Still, Putin held great power during that time and it was always known he'd return to power, though we can't say whether he had a hand in Volkov's release, or not. The family name means *wolf*, and he has certainly seemed to live up to that image at times, though he's recently been a lot quieter, especially since his release from prison.

"Married to a popular Russian actress, Sergej and Svetlana Volkov now spend their time between Moscow and St Petersburg, though they travel extensively throughout the world as well. They own a number of travel firms, a bank, a car manufacturer, as well as being involved in shipping, oil and the nuclear industry. They say the day he married Svetlana, his net worth doubled—not really because of her wealth, though she wasn't poor, but because of the positive image it gave his empire, a personal endorsement of the highest order. And that coming two years after a full Presidential pardon. He's certainly got someone watching out for him, that's for sure."

The two British agents scanned the list of names, none of them meaning much to either of them. They'd come across the few high profile Russians that now lived and owned much of London, but these names were nowhere to be seen on the information Sasha had provided them. They would digest it all properly at another time, maybe once they were back in London.

For now, they were content to talk more with Sasha, finding out what connections he knew, discussing what to do next and planning some sort of joint action, whilst keeping it all off the radar of either of their employers. Sasha had the most to lose, as they were all well aware. Sasha was a valuable asset, far too valuable for them to risk losing him, which would be inevitable if anyone within the FSB were to know what their agent was getting up to.

They spent the rest of the morning walking around the land surrounding the dacha, a pot of tea never too far away. Food was prepared for lunch over the fire, chunks of meat which Sasha had gone out to buy from the nearest shop. He had taken them from the plastic bucket they came in, skewered them onto metal spikes and left them to cook thoroughly over the burning logs. It had tasted good.

They'd declined the suggestion of heating up the banya, Anissa not really into too much heat and besides, as the afternoon moved on, the need to start thinking about heading to the airport became more of an issue. They finally set out rather later than either Alex or Anissa were happy with, but they were unaware of how close the airport was to the dacha, and they still arrived at the airport in enough time. Sasha saw them through security, reentering the airport through no doubt the same labyrinth of doors and rooms Sasha had used when they first arrived. Just as it had been then, no one was visible, Sasha's FSB authority and rank clearly enough to make anyone who might have been there suddenly scarce. It worked, and the two MI6 agents were the last to board the British Airways flight to London's Heathrow Airport, taking their seats in Business Class before the doors were locked, and the plane started to make its approach to the runway for take off.

Lifting up through the sky five minutes later, Alex looked down at the trees and houses that made up the countryside around the airport, the edges of the city visible from there too, with their high rise blocks of flats. It was a three hour flight to London, both agents taking the drinks when they were offered, and trying to catch a little rest, everything that they'd done that day now taking its toll on them both.

14

Dmitry Kaminski left his office in the centre of Moscow, just a three minute drive from the Kremlin. The historic Red Square sat between the two places where he spent most of his time—and where most of his influence lay. He was due to meet with a group of politicians in twenty minutes, having left a business meeting with various of his company executives early in order to make a short stop off en route. A three minute drive was near enough to walk, though few of Moscow's elite ever did that, the streets not being as safe as maybe they once were. Besides, today he needed to meet with someone from his team, a man few others knew about.

Pulling over at the agreed meeting point, away from any obvious watching eyes—he'd been careful about checking that out years earlier when these meetings had first been necessary—he stepped out of his car. Moments later he was approached by the person he was waiting to meet with. The man handed Dmitry a portfolio, leather bound as always, containing three individual pages on detailed information.

"So, who do you have for me this time?" he asked his chief Spotter, flicking briefly through the sheets, but expecting to be told the key information right away.

"Martín Torres, fifty-three and a Spanish national, currently residing in London. Fits the profile in every area you were after, scoring highly in the areas we've especially been seeking. The enclosed report will detail this for you." Dmitry would look at that later, and closed the portfolio as his employee continued to brief him. "The documentation is being prepared, we'll proceed to stage one within the next month and have him primed for whenever you deem necessary, sir." Stage one was the first of two processes the Spotters went through, at the orders of their Host, to fully entice a would-be Contestant into entering their world.

It required the right type of incentive—for some, that was just money, or the thought of getting more money. They could be blatant with these types of people. Others required a little more subtlety, the sense of greater power, connections or influence enough to edge these people into the trap. For others it was often another angle, never anything noble, still always some basic, primeval greed that needed exposing—lust, envy, pride. If they had an angle to exploit, the Hosts would do so, as they were desperate to get a Contestant worthy of their Hunt, someone that would divide the room of oligarchs, making it hard to know which way to bet. In those rare situations, the wins could be huge, especially when you controlled the Hunt. Have enough people betting against you, you could pull out all the stops and shut down the Hunt as quickly as possible. If enough people were betting with you, then it might be worth sabotaging your own Hunt in order to win a greater good, swallowing your own pride in defeat, aiming to get it all back in what was nicknamed *the after party*—where any losing Host would do everything they could, usually within the law, to get back every ruble they had lost.

"Very good. The stakes will be high for this one, so we have to be on our game. No mistakes," Dmitry said, turning away from his man and returning to the car with the portfolio safely placed into his own personal briefcase. He switched on the engine, pulling back out from the small, hidden side street, and five minutes later was cleared through the front gate into the Kremlin, an afternoon of meetings ahead of him.

In Kiev, Ukraine, Rurik Sewick, known widely as *Mr Grey*, was relaxing at home. A member of the newly formed Ukrainian parliament, he'd spent years in politics. A wealthy man through his life, he'd funded his own failed run for President three elections ago, from his own reserves. Whilst failing to get enough backing in that election, finishing a very respectable second place in the final result, twelve percent behind the eventual winner in the vote count, he had not bothered to run in the following two elections, though his influence had grown hugely and had he run for the Ukrainian Presidency the last time, he would surely have won it easily.

Life had changed a lot in his country over the previous decade, and his connections with Russia, besides his business life, made it a hard position to be in for him at times. He'd opted out of running for President because of this, and whilst Ukrainian to the bone, he did move in circles that included many of the richest men in Russia.

Youthful for a man in his sixties, *Mr Grey*—a translation from Ukrainian of his surname—had nevertheless embraced his premature silvering by dying his hair twenty years prior. The nickname had become his image to both acquaintances and the media; only in political circles was his original name used. Elsewhere, he was this character of intrigue and influence.

Sitting in his drawing room, dressing gown still on, his maid came in to inform him that his visitor had arrived, a man appearing behind her as she spoke. Mr Grey indicated to the man to come in and the maid closed the door behind her as she left, leaving the two to discuss whatever they had to discuss. She always made a point of keeping her nose out of things when it involved her employer, sure that she wouldn't like what she might otherwise find out, which would put her in a position she didn't want to be in. She needed the money more than a clear conscience.

"Come, sit down," Mr Grey said, the man coming forward, leather bound portfolio in hand, which he handed to his boss. Rurik took some moments to go through the few sheets that were included, the room in silence as he read, his guest saying nothing, sitting there and waiting for his employer to finish reading what he needed to read.

"Very good. So, what makes this one, this Ms Patrícia Simones, my ideal Contestant, someone I could risk millions of euros on and sleep well at the end of it all?" It was a question he always asked, wanting to know more than just bare facts, as helpful as that was to him. He wanted to know what made this Portuguese lady tick, what made someone in her late twenties suitable enough to be considered in the first place, aside just the desire for money.

"Besides the criminal background, which we've detailed for you, there is a rugged determination about her, a feistiness that won't let things go. She's open to make a quick buck, like they mostly are, but will dig deeper if the reward is sufficient. We believe she's behind a number of long cons that have plagued many in Porto over the last few years, no one has ever been arrested for these crimes."

Rurik stood up, pacing over to the window. He'd come across similar Contestants in the past, and other oligarchs had certainly used former criminals in their portfolio, but he'd been less than sure. Someone with too many of the wrong connections could become a liability. Should they actually take the money, they were more likely to move it on or involve people that would make getting it all back that much more messy. It was a risk, for sure. But as the Romans knew, the greater the fight, the greater the gladiator that was needed.

"Fine," he said, turning from the window, his Spotter standing up as he was being addressed, "get stage one underway with her, and let me know what happens. If she proves worthwhile after that is done, I'll consider taking her. Keep me updated."

"Yes, sir," he said, turning and leaving the room.

∞∞∞

Rurik downed the last of his coffee, leaving through another door, which took him into his own private wing of the house, where he showered, dressed and prepared himself for the day ahead.

Motya Utkin's private jet touched down in Geneva, Switzerland, just before noon that same day. He'd been handed a portfolio by his Spotter, and whilst officially in the Swiss city on business, always made a point of personally watching the people his team were bringing to his attention. Roger Roche, a forty-year old Swiss national with Italian/French parents, had lived in and around Geneva all his life, speaking three languages fluently and comfortable in another three as well. Motya had read with interest the information presented to him by his team, a group of people he valued highly, and they'd never let him down. He now rarely questioned their selections, his visits to see the Contestants in the flesh done for purely personal reasons.

For him, there was nothing like getting a feel for a person by watching them when they weren't aware. That way he could begin to understand them, and if that was achieved, he'd be better able to react to their actions in a real time Hunt scenario, second guessing their next move, in order to stay in control. He'd never lost a Hunt yet, and he knew that was largely down to the selection of the right kind of Contestant, which was totally the work of his team. He also knew that understanding their behaviour was vital and he felt he was better than most at being able to read a person just by observing them. He now always travelled to wherever was required in order to watch his future Contestant.

Motya's money came from gambling and strip clubs. When Russia had made it illegal to have casinos just anywhere, a law he'd been central to help implement, it closed down most of the competition overnight, and left his perfectly placed businesses to pick up the slack. Rich before that change in legislation was ever ratified in the Duma, the move doubled his net worth within three years, and his empire grew massively, moving into a number of other new avenues, too. He was worth just short of $1 billion, and mixed with Russia's elite as a result. His entry into the Games had only helped him elevate his influence to another level. He was a popular Host, with the only one hundred per cent record across either group. He wasn't about to let that particular record end easily, in what would be his tenth event as a Host.

Motya Utkin, known within the Games circle simply as Seventeen, sat down in a restaurant, one of the most exclusive places in Geneva in the most expensive part of the city. The waiter who'd shown him to his table, now came back with the menu and a bottle of wine, usual compliments of the restaurant.

"I am Roger Roche," he said, in perfect English, "and I will be serving you today, sir. Let me know if there is anything you need me to do for you to make your lunch with us all it should be. May I recommend today's specials, which are listed for you here," and he pointed to the part of the menu which was updated daily. "I've personally tasted them all and can therefore attest to their quality."

∞∞∞∞

Twenty minutes later, the main course just arriving, Motya already had a good insight into the man he'd come to study, watching him constantly in his peripheral vision, catching every syllable, the way he greeted his guests, everything about the man Motya knew would make a fine Contestant one day.

Just over four-hundred and fifty miles north west of Geneva, two men were travelling through the Paris metro, watching Matthieu Dubois, a French national with Belgian heritage. He had recently been discharged from the army— reason unknown—and was currently jobless, a situation affecting many former servicemen in his position, a large influx of foreign nationals not helping the issue, nor the stability of a city on the brink of violence. A hard man throughout his life, the army had given him ample opportunity to exert that energy, while building in him the ability to focus those feelings, which in his early adult life, had been his downfall too often.

Once off the train, not realising he was being followed, Matthieu walked through a park in the centre of the city, the only part of Paris Parisians really counted as meaning you actually lived in the capital. The two Russians made a video call to their employer, Stanislav Krupin, connecting almost immediately—he'd been waiting for the call.

Stanislav, known as Twenty when it came to the group of people he was hanging onto the edges of, was worth $500 million, rich by most standards but the poorest Host in that rich group of friends. He was also the most connected to the street, his organisation of criminal gangs and mafia personnel effectively policing most of the Moscow streets—his men moving into St Petersburg three years ago, a turf battle underway for control of that city, a dozen dead so far in an as yet undecided contest.

Stanislav liked his Contestants to be as he himself was; tough, hard and willing to do anything to escape. He viewed them as equals until he could prove them otherwise, delighting in finally breaking them, taking more enjoyment than most did, though he wouldn't ever let that show. He intended on making real progress with his next Hunt, the chance to Host coming around not that often, and less so it seemed for him than others, this being his fifth time. In his last attempt one of the

Contestants had even managed to beat him. What he'd done to destroy the victor, which ended in two suicides, including that of the Contestant who'd managed to get the better of him in the original Hunt, had pulled Stanislav into conflict with the Chair. His place in proceedings was almost ended on the spot, until another oligarch had come to his rescue. Stanislav didn't understand the reasons for this move, unclear whether it had been a sign of weakness in a fellow oligarch, or if there was something else going on. Maybe they just needed to buy his silence, to keep him happy by not evicting him? If he was still involved in things, he'd have nothing to say to anyone else. Eject him from proceedings, and maybe he'd talk to the wrong people, sounding off his feelings, exposing to the world what these other, very secretive men in this regard, were doing.

Whatever their reasons, and Stanislav didn't really give it too much thought, he was glad to still be involved, and had only cleaned up his act as much as the others could see. What went on behind the scenes was up to him, and he used every piece of information he could to control, threaten and weaken his opponents, bringing in thugs to carry out retribution when it was needed.

They chatted on the phone for a few minutes, the video feed then trained on their man—on this disconnected Frenchman as he walked through a park in the city of his birth—with hardly a euro to his name, despite serving his country proudly for nearly six years.

"Perfect," the Russian said after watching for a couple of minutes. "Start stage one and keep me informed. I don't think you'll have too many problems with this one, given what you've told me about him." He ended the call, leaving his men in Paris to do their thing. That would result in this man—this Contestant—at a later point boarding a flight to St Petersburg voluntarily. He would already be convinced by that point that he was walking into something special. How that was communicated varied—it was rarely the same thing twice. The ticket was almost never mentioned; the first any Contestant would know about it was the appearance of a note, usually slid underneath their hotel door once they were already in the city.

In his offices in Moscow, Stanislav knew he had another Contestant, another person ready for when the dice would get thrown once again, and where luck could work just as easily in your favour as it did against you. In Matthieu Dubois, Stanislav knew he had a man who would use skills learned in combat to get himself out of a tight situation. He knew this was a man who had clearly crossed the line many times, the gap between right and wrong blurred by years of moving between the two. Most of all, Stanislav knew he had a man just like him—therefore, a worthy opponent.

15

It was now April, spring was in full blossom across much of the UK, only the most northern parts were holding onto the cold and occasional snows of winter. Alex and Anissa, working together on a range of unconnected cases for MI6, had been keeping a close eye on things in Russia whilst not being able to get anywhere with regard to a clear breakthrough. Keeping everything off the radar from those within their own security service also didn't help and risked wrecking their entire futures should it become known what they were actually involved in.

When they'd arrived back from that first trip to St Petersburg, there had been some hope. Anissa went straight into things in the office and her absence was not questioned by anyone, to her delight—she was a terrible liar. Alex was still not due back from annual leave for another few days so he'd taken that time, mainly resting, away from everyone. Whilst his plans for seven nights in the middle of nowhere had been originally cut short, the chance of a few nights doing nothing in particular was certainly not to be missed.

He managed just over twenty-four hours, the bloodhound in him opening up his laptop and using the free time he had left to read up as much as he could on the Russians Sasha had highlighted, as well as anything else he could find that was related to his investigation. Over the coming weeks he would remain in contact with Sasha, albeit covertly, asking him to probe certain areas that otherwise might be off limits for them at that moment.

Globally, the spotlight was moving away from Russia and onto more critical issues, which meant over the weeks that followed, Alex and Anissa were pulled in multiple directions, though between them they kept a close eye on their Russian based sideshow.

The Irishman, Dubhán, had been flown back to Dublin a few days after he died, his family contacted, arrangements being made between the various authorities, the death put down to a tragic accident, with excess alcohol consumption noted as a key factor. There were no criminal investigations taking place in either country, the Russians happy with what they'd decided upon from the initial investigation, the Irish with no reason to suspect anything.

Alex had noted, in a newspaper that had been published by Dublin's Evening Herald, that the family had no idea why he was going to Russia, besides the fact he'd told them two days before leaving that he just needed some time away, and felt somewhere like Russia offered just that. The interview had been published three days after the funeral. Nothing more was said, or if it had been, Alex hadn't been able to find any evidence of it.

Twila had returned to Leeds, getting on with her life, though she resigned from her job at the fitness centre exactly seven weeks after arriving home from Russia. No reason was given to her employers at the time, other than she had just wanted a fresh start. Anissa had made a visit herself, dropping into the gym whilst passing through the area on a family weekend away, her husband aware and supportive of her on-going investigation. They'd not been able to get anywhere directly with Twila herself. Alex had sent someone to enquire and Twila had threatened to report them to the police should she see or hear from them ever again. Alex couldn't risk anything going on the record about her, still unsure as to who or what might be watching her. They let it drop. If she was likely to have said anything, surely she would have done so right back in St Petersburg when Sasha had picked her up after her arrest at the border. The thought that she *had* said something during her time with the FSB agent but Sasha had chosen not to tell them, for whatever reason, was something that crossed Alex's mind at first. He dismissed the notion as unlikely, however, given the way Sasha had helped them so much in St Petersburg in the first place.

In Spain, with the limited connections Alex and Anissa had on their own, it seemed Teo Vela had largely dropped off the radar. Little more was known about him. He'd been reported around his home town in the days immediately after his arrival back from St Petersburg, but nothing had been seen or heard from him since then.

Annabel Herbertson, on the other hand, was another story entirely. She'd gone public and had been very much in the news since announcing her late win but no clear answer was ever given to the many questions that circled around why she'd left it so late to claim—working two jobs at the time and living in rented housing—when she had millions of pounds waiting for her. She'd moved house twice, the first move within days of arriving back in London, taking her son out of his school and taking a home, still rented, in a more expensive part of the city, whilst she worked through her next steps.

Once more the papers tracked her, letters then started arriving, pleading for some of her money, pulling at her heart strings. The second move took her off the grid entirely, though Alex had been able to track that one, too, to a country house in Surrey. A court order had been secured to stop any newspaper publishing anything at all about her, or where she now lived, if they ever tracked her down. Her face had been splashed across many front pages, it had been a big story when it broke.

She knew it wouldn't be long before people in her new setting started to work out who she was, but in an area of wealthy people, most of them city workers on huge salaries, they would want to keep things as quiet as possible for their own sakes, most probably resenting her arrival and any disruption it might bring. Plus, she was a working class woman who'd come into more money than she clearly knew what to do with. She was not a fit for the area she now called home, and they all knew it. She was therefore left to herself.

By the April it was all over for her. Payments she'd promised never made it to various parties and the bailiffs were called in; stocks and investments—mainly in Russian companies expected to be the next big thing, or so she'd been advised—suddenly collapsed, overnight it seemed. Her financial advisor vanished into thin air. She was declared bankrupt just sixty-three days after arriving back on British soil with the lottery ticket. It was a new record within the Games, beating the previous best effort by well over five weeks.

Osip Yakovlev, known within the group as Nineteen, the Host and recruiter of Annabel in the first place, had come out top once more, saving face and what pride he had left, though the manner of his victory might do more for him in the long run than if he had not lost in the first place. He'd been pulling strings since the moment she landed at Gatwick, aware then that she was most certainly going to claim his €15 million prize herself. He had a good idea what her next moves would be, and had driven the press to her door, as well as the money chasers, in order to keep her moving. He'd supplied her with the financial advisor, a man who'd made her several small gains initially, sucking her in so that she would entrust everything she had to him. He'd said she could be set up for life, and she'd believed him. She was desperate to give her son a future he could build on.

Her collapse, sudden and dramatic when it came, was something of a surprise even to Osip, a man who wouldn't knowingly cross the line. The share money that had been invested was for shadow companies his group owned, the money buying back bad debt so he was paid off and did well out of it. He entered the second week of April a very contented man, able to hold his head high among his peers the next time they were to meet, which was within a month. Their events always coincided closely with various national holidays. Victory Day, celebrated on May 9th in Russia, was very much one such day. The biggest was always New Year, the highlight and culmination of the year. To get the honour to Host a Hunt for that event was purely at the Chair's invitation. It was possible that in May, the Hosts for that December event would be announced.

∞∞∞

Alex and Anissa had grabbed lunch together during that week in April. Another MI6 agent joined them, and whilst they did not tell him exactly why they were asking him the questions, they were glad of his input.

Charlie Boon, the agent in question, had a long history with Russia and would usually have been contact man for MI6 for anything Russia related. He spoke the language himself and had served in St Petersburg also, though entering Russia for him at the moment was not possible. The dust had not yet settled on a situation that left one female FSB agent dead and Charlie, her former boyfriend and currently a British agent, was still reeling. He was also under light surveillance within MI6, following his pursuit of those ultimately responsible for the murder.

Charlie had warned them about Russia, how the power flows, how the minds work. He had mentioned, and spoken well of Sasha, which pleased them both. They'd come to think the same of this unusually helpful FSB agent, though they couldn't let on to the fact. Neither Alex nor Anissa wanted to involve any more people from their world at Six than they currently did, for everyone's protection. They parted company, Charlie heading back out of the restaurant, the two partners chatting over coffee, working through their next options. Fitting everything around a busy working life was not always easy, and Alex could see that because Anissa had a family to think of as well, it was doubly difficult for her, juggling everything as she clearly needed to, but doing it in a way that just got on with it. He respected her highly for that, and envied her enormously. She seemed to have everything he didn't, but he didn't begrudge her one bit of it, he admired her. It only brought into focus his own shortcomings in that regard, his often childish behaviour that had driven women away, so that now all he had was his work.

It was that same afternoon when the only other person that knew what they were up to, the same technician within MI6 who had shared the report from Andre with Alex in the first place, contacted Alex with news about Annabel's bankruptcy.

"My goodness," Alex said, going on to tell Anissa what he had just heard.

"That's terrible, the poor lady. She has a young son, too."

"Do you think she'll speak with us now? I mean, if this was not her doing, if she's been cheated of this money by the Russians, maybe she'll be happy to turn on them, to talk to us?"

"To what purpose? There would be nothing in it for her, the money's gone."

"It might be more than that for her, now. She's lost everything."

"I don't know. Let's not do anything yet about that one until we've heard a little more. I don't want her running to the police the minute we show up. We've worked hard to keep this from anyone who might be working for the Russians. We are no nearer to getting on the inside, but we are seeing more aspects of their activities all the time, more evidence of this organisation's existence."

"If we can really call it an organisation," Alex added. "All we have is the name Igrii which they go by. We've seen that they obviously hand pick the people they want to use within the process. We know nothing as to why or how they do this. We have a first name for one of these people, we presume—this from a man that has since not been heard of for over four months. We've been on the edges of an actual event, people really finding winning lottery tickets somewhere around the city in St Petersburg, genuinely making a run for it, trying to get back in time to claim for them a small fortune. And now we've seen the apparent lengths that these oligarchs will go to in order to get back their money, if they have lost it."

"We have no proof that this was actually the case, though, Alex."

"No, but we'll find it. No one burns €15 million in just two months and is then left with not a cent to their name. No one can be that naive to waste it all so quickly."

"You're probably right, I just don't want us seeing everything one way when it can't all be them."

"Until we know what it all means, I'm going to assume the worst. You must feel that, too? It's why we've not told anyone else about this whole investigation."

"That'll have to change at some point, Alex."

"Why do you say that? We would risk everything if word got out, we'd be finished for sure."

"I don't mean we bring everyone in, but as we are, we haven't the resources or the information we need. We need to be using the database at HQ, for example, more than we can at the moment. We need to be using the skills within that whole department to make links that we haven't been able to find. Join the dots that we've missed because we've been too close to it all. We'll have to bring someone in, a team of people who can run data for us. Otherwise we will always be following this from behind, aware of what's going on only because it's already happened—behind, never ahead of the events."

"I might have an idea that could help."

"Go on, I'm listening."

"You know how you are always saying we should be doing a little more to help out within the service. Let's volunteer to run security for the forthcoming business conference in London."

Anissa smiled as Alex said that, not least because he'd always hated doing the extra stuff, which was tedious at the best of times and fell, he always said, way outside the job description of a real agent of Her Majesty.

"You mean the meeting of the owners of the UK's top one hundred traded companies on the London stock exchange, a group that includes at least twenty Russian multi millionaires, several of whose names appeared on Sasha's information?" She knew this was exactly what Alex meant, who just smiled in a very smug way, the only answer he needed to give. "I think that would work very well. It'd give us legitimate access to run our own background checks on all one hundred attendees. We can pull in additional resources to run those checks, going deeper on certain people. We could also then meet these people face to face at the event itself."

"Oh, Anissa, I think you just might be spot on with that last comment. Nothing like looking a man in the face, locking eyes together and delving into someone's soul to really understand who a person is. I'll make the suggestion straight away. Might win me a few brownie points, too, in the process. You know my reputation with regard to these sort of mundane jobs."

"You are famous for it, Alex, I can assure you."

They both laughed at that thought, Alex picking up his phone and calling the office. Five minutes later it was done. To be able to have two senior MI6 agents personally assessing the security angle for an upcoming conference of key business figures, was no small thing. Whilst some were surprised to hear the news, few would voice anything but support for the idea. The conference was two weeks away, both agents heading to the office, a lot of work before them both.

16

It was a wet day in London, the winds picking up from the west, the tail ends of a strong weather system that had been sweeping up from the Caribbean the week before. Phelan McDermott lived with his wife and three children, the oldest of whom was nearly ten.

Born in Ireland, growing up on the edges of Cork, he'd travelled to the UK for university and after meeting the woman that was now his wife of eleven years, had never really gone back, besides the occasional Christmas and twice for a family wedding.

They lived a modest life, their three bedroomed mid-terrace house often feeling a little squashed, especially when family were visiting them, and certainly since the latest McDermott popped out, the pregnancy having been somewhat of a surprise at the time. They weren't able to move, their home in negative equity. They got stung, badly, during the economic crisis from a few years before, and were slowly working to turn around their fortunes.

Outside, in a blacked out transit van, three men and one woman were sitting listening in, a series of bugs and a few miniature cameras fitted inside the Irishman's home two weeks before. The team worked for Dmitry Sokoloff, a man known as Twelve within the secretive community that existed among the group of Russians that made up the Hosts for the Games. They'd sourced Phelan from a number of potential candidates, a very interesting potential Contestant, a man clearly living well below his capabilities, if the reports were to be believed.

A graduate of Oxford, one of only a handful of Irishmen from his year who got into that prestigious university, where after three years of diligent study, he graduated with First-class honours, the highest scoring student in his subject. He married young, the wedding to a local girl and fellow student of Oxford happening just three weeks after he received his results. Phelan's new wife was in the year below him so she completed her final year and then they went travelling in their second year of marriage. Their first child was born at the end of that second year, the pregnancy occurring during their travels and shortening their trip by a few weeks. After months on the road, which had concerned her parents, they were happy to settle back down into something of a normal life once more in the Oxford area.

Five years passed, Phelan worked on a doctorate and impressed his supervisors so much that he was offered a post-doctoral research post, a rare opportunity. Meanwhile, during those five years back in Oxford, his wife took care of their child at home, a second boy being born two years after the first. Life was good for them.

Then they suddenly moved away from Oxford, travelling a while before settling a little closer to London, in the home they still lived in. He'd given up his academic post, taking an office job within a large firm in London, much to the surprise and concern of many at the time, though the pay was good. Over the years he'd been working there, he had made progress within the firm, travelling a little more with his own team to manage and even his own secretary to organise his diary. It was a dramatic change from his research post he'd held in Oxford, a career that offered a high level of prestige compared to what he was now doing.

His wife had never questioned what her husband wanted to do, as she loved him dearly and was happy to go along with whatever he wanted. She worked part time with an online publication firm, putting her skills to good use, so as long as she had space for a desk to work from, she didn't mind where she lived. Her parents, still living in Oxford weren't too far away for them to come and visit them in their new home. She never passed on their concerns about why their son-in-law had seemingly made such a big step down when everyone else was seeing so much potential for his future.

Breakfast times were always noisy, the youngest now going through potty training, a process that had proved stressful with the first two, and was proving the same this time, too.

Outside, in the van, the four person team lowered the volume a little, a video feed picking up a visual display from the dining room. There was another camera in the lounge, which just showed the family pet, a cat, sleeping on the rug in the middle of the room. As well as the audio mikes in the same two rooms, they had two others upstairs, including the main bedroom. There was also a mike in his office, though so far he'd never actually held a meeting within his own four walls of his working environment, instead meeting people around a canteen table, or nearby café. He was an extremely sociable person, and for his part, seemed to be well liked and popular.

The Russians had certainly picked up a sense from the office crowd that a number of the female staff thought of him as a rather handsome fella—the talk often coarse and frank—when they thought no one else was listening.

Phelan was in the hallway of his home when a text message came in, the kitchen doorway behind him, the family in full voice as was usual at that time of the day. The two oldest were running late for school, their mother pleading with them once more to finish up and brush their teeth.

Phelan stepped out of the front door, briefly, phone now at his ear. The man in the driving seat of the van parked the other side of the street facing the Irishman, placed a directional microphone on the dashboard, turning up the receiver on the device to pick up what was being said.

"Yes, I'll be able to come and see you…no, of course my wife doesn't know and we both know that has to stay that way…no, I've not changed my mind…yes, I'm still interested in you, of course…don't worry, it'll all be okay, you'll see… okay, be in touch soon…yes, I'll come and visit you as soon as I can get away…no it won't be a problem, just leave it with me…look, I need to go, she'll wonder where I've been…yes, don't worry, it'll all be over soon…just trust me…" and he ended the call, stepping back inside the door carefully, the door closing quietly behind him. Those in the van looked at each other, nothing being said, the two men in the front seats just smiling amongst themselves.

∞∞∞

Later that day when a fresh report had been sent in from his team of Spotters watching this promising and unusual Irishman, Dmitry Sokoloff sat in his penthouse apartment in Moscow, his guest sitting across from him. It was not unusual for two oligarchs to meet each other outside of the setting of the Games, but usually these were in normal public meetings, like they would face the following week when they were required to travel to London for a gathering of the one hundred most valuable companies in the UK.

His guest, Aleksey Kuznetsov, known as Fifteen on Games day, was therefore ranked three below his own ranking of Twelve, a fact that meant the guest would always play second fiddle to the man he'd come to see, wealth and ranking amongst this group of very status conscious men meaning everything.

"I think I have a Contestant who'll be ideal for the big one this summer," Dmitry said, keeping most of the details to himself. No other oligarch ever shared names with another man before the actual event. If they did, all the other oligarchs would be able to watch that individual, all able to work out themselves what the Contestant would do. The bets would be off, as there would be no real element of surprise. The Hosts valued the secrecy of their potential Contestants as much as they did any other part of their own security, protection and empire. "He's an Irishman," Dmitry let on, grinning at his guest, whose own Irishman in the previous Hunt had proved a complete waste of investment.

"Well, let's just hope I don't have to do to your guy what was needed to mine."

"So you were involved, though I never doubted that for one moment."

"As if you haven't done twice as much in your time! Why am I here exactly?"

"You needed my help, you said. I run most of the services you need to expand into the rest of the country. Much more if you want to grow throughout Europe."

"And what is it you need from me?"

"There is nothing I need from you other than your vote for me to get a slot at the summer event." Aleksey knew exactly what he meant, his own influence and wealth in the business world was nothing compared to the man in front of him. He could do nothing for him in the outside world, but as an oligarch within the Games, his vote was worth as much as each of the other ten. Having just hosted a Hunt himself and failed, he was desperate to get back to the table and show what he could really do and yet he didn't have anyone to put forward as a Contestant. But, if it meant that much to the man now sitting in front of him, then Aleksey would gladly give him his vote. It would mean his own empire could grow rapidly without even having to win a bet within the Games. He might even then be able to win more from him if Dmitry was to fail during that particular Hunt.

"I'll get the people on board. Twenty owes me a favour and I think Eighteen could be persuaded. That would surely give you enough votes to be included in the summer event. I think they are considering multi-Contestants once more. It gives more interest than just a single Hunt. More chances of one of us failing, I guess."

"I don't fail, and I thank you for your backing in this regard. I'll get the contracts drawn up that will allow your business to expand. We'll sign them the day after I'm voted into the summer event. Now get out of here, I have much more important things to get on with."

The meeting suddenly over, Aleksey stood and left without saying anything else, their relationship nothing more than a business one. Within the ten men, despite the fact they were all very wealthy, there remained very strict alliances and cliques, most often based on their rankings, the richest sticking together, the poorest too in their own grouping, as well as people that might have business connections that overlapped. It was therefore only in that regard that Aleksey had obtained ten minutes with a man worth an estimated $2.2 billion, despite being worth over $1.8 billion himself.

∞∞∞

With the vast resources of the MI6 and therefore MI5 database now fully at their disposal, Alex and Anissa felt that for the first time in months they were making some progress. Within the Service, their voluntary involvement in this type of often avoided side-project was seen as a good example of experienced field agents getting involved where usually—Alex Tolbert being a prime example—such agents thought of themselves as too important to be tasked with such a menial assignment.

Due to the profile of those in attendance, the British Government always insisted upon MI5 and 6's involvement—the task usually then just handed within the Service to the most junior agents available. To have Alex and Anissa both stepping forward was therefore a delight, and the Service also saw the value in these two agents brushing up on the technical side of things, the role largely calling for a careful study of much cyber information, often the first signs that anything of a sinister nature might be planned for this particular meeting.

The participants, the one hundred members of the FTSE100, changed a little, being a group of the top one hundred companies listed on the London Stock Exchange with the highest market capitalisation. The top seventy or eighty were mainstays, and covered a wide range of industries and sectors—oil and gas, consumer goods, banking, tobacco, pharmaceuticals and so on. Those twenty or so firms making up the rest of the list might move around from one year to the next, sometimes in the top one hundred, sometimes not, depending on the state of the market at any one point. Attendance for the annual gathering was always fixed after first quarter results were published, from which a top hundred was established. What the actual share price was doing at the time of the conference was largely secondary, sometimes the companies present were no longer listed on the Footsie, as it was best known.

As it turned out, seventeen of the firms that would be present at the London gathering had links to Russia, their owners and often billionaire oligarchs would most certainly be attending one of the highest value networking events the UK put on. Security was paramount, a violation of any type—no matter how small—would have repercussions for years to come. London had been through enough, they couldn't allow something to happen to these key people.

The venue was kept a secret, though it mainly rotated around three locations. The event itself was kept out of the press as a whole, the occasional reference mentioned in some of the financial papers as an afterthought, but anything that was shared publicly was always low key.

Two days after putting themselves forward for the task, Alex and Anissa were heading up their own team of five junior technicians, supported by a senior technician—the same man who'd contacted Alex having received the message from Andre in the first place. That had made sense to the three at the time, Anissa agreeing that having him lead the team working in the background would give them a heads up on anything they might need to be aware of within MI6.

A full day had been spent detailing every key piece of information they held on the hundred companies represented, the five computer experts each taking twenty companies, each report already coming together. Alex and Anissa took the seventeen that interested them most, not knowing which of these might also be a part of the Games events in Russia, though sure that some of them were. It gave them a good background to each person, a list which also included three women from the Russian ranks.

Alex had also tried, unsuccessfully, with the Lottery Commission to obtain information about some of the previous winners who had claimed very late, usually doing so on the last day possible and then remaining anonymous. The Commission had refused to give them that information, quoting their right to defend the winners' identities. Without something from the highest courts, they couldn't disclose anything about any of these people.

The same had been true for the European wide Loto. Alex knew he wouldn't be granted this permission, nor did anything he was working on—that MI6 knew about—warrant even his interest in that information. He put it to one side, knowing when to walk away quietly in order not to draw the attention of anyone within his own organisation to his actions and that of his team.

What Alex had been able to task the team with—and they'd taken to it without question like any other task—was mapping, not just in the UK but right across Europe, every single lottery result for the last five years, a huge grid drawn up with claim times and undeclared tickets, looking for any patterns in the system, anything that would give them an idea on what had happened and when.

The dates that Andre Philip had originally given them were added to the side of the board, their meaning to anyone else just random numbers, apart from the three people in the room who understood why they were there. It was then, once the results had been collated, the dates written out in front of them, that patterns first started to emerge. Unclaimed tickets for large amounts were mostly from the Continent in any of the dozen plus lottery draws that there were made each week, whilst still a significant number were from the UK. The Euro Loto—EuroMillions to the British—a European wide draw that usually offered the regular, really big winnings, featured most, however.

With the benefit of this wider information, what they were seeing was a connection to each of the dates they'd been given by Andre back in that original—and last—transmission. Be it a Greek ticket, or the Spanish National Loto, French Loto or Irish Lotto, the Italian Super Enalotto, or any number of others in countries right across Europe, there were unclaimed tickets that coincided with each of the dates that were listed. The gap between draws and the date depended on each country's rules regarding how long a winner had to claim—some as little as ninety days, others as much as one hundred and eighty. An internet search had shown that Austria, with three years for claimants to come forward, gave the most time, but as far as they could tell, there were no Austrian tickets that matched any of these events.

The sums involved in each of the draws that coincided with a date were now written onto the board in red ink. All the other times a ticket had been claimed after a sizeable gap were written in black ink. Now they had a clear pattern. Every red ink number, with just a few exceptions, was one of the higher amounts. The red numbers that were not that high, keeping roughly with the average value of the black numbers, had no higher value draws around them at the time the ticket was presented.

"Do you see the pattern?" Alex said, taking Anissa to one side as the team of enthusiastic juniors kept building the picture for them. "There are no huge black ink draws. All the ones in black are small amounts, and there's a red ink number that's significantly higher from around the same time. It tells me the Russians are watching these draws in much the same way we've just been analysing them. If there is a large amount won, they must target it. They either get to the winner before they make mention of their luck—thereby bringing it into their game—giving us the red numbers we have displayed on the board…"

"Or the winner claimed the prize before anyone was able to get to them, so that we don't see it at all on this board," Anissa said, aware of where he was going with his logic.

"Exactly. It gives us a way in, in real time. In any one week, there must be two dozen draws across Europe, probably more. Most will be small amounts, which only come into play when there are no other options. Some will be big, especially when there has not been a winner for the previous few draws. These prize funds always get increased attention, the jackpot rising higher the more weeks it goes unwon. So when we see this happening, knowing that these Russians we are after are needing a constant supply of tickets, we'll get some knowledge as to where they'll be looking to source their tickets."

"But how do they know where to look, besides some general information?"

"I don't know, but clearly they do. I don't believe they could possibly have a network large enough to have people in every country. So there will be some movement of key personnel. If we can pinpoint who these people are, we have a start. Let's get one person working on that," and he made a note to follow that up with someone later. "We also know they must have a way of recruiting people into this thing, though for that I don't have any ideas how we'll know about who these people are until it's too late."

"Yes, I've been thinking that one through, as well. Without getting an idea on the people they are using to watch these victims, we won't know where or whom they're watching."

"Coming back to these dates," Alex continued, more animated than she'd seen him in a while, blood pumping through his veins as he finally felt they were getting somewhere in the investigation, "we now know when previous events took place, including the one that was happening the last time we were in St Petersburg two months ago. I'm going to get two, maybe three, people from the team tracking the whereabouts of some of these hundred names on the list, mainly the foreign nationals, and I'll include all seventeen Russians. If we are able to place even a handful of them as travelling or away from home on any of these dates, we potentially have some firm evidence that these particular people might be part of the Games. If their travels match up with several dates, we can put people on them, keep a closer eye on them. Maybe that way we'll come across some of the people they have working for them in the roles we've just highlighted as essential." He made another note, deciding to put at least three of the remaining four people on that task, with the additional input of the senior technician. Getting half a dozen names of people likely to be part of the Games before the next week's conference in London would enable the two British agents to attend the event and meet these people face to face. Alex went around the room, tasking those there with what he needed them to do, no explanation needed from him as to why he was asking them to do anything, their job just to follow orders.

The office they were working together in kicked into life once more—fresh impetus to the task in hand giving them the boost they all needed.

17

The London FSTE100 Conference was a big deal within the business world, though it had been decided before the first ever event took place many years before that it would not appear on any publicly circulated business calendar. It was not for the outside world, but a key coming together of the top one hundred business leaders in the country, a place where even the press were kept at arm's length. Many of the most respectable papers knew about the event, of course. The tabloids could only try to find out what they could, and were more of a nuisance in the early years, though they had lost interest somewhat in it all lately, rejected once too often, perhaps. The financial papers that did include anything on the conference did so without making specific references.

The venue also changed from year to year, now on a three year cycle with the three most suitable—and securable— facilities in the capital. MI5 and 6 had been tasked with overseeing the security arrangements from the beginning of the event, despite it really being something the police force themselves could have handled—maybe Scotland Yard at a push. But due to the sort of people involved—and their willingness to pay for greater protection—it was left to the security services to work together to oversee the safety of each annual event.

Working together was never easy, which was why those in government liked to insist it happened. Finding personnel to take to the task was also a challenge, though this year was an exception. Alex and Anissa volunteering to oversee the project was a welcome relief, letting off the hook those who might have been landed with the task.

The venue that year was in a part of London which had once been rundown docks, before a vast revamp had taken place. The iconic Canary Wharf had once towered above most other buildings, though a few of similar height had been added in recent years, giving that part of London a slight New York vibe. The conference facility being used was in the shadow of London's tallest building.

A spacious entrance way, cameras watching everywhere, mostly out of view of the general public, gave way to a wide staircase which spanned the width of the building, taking visitors up about two dozen steps onto the main concourse. Lifts took office workers up to the floors above, the spaces on those higher floors used exclusively for meetings, mainly for people working in offices that didn't have their own conference rooms. The entire building was booked out for the FTSE100 event, so these floors were to remain empty throughout the days ahead.

Beside the lifts, there were four sets of double doors which opened into the main conference auditorium, the venue for the next few days for the one hundred business CEOs, and the small teams that each person tended to have tagging along with them. Mixed with the crowds were a team of highly capable catering staff, bringing drinks in and out constantly, serving food and other refreshments when it was time. MI5 and 6 completed the set up, their personnel blending in as best they could, but most could spot them easily.

Alex had arrived first that morning, a set of cleaning staff just finishing and leaving the place. He'd proceeded to do a complete tour of the building, understanding where each room linked up, where the kitchens were located, noting all entrance and exit doors, fire escapes, etc. He checked out the higher floors, mainly focussing on the floor above the auditorium, figuring anything higher than that was largely out of reach. He was doing his job, tasked with the security element after all, and he had several extra people drafted in to continue round the clock monitoring of the building.

He had to be seen doing what was expected of him, but really he and Anissa, who joined him now as he emerged from the lift on the ground floor—his tour finished—were there to meet the Russians they'd been getting to know more about over the last few months.

The previous week had been intense but helpful. In the end, a pattern of dates and names semi-emerged, the information a little sketchy in places and a few assumptions made, but they had five names of Russians attending the forthcoming conference that they had a strong suspicion were involved in the Games. That was a huge head start. By the end of the week both agents were falling asleep with the facial images of their key targets burnt into their minds, their faces still visible when they closed their eyes. They had determined to learn as much about the people as they could, to be able to instantly recognise these five men in any crowd, to be able to spot them as soon as they arrived. They had to have the information learnt and stored for quick recollection at a later point, without it becoming too obvious that they were paying such close attention to any one particular party.

Alex strolled around the main room, just the two of them, the occasional person from the catering team walking in and out, it still being three hours before the first guests were expected. They were going over the names they'd learnt, taking it in turns to test each other.

"Lev Kaminski," Alex started, Anissa taking a moment before speaking from memory.

"Known among closest friends as the *Lion Man* and the richest Russian here today, latest figures suggesting his net worth is $12.5 billion spread across steel, telecoms and investment businesses. Owns a firm in the UK that's been in the top seventy for over a decade, been to every event the FSTE100 have ever hosted."

"Appearance?" Alex added, going over the same information as she was speaking, each now able to run the information off the top of their heads without much effort.

"He's sixty-two, round face, receding greying hair, well built and six feet tall."

"Valery Holub," Anissa said in return.

"He's fifty-nine, also in steel but has vast transport links too, has amassed a fortune that Forbes calculates being worth $9.3 billion. Black hair though it's showing his age a little around the edges, not balding yet. Facial hair is grey, he usually has at least a short cut beard, sometimes growing it out across other parts of his not overly plump face. Akim Kozlov."

"Akim is forty-nine, worth $2 billion, made through aluminium and State utilities. Lives in Moscow mainly, owns a metal supplier here in the UK, hence his appearance today. Good head of brown hair, most usually clean-shaven. Married with two kids, has a degree in Arts & Science from Moscow State University. Dmitry Kaminski."

"Worth $1.7 billion, mainly through a number of financial institutes. Now owns the Futures market here in London, under a much larger investment portfolio. Has political aspirations, too. Forty-eight years old, good head of jet black hair, brown eyes, well built and about five feet ten."

"Last but not least we have Osip Yakovlev," Anissa said, "worth $1.2 billion, making him Russia's 55th richest man. Owns cement suppliers and airport builders. He's fifty, married with two kids, and graduated from the Leningrad Institute of Physical Culture a Bachelor of Art & Science. Has blonde or almost ginger hair, keeps himself in shape, and stands five feet eight inches tall."

They were now back at the main doors, proud that they'd got the key details down for these men they were anticipating later. The room seemed to be prepared, ready to welcome the first guests, and these began to arrive after forty minutes, those closest to London arriving first, others who might be flying into London's City Airport arriving only in time for the start of the first session.

∞∞∞∞

As lunch was brought out for all the delegates later that afternoon, Alex had spotted all five of the Russians they were expected. They tended to stay together, though usually in two groups, Lev with Valery, and the other three by themselves. Alex couldn't tell if that was a net worth kind of thing—the first two being by far the richest of the five—or an industry thing as both the former two were steel magnates, usually in direct competition with each other, as they certainly were in the UK market.

Only one of the one hundred delegates was yet to make an appearance, their flight delayed leaving America, the private jet not now expected until later that afternoon, in time for the evening's hospitality.

It was always a difficult thing to do—put on an event for billionaires.

Somehow, and so far, the Hosts had once again managed to pull it off, but it was mainly the company, being in a room of one's peers, that was the biggest draw.

Both British agents mingled freely with the crowd, the organisers keen to introduce the two MI6 agents to anyone they were able, it being somewhat of a coup to have anyone of their experience amongst them.

"Alex," the organiser said, not for the first time that day, taking him by the hand and introducing him to another delegate. "This is Lev Kaminski," he said with a certain element of pride, as if the name would have meant anything to Alex had he not been learning so much about these men.

Alex took the outstretched hand, the handshake strong and forceful, the Russian exerting something of his personality towards someone he assumed was of little importance, most probably security personnel, given Lev knew all the other delegates, and Alex was not one of them.

"Lev, this is Alex Tolbert, he's heading up the security operation for this conference."

"I hope we aren't making you too busy, Alex," the Russian said, his English clear and understandable, though his heavy accent suggested he had not learned the language until he was an adult.

"Lev is Russian for *lion*, isn't it?" Alex didn't see the danger in stating something that many might know.

"You speak Russian?" Lev replied in his native language, before repeating it, a smile on his face, in English, once Alex had given him a confused look.

"No, I just hadn't come across the name Lev before, and couldn't tell where it was from, and it came up on a translation site as meaning *lion*."

"Lev is one of a handful of Russian guests with us these few days," the organiser added, as if giving information that might otherwise not have been known. Lev could tell Alex was well aware of every person present, his eyes giving away the fact there was more going on behind his calm expression than he was letting on.

"Are there now, how fascinating," Alex replied, weakly. At that point, Anissa walked over and joined them. Greetings were exchanged, the organiser once more introducing the agent to the Russian, the formality repeated.

"Well I hope these days, for all our sakes, are very uneventful for you both," Lev said, ending the conversation that had kept to general topics without much substance to any of it. It left the Russian with a vague sense of caution, but he didn't know why. The organiser went on his way too, mingling with the crowd as everyone enjoyed a three course lunch, the two agents left to themselves once more. Alex and Anissa walked over to an area of seating that was raised and currently deserted, before speaking with one another.

"So what did you make of that?"

"Lev, you mean?" and Anissa nodded her head, both agents watching the crowd, sitting side by side but not facing one another, speaking in hushed tones, their hands often in front of their mouths blocking anyone that might be watching them from understanding what they were saying. "I think he's a very observant man. He knew exactly who we were before we were ever introduced."

"I thought that, too. Do you think he has been told about us being in Russia?"

"No, I doubt that, he's not got those kinds of connections, from what we've learnt, anyway. I guess it's just the nature of his life, he must come across a lot of people like us. He's probably just accustomed to people in our walk of life."

"Yes, I guess that makes sense. Have you spoken with any of the others?"

"No, not in the same way as what just happened. I've been around them all, listening in as I can. The three Russians, when together, speak with each other only in Russian. They do speak English with others, but they've said very little. They all seem on edge."

"Yes, I was going to say that. More on edge than most here, or is it just my imagination?"

"Maybe—these are all very rich people, after all. Some are multi-billionaires from various backgrounds, others have just crossed the line into their first billion. I guess that dynamic alone is enough to put anyone on edge? Especially if you are the ones at the bottom of the pile."

"Crazy, isn't it. To be that rich and yet in a room like this, be considered one of the poorest people present. What a messed up world we live in."

∞∞∞

By the evening of that first day, all one hundred delegates now accounted for, Alex had managed to meet with most of the people present, many having positive words to say to him in the process, happy for MI6's presence at the event.

He'd been close enough to all five Russians, their English ability passable. He imagined they understood more than they spoke, no one present needed translation—though he wondered if any self-respecting billionaire would even ask for help if they had needed it. It was an interesting thought.

People started leaving just after ten pm, those that didn't own property in London staying at any number of executive hotels in the city.

Once the last guest had gone, Alex and Anissa did a final sweep of the building, going through the motions but keen to be seen doing their job, before they too left for the night.

Tomorrow's first session was due to start at ten-thirty, the two agents needing to be on-site at least two hours before.

They parted company, Alex heading to his home where he lived by himself, Anissa back to her home, where the kids were asleep and her husband was watching the closing stages of a film that was on the television. They talked a little, but Anissa being tired and drained from the day, took herself off to bed with a mug of peppermint tea and a book, just before eleven.

18

Frustratingly, the longer the second and final day went, the less obvious reason for Alex and Anissa both being there existed. They saw out their role well, there were no incidents of any kind to report. Hardly the need for such senior agents from the Security Service to have been there all the time, but they'd put themselves forward, no one had made them. They had been able to get close to the Russians somewhat, but it was as close as anyone is to someone who is part of a crowd. Nothing more was really learnt, the Russians only talking freely when it was just them and no one else was around.

Alex had taken a risk and installed two mikes in the ceiling area of the main auditorium, in the area of hall where the group of three Russians tended to meet, away from the serving area, away from the food—alone. He hoped they'd be able to at least pick up some of the conversation which could be translated later on, their words analysed and understood. Anissa had also worked on her own idea; an altered front page of one of the main newspapers made to feature an article about the bankruptcy of Annabel Herbertson. The bankruptcy was going through that week but had not actually made the front pages.

On the newspaper which Anissa had got the team to photoshop, there was a large full page photo of Annabel with an equally captivating headline running across it. She'd brought the copies to Alex, who'd seen them and instantly appreciated the effort and idea. They made sure the papers were placed in easy reach of the two groups of Russians, and they watched to see what reaction they would create.

Much to their initial frustration, the first group of Russians—the two wealthiest who mainly socialised with each other when not with bigger groups, avoiding the other three Russians present at the conference—made nothing of the image. Neither man appeared to even notice the paper. It seemed the photo on its front cover, and maybe the brand of newspaper itself, were of absolutely no interest whatsoever to either billionaire. The same was largely true of the other group of three, though there was certainly eye contact from Osip Yakovlev, the briefest of glances which made the others look, their own responses suggesting very little as to what, if anything, it might have meant to them.

The conference was now over, the various parties, their teams in tow, leaving as swiftly as they had arrived. It had been a useful time for them all, once again. It was a conference light on actual content as the real purpose was peer-to-peer connection, no one firm or individual taking all the limelight.

In previous years iconic figures had been shipped in—film stars, a retired president, sports people. That model had been scrapped for this year, the firms preferring to keep their business in-house, their gathering a little more low key. Away from too much attention, they could be left to size up the opposition themselves, though many made meaningful connections also, the time and space available offering the opportunities that busy diaries for globetrotting entrepreneurs just didn't otherwise allow.

As everything was packed away, the conference venue now deemed clear and the offices allowed to be rented out again, the two agents left, the organiser of the conference thanking them for their involvement and suggesting they do so again in the future. Neither Anissa nor Alex responded to the suggestion, thinking it best to say nothing rather than let on how it had been anything but a success from their point of view. At least there had been no incidents, which from a security viewpoint, was always the main goal—it just hadn't been their goal.

The recordings were sent on to the team, a freelance translator brought in to work through what was said, giving them a written transcript of everything that was spoken between the voices, their names and identities kept secret, even from the team within MI6.

The typed transcripts had just been finished when Alex and Anissa arrived back at the office after their three days' absence.

Alex touched base with his team, on what was the final day to tie up any loose ends from the conference. The manpower needed to dig into the lives of the super rich and powerful were no longer available to Alex and Anissa for their own purposes. Anissa called over to Alex, papers in hand.

"What is it?" he said, just the two of them, their voices low.

"Look, here," she said, pointing at the papers she had in front of her, the transcript from the illegal mike they'd placed in the conference centre. "They mention Annabel's name, just briefly, as part of their conversation." Alex read the sentence Anissa was pointing to, the two of them then scanning through the entire sheets that made up the whole transcript, but there was nothing else, no other reference. The sentence itself wasn't anything definitive—nor could they have used the evidence anyway since the source of the information was far from authorised.

"They knew of her," Anissa said, almost a revelation to herself as much as anything else.

"Exactly—we have it! The paper worked, it sparked something, just a comment is all we needed. Her picture in a paper made total sense to these three Russians. They have to have been involved in the event that she won."

What the transcribed words on the sheet before them could not do was express the style, the flow of speech and how it was spoken. For this, they listened themselves to the recording, not understanding the words being spoken at all, but by using the detailed tracking system, the timing of each section corresponding to the words written down on the paper, they found what they expected to be the section in question, and played it through several times on repeat.

"There's definitely a laugh there."

"Unmistakably," Alex said.

"Who is speaking?" Neither could be certain, having only had a few words with each in English, the three on the recording speaking confidently and fluently in Russian, their style and voices therefore sounding different. Without someone working through the whole recording, knowing who was who, it would be impossible to really identify the speaker.

"I guess it doesn't matter too much at this point, but this is an in-joke, shared by all. What they said would not make sense if you didn't know all about Annabel and what she otherwise meant to those involved in the Games. The fact all of them shared in the joke—regardless of who was actually the one speaking at the time—can only tell us that they were all there at the event, all involved in it."

It was the only thing they had that came out of the entire three days spent at the conference centre. That and a few face-to-face meetings, which now, given the fact they were most likely to run into these people again but in more hostile situations, probably wasn't a good thing at all. But it was another piece to the puzzle.

The information they'd gained before the event had also been helpful, and for what it was worth, confirmed what happened with the three Russians during the conference. The travel dates and times for the other two Russians hadn't quite matched up with the other three—who had matched almost perfectly. Clearly they were not part of what the other three were and could largely be left out of it.

Now, though, Alex and Anissa did have three names they could focus on, three men often in London and other European countries, men they could now watch from afar, tracking those that they might associate with, watching for any more connections to what was really happening behind the scenes.

Alex and Anissa left the office contented with the fact that they had made another step forward in this painfully long and arduous journey.

A little over four months earlier, they had nothing—besides a rumour—an urban myth about such an organisation working amongst a select group of Russians, secretive people who made no mention of anything to anyone, each oligarch sworn to total silence.

That had changed with the confirmation from Andre—with his list of names and dates—and now finally, months into an investigation that needed to be kept off the record for fear of who might otherwise be watching within their own ranks, they had three names, proof of previous trips and what they hoped was a way of predicting when, if not where, future events would be taking place.

It was certainly something worth celebrating, the two going out for some drinks, their working day over. Anissa had called home, clearing it with her husband, the kids already in bed and a football match about to start on the television, as the two agents walked into a popular bar not that far from the office, but far enough to avoid any of the usual work crowd that might otherwise have shown up. They each ordered their favourite drink, found a seat in the corner, and toasted one another.

"To progress," Alex finished, and they savoured the taste as they each swallowed. They would order a few more before it was time to go home, which they did just after eleven that night, Anissa taking a taxi, Alex able to walk, delighted with the fresh air since be had been inside for too many days.

Around him, in the shadows of the night, a team of three kept their watch on him, as they'd been ordered to since he first got introduced to their boss on the opening day of the conference.

∞∞∞

In Moscow, Sergej Volkov, with his wife Svetlana, were just leaving the residence of the President, having spent three hours with him and a number of key government officials. For his glamorous wife Svetlana, who'd made the transition well from pin-up actress to political circles easily enough, it was just another role she got to play.

The couple didn't have any children, and hadn't been married for that long, anyway. And besides, she was still making movies, and becoming a mother did not quite fit in with her current commitments.

She'd spent time amongst many of the other wives—many of whom were former actresses, models, the usual type that end up marrying into vast wealth and power.

She was also happy within a male environment, not hiding away when the President walked over to her husband, staying by his side, even striking up her own conversation with her country's leader. Sergej had especially liked that side of her, and his influence amongst those he rubbed shoulders with was noticeably increased as a result.

In his earlier years he'd had a rough reputation, his nickname of *the Wolf* going back, and largely appropriately, to his first two decades in business, when he took hold of the companies he'd been handed responsibility for and turned them into successes in just a few short years. Back then, he took no prisoners, and so the legend around him grew.

In recent years—certainly publicly and especially since his marriage to arguably Russia's most iconic current actress—he'd shown far less of that side of things that had so shaped his first years and forged his reputation.

Now, they were seen as a model couple, two people bringing so much to the nation, working together, often seen publicly, the wife beside her husband. It was a positive message the Russians wanted broadcast across their nation, two people working hard for one another, standing beside one another, equally supporting each other in the talents they possessed.

The President, too, was most impressed, knowing Sergej personally from their time at university together, and then a few years after that when they served in the same team within the former KGB. He'd only met Svetlana recently, in the years since her marriage to Sergej, though he knew of her as any President would, since she was a leading performer with a worldwide audience. Like many sports people, as well as the successful business leaders, anyone bringing attention to the nation naturally came onto the radar of the President's office, and he was delighted to see this particular match when it had become known, the wedding big news in certain circles—those in the know understanding it would only cement Sergej's position within the hierarchy.

As much as Sergej's earlier years had been marked with threats and insults, Svetlana represented the complete opposite, the picture of peace—of tranquility—most often seen in public in white fur, the very image of tranquil beauty.

They got into the back seat of their car, the driver closing the door behind them before taking the wheel in the front seat, the glass partition between them closed, their privacy secured.

As a couple, their combined wealth made them amongst the richest couples in the country, and everything about their lifestyle confirmed it. Their main residence was in Moscow, though they had properties in St Petersburg too. The couple had to make regular visits north, for various reasons and so it was all the more important to have their own places there.

Small teams of people ran each property for them, everything cleaned and ready for whenever they were to arrive next, often on different jobs.

Sometimes she'd have an acting job that would take her away for a few days, sometimes he'd have some business that needed sorting. They travelled together, very often deliberately arranging meetings in the same cities at the same time, making the most use of each trip.

They had people who ran their diaries, keeping them up to date on what needed doing when, and it was a set up that worked exceedingly well for them both. So when Sergej announced that he needed to travel once more to St Petersburg, Svetlana was already clear in her diary, plans underway for what she would do with her time in the city. It was as if she too realised that the connection and influence that their marriage brought was as much for her as it had been for her husband. They both used it to their advantage.

19

The days following the conference in London had become quite productive, the offices of MI6 busy with activity, as Alex and Anissa worked with one or two people pulling together what they could.

Alex had been asked to give a debrief following his involvement at the FTSE100 conference, which had seemed like overkill, given the low key nature of the event. It was also confusing that in the listening crowd there were such senior figures present from MI6 as Alex ran through his notes, in barely twenty minutes. He covered the entire three days, not going into any real detail, and thankfully not being asked anything else about it.

Meeting over, he returned to Anissa, a little taken aback by everything that had just happened. He was sure that someone within that room was keeping an eye on him—which was disturbing—since it was only MI6 personnel present.

Going over the information they had on the three Russian businessmen and oligarchs they were now focussing on, a link had been made with one of them—Dmitry Kaminski. He had a connection to a number of private firms that offered immigration services for those based in the UK and Ireland for people who wanted to visit Russia. Applications were not dealt with at the Embassy in London or Dublin, they were processed first by third party companies who would collect all the information needed, before forwarding on the passport and details to the Embassy, the main work already carried out.

It was these first contact companies that Dmitry ultimately—through a complicated number of connections—had control over. That made it possible, though most probably untraceable, for him to sanction the applications for visas to be made in the names of the three people they knew about, to travel to Russia in the first place. Because of the connection to the Russian, Alex and Anissa didn't attempt to contact the handling agent that had dealt with the initial application, wary of the risk of word getting back to Dmitry should their request be declined. They had no idea who made the application therefore for Annabel, Twila or across in Dublin for Dubhán, but they were sure they were fast tracked without the usual processes—and probably without the three actually making the application themselves.

For the moment, they would be happy with making this one additional connection, the information going onto the shared file, which was the safest place for the small team to share information with each other. Nothing existed within the office, no paper trail that would lead anyone back to them should someone come looking. They intended to keep it that way.

Anissa was walking with Alex around the park, they'd been going over everything for a few minutes, no one around them, the park noticeably empty for that time of day.

"So, we have a confirmed link to migration services in the UK. We must assume similar links exist within other countries, too. That enables these people to get a visa for Russia for whoever they want, presumably at short notice if needed. They must safeguard the application, in some way, meaning the normal checks and processes are not required, or they are just overlooked. We can't underestimate the chance that maybe they have someone within the embassies, too, who is working with them."

"I'll connect with Sasha again, see what he's managed to rustle up."

They walked for a little longer, having the occasional word but really they were each deep in thought, working over what they were involved in, looking for gaps—areas to explore. Other projects within MI6 were increasingly keeping them busy, their entire Russian operation solely kept in the shadows—deliberately off the radar—and therefore fitted in here and there as time allowed.

"One more thing," Anissa added, catching Alex by the arm to stop him walking away. "I've made contact with the three Russian firms that we now have our eyes on, posing as a conference organiser looking to get motivational speakers to come and share at future events. I'm only dealing with the secretaries, so the Russians should never know about it."

Alex wasn't so sure, adding, "Go on."

"We now know what the Russians are targeting—unclaimed lottery tickets. By unclaimed, I mean ones that as far as we know, the winner has not come forward. In fact, the Russians might have already given them a cash prize in exchange for the ticket—how else would they get it? Anyway, that knowledge gives us some idea as to when a future event might take place."

"By seeing what tickets are yet unclaimed and working out when they expire," Alex said aloud, intrigued with where Anissa was going, though she hadn't even got to her main point yet.

"Exactly. We don't even have to work much out, all the websites for these various lotteries give this information freely. Of course, most of these tickets are simply lost. It's only a few that interest the Russians—often high value tickets—though there is no absolute pattern to prove that. Either way, we have an ever increasing list of dates spanning up to six months ahead, any one of these being possible dates when this group of Russians will meet again in the future. Now, with the last event we know about, there were two from the UK with one each from Ireland and Spain. The date must have been set around the time the two UK tickets were purchased. They both had a one hundred and eighty day limit on them. For Spain and Ireland there were just ninety days."

"So these tickets must have been purchased later?"

"Yes, much later, when a date was already known. Kind of like a bonus play when they became available."

"So tracking UK draws is the key?"

"Yes, UK and Switzerland in fact both give the longest time, with Belgium at one hundred and forty. I've started to make notes regarding draws across the various lotteries available to British citizens, and where two or three possible tickets intersect, I circle that date. These are the dates I made a note of. We won't know until three months in if any other draw around Europe will give up winning tickets, but with so many available, and winners announced all the time, it isn't hard to add tickets to any one event later on."

"If you can get hold of them."

"Of course, but they obviously do, so I don't suppose it matters who they are dealing with, the set up is probably the same, their approach now no doubt finely tuned. Anyway, my main point in contacting these businesses is this: I've suggested conference dates for all our circled potential ones—we wait to see if the secretaries claim they're already busy, and whichever ones they are free on we can cross off the list."

"A bit like a game of battleships, you mean?"

"Sorry?" Anissa said, not understanding what her colleague was meaning at all.

"The dates you are suggesting are like the ships you place on your board when you play battleships."

"I never did."

"You've never played battleships, not even as a child?" Alex laughed, before clarifying; "Basically if one of your circled dates meets with the unavailability of any of these Russians, it's like you've made a strike. We're onto them."

"Yes, and I heard back this morning. We have two dates that none of the three men can make."

"That's some coincidence."

"Alex, that's much more than a coincidence. We have their next two event dates, and now know three of the people involved. I'd say it's a massive leap forward."

20

It was the warmest day of the year so far, St Petersburg in its slower paced summer season—when tourists threatened to outnumber those Russians that hadn't left for the countryside. School holidays had kicked in a month before, the long nights of summer fully underway, allowing those still walking the streets late to lose track of time altogether. There was a serene, melancholy feel to the atmosphere, people in less of a hurry, though that was the norm with the evening crowds. The streets, though less packed than the rest of the year, would still be full of cars come the morning.

At Temple Mount, the aptly named five-storey mansion owned by the Volkovs, the oligarchs had started to arrive. The mid-summer event was the second most significant gathering in the year, behind the massive New Year contest. Nothing outstripped these two occasions for all that they were and meant to those involved. There was something so beautiful about being in St Petersburg in the summer.

Most guests used this event as the chance to grab three days away from the heat that gripped Moscow at that time of year. Nearly everyone would be staying at Temple Mount over the next two nights, the annual tradition being that they spent one day together, the Games took place the following day and the third day was just left free.

The summer event didn't always fall exactly on the shortest night of the year—though it was happening that year. The dates were always determined by the lottery tickets they were using to make normal people do crazy things.

With everyone inside the building, the Chair spent five minutes speaking to them all, holding their attention, every word spoken with purpose and meaning—nothing said without a reason.

The gathered crowd of ten wealthy oligarchs were reminded of the competition rules, reminded of the fact that though this was a contest and for many there was a lot at stake, it was against the rules for any one oligarch to directly interfere with or go against another Host. No oligarch was allowed to invest money to stop another Host succeeding, they could simply watch and bet based on what happened before them all.

They all knew the rules, they didn't for their part need to be reminded of them, but these unwritten laws now being voiced reminded them how often they ignored the very structure that was designed to keep them all working together.

The main thing that kept them there were the connections and influence it brought them, each man certain that though they'd experienced losses at times, their involvement in a league of such people had only had multiple benefits to their entire empire. Only one man, his losses so great—as he'd got drawn into a very public argument with another Host—had ever been asked to leave the group. That had happened three years before, his silence guaranteed by the information the others had on him. His place had been taken by another, now richer, man who accepted the invitation to join, becoming the new Seventeen, the previous holder of that number becoming Eighteen, and so on. The numbers hadn't been revised in the last three years.

That evening, food was provided in the house, a firm of catering staff offering a high quality range of only the finest cuisine. The identity of those present was kept from the caterers, the food prepared and staff long gone before the first oligarch entered the dining area—secrecy, as always, paramount.

The following day, the sun rising just a few hours after it set, the weather was clear—another warm day expected. Most Russian visitors to the city celebrated Mid-Summer by dropping in on friends and relatives or visiting one of the many sites that made St Petersburg such a grand city.

Sergej and Svetlana Volkov were hosting a number of their peers on their own boat. They spent most of the morning until well after noon travelling along the main river, taking in some of the more sizeable canals, leaving the smaller ones alone. The conversation was flowing, Svetlana mixing well with everyone, her husband keeping a close watch on the others, but their comments to her were always respectful—he couldn't really fault them on that.

Lunch was served on a riverside pier, the boat docking at an arranged time, the guests tucking into all that was provided.

∞∞∞

In London that same morning, Phelan McDermott set out from his home, a taxi waiting for him out front. He was travelling to the airport having suddenly announced his need to take a trip. He didn't like to leave in that manner and he now regretted it. He wish he'd told her sooner, but it was too late now. He would have to piece things together once he returned home.

At Heathrow, he was checked in at the British Airways desk, his ticket in hand, as he looked through a few shops, considering the various chocolates, perfumes and then ladies' underwear they had on offer. He resisted buying anything right then.

The call came through for his flight just before eleven, and he was one of the first to board. Excitement was growing inside him—a nervous energy—unsure of why he was actually doing this.

As the plane lifted off the tarmac in London, he knew there was no turning back. What awaited him was another world, a city unlike any he'd seen before.

He'd travelled quite a lot, and had been to many interesting places, but had never been to Russia. The mysterious nature of his trip was beginning to worry him. He ordered a glass of wine when the option came—insisting on just one to settle his nerves—which it only did a little.

He slept for a while, waking as the call came through for passengers to return to their seats, as the plane was coming in for landing in Moscow.

∞∞∞

Svetlana walked with her husband, their minders never far away, almost daring someone to get too close to such a powerful couple. They were in deep conversation, walking past the front of the Summer Gardens across the river from Peter the Great's fortress and what was now a summer beach. There were many boats along the river, tourists flocked across the various bridges and a coach load arrived for the park as they passed.

No one gave the couple too much attention—it was what they liked about St Petersburg compared to Moscow—being able to walk around without being pestered by too many fans. Besides, most people around them at that moment were tourists, and despite Svetlana being an internationally known actress, her everyday appearance—whilst elegant always—was quite different from her on-screen glamour; enough to make her seem just another woman, to the casual observer.

∞∞∞

It was late as Phelan left a hotel in the centre of the city, having spent two hours inside the opulent building. He looked around, as if someone would notice his exit, as if his wife might see him—forgetting for a moment that he was thousands of miles from home.

Home, he thought. The kids would be busy around the dinner table. Her mother had come to stay, helping out at short notice—Phelan only springing the news on her of his need to take a trip two days before.

He'd said he was heading to Germany. He didn't know why he had lied, but he would sort it all out when he got back, he determined. He had to do this to get it out of his system, three days away from home, where anything could happen, before settling back into the normality of what his life had become. Maybe it would all be different from now on? Maybe he'd finally found that excitement, that edge he'd been searching for his whole life? Moscow, it seemed, with its vast contrasts offered that very thing.

He'd been around many beautiful women all evening, their fragrance carrying with him as he got into the waiting taxi, it taking him to the main railway station in the city. Everything had been provided for him for his onward journey north, which he was very pleased about as he didn't speak a word of the language he was hearing around him—not a single word made any sense.

He boarded the train at half past eleven, an overnight sleeper that would deliver him to the centre of St Petersburg by nine the following morning. He found his compartment—in the first class section—which he had to himself. He settled on his tiny bed, determined to get a good night's sleep, dropping off quickly, the journey north happening steadily throughout the night as he got some much needed rest.

∞∞∞∞

It was Games day at Temple Mount. The previous day's more leisurely pace had done a lot to relax the men now standing scattered around the room. A few technicians worked on screens in the background, but they knew how it went by now—never speak, never let your presence be noticed, pretend you don't exist.

They were just there to keep the displays running, like a television crew working behind the scenes to broadcast the next big event. They weren't the focus, it was the ones appearing on the screens who mattered. The oligarchs were the focus, though it was particularly the Hosts who were in the spotlight. They were the ones who were supplying the Hunt, they were the ones with the most on the line. Reputations could be made as well as broken within these four walls. It was never about the money, it was always about the Hunt for these men.

There were two Hosts for this latest event, one man failing to take up his option of becoming a third Host by not being able to come up with an appropriate ticket in time. That happened fairly regularly, which was why they now had multiple Hosts, though the first ticket was always secured before a date was set—ideally the first two.

Hosts for this Hunt were Twelve and Twenty.

Dmitry Sokoloff had indeed got his wish to Host during the summer event, and his Irishman was already one of the most keenly anticipated Contestants they'd had in a while.

"Gentleman," the Chair announced, drawing the men together into a circle around the central staging area, "we are ready to start, so let the Hunt begin. Today we are in the hands of Twelve and Twenty. May your Hunts be successful."

The usual reply was given.

The screens displayed where the two Contestants were, neither having yet taken a ticket, the Hunt only starting once a Contestant had fully understood what they were being offered.

To the side the Odds Maker had been calculating the bets, setting odds for the outcome based on when a Contestant might be caught—though rarely was money ever used.

Today, however, the bets were starting stronger, three hundred million dollars laid down already, which whilst not unusual, was certainly uncommon so early on in a contest.

Twelve walked around, speaking with the Odds Maker, taking in what was being bet against him—the idea that his peers within those four walls were banking on his downfall only spurred him on to succeed. He matched each bet, covering them for the other outcome: the Contestant caught before evening, no foot set outside of Russia.

Fifteen, who'd helped secure the Hunt for Twelve in exchange for some trade deals, was in buoyant spirits.

"I bet his European market that he'll lose this one," he stated, the Odds Maker speechless for a while, before calculating the value in his head. He was talking possibly nine hundred million dollars worth of business.

"And what do you have to wage against such a bet?" Twelve said, picking up on the fact such a rash bid had been made against him.

"Mining rights throughout Siberia, Kazakhstan and Mongolia."

The Odds Maker took the reply in, Twelve turning to him as he wrote some things down, a nod of agreement meaning he saw the bet as viable.

"Very well, on your own head be it," Twelve said, turning away, more aware than ever he needed to be on top of his game today. It was the biggest exposure any Host had ever faced—

though the opportunities it offered were already running through his mind. It would give his empire the natural resources he'd been negotiating hard for, so far without success, and put them under his own control—it made global expansion possible.

∞∞∞∞

Phelan left the train station just after nine, a team of Trackers on his trail as soon as he was located. Outside the station and once he'd moved away from the three police vehicles that were sitting there—alongside several other cars as well, which he presumed were taxis—he saw a large roundabout with a huge column at its centre. Vehicles were packed around each exit point, blocking other roads entirely.

He stood there, taking in the sounds and sights, the drivers navigating their way through what looked utter chaos to his untrained eyes. Two different people approached him trying to sell him city sightseeing tours. He politely declined them both, recognising he obviously stood out as a tourist.

Across the other side of the roundabout there appeared to be some form of café, and as he approached he was happy to have his initial thought confirmed. From the pavement in front of the building he could see people inside sitting at the tables. He entered, looking both left and right—the café extended in both directions—before deciding to go right, as most of the food visible was in that direction, the other side solely offering extra seating should it be needed. It wasn't needed as it was early and there were plenty of seats in the right hand section. He found a table easily, a tray of various pastries in front of him, no idea what exactly was in any of them. He figured if they were good enough to sell to Russians, then he would be able to stomach them as well. Besides, he was now feeling really hungry as he had not had any breakfast.

Entering the café as well had been two of the Trackers, the rest staying on the street outside. With only two Contestants in the Hunt this time, there were more personnel to go around, and they wanted to be more prepared than they had been last time—when two people had got away from them because they had not been able to keep a constant watch on the Contestants.

The two in the café sat down three tables from Phelan, with no one in between them, but their appearance did not register one bit with the Irishman who was tucking into what turned out to be three very tasty savoury pastries.

Normally the Contestants arrived the night before, a note being slid under their hotel room door the preferred method of alerting them to what was on offer. That had not been possible with Phelan, who'd only just arrived on the train. Something else was in store for him and it went smoother than they had imagined, a waitress coming to clear something from his table—a small conversation taking place—and an envelope placed under his tablet whilst the tray was cleared.

Finishing the last of his cup of tea, Phelan started to collect his things together, spotting the envelope as he picked up his device, its contents soon examined. He looked around briefly, seeing if anyone was watching him, but focussed quickly on what the message inside said. A photograph was attached to the back of the note—and those in the Games Room watched silently on the main screen, the anticipation growing with every minute.

"Stand by," the Tracker said into a hidden mike as he sat watching in the café, Phelan standing up, looking around him once more before moving towards the exit. "He is on the move—black jacket, dark jeans. He has the details and we must believe he'll be in possession of the ticket in a matter of minutes."

Phelan was back out onto the street, the note giving him directions that suggested he go around to the back of the building, a photo hinting at what he might find. He'd been expecting something to happen since arriving, but the way it had—so sudden and subtle—had surprised him. Now he wanted to find out what was coming next.

The traffic had increased even more since he'd been inside, buses and cars cutting each other up it seemed for the sake of a few metres. He easily outpaced them as he came out of the café and round to the right. He went down the side of the building for about thirty metres then right again round the back.

Behind him, in an upstairs window of a building with a good line of sight, one of the Trackers had him on camera, as he made his way to the spot the note was indicating. Once there, Phelan easily spotted the piece of paper attached to the lamp post, something that might have seemed like just another advert illegally taped to the metalwork—had it not been a lottery ticket. He stood there taking it in, looking around once more, turning a full circle before standing there, in the shelter of his current position.

"He has the ticket," a second person confirmed, a woman at ground level further down from where Phelan was standing, his back facing the camera in the upstairs window blocking their view somewhat.

"Game on," rang out in the Games Room at Temple Mount, the interest picking up immediately.

The other Contestant, a Frenchman by the name of Matthieu Dubois, had also not long ago started his Hunt, so with two active Contestants, it made for a good day.

21

Phelan McDermott, pulling on his hood against a little wind that was picking up, the day otherwise sunny, started moving along the streets, clearly working through what he needed to do. He'd jumped back into the café, the Trackers watching him, knowing he was about to do what all Contestants did—check the credibility of the ticket he was now in possession of. He did, pulling his tablet out, a Wifi signal located, and within minutes he had found the confirmation he was looking for.

"Sweet Jesus," he whispered under his breath, his Irish roots and accent showing in moments of extreme stress. He'd discovered this during the birth of his first child, when his wife screamed at him in the end to cut out the accent, something he'd not even twigged he was doing.

He entered the toilet before jogging out a minute later, hood pulled up high, cap on his head—a man clearly on a mission. The team of Trackers followed him across the road, as he headed back towards the train station.

Inside the Games Room, Twelve was in full control of what he now expected would be a very successful Hunt for him—and a very profitable one at that. Through his bluetooth headset he was in and out of calls in seconds, instructions given to his team of people now keeping a close tab on the man filling the television screens they were watching.

"Take out the next two trains to Moscow," he ordered, wanting to limit that route should Phelan opt for it.

They followed the man into the station where he was indeed seen trying to work out the ticketing system, the boards now displaying the lack of trains, the ladies behind the windows not speaking any English, either, it seemed to him. Frustrated, he pulled out his tablet, though there was no signal.

He made an interesting figure as he stood there—feeling helpless in the huge concourse of the station entrance way—his body wrapped up and protected from anyone that might come and take his prize, eyes glued to his tablet, for which he couldn't get any sort of connection. He placed it back in the rucksack that he'd carried on his right shoulder the whole time, and proceeded to leave the station.

"Take out the internet in the café," Twelve said, knowing his Contestant's next steps before they were even certain—his company the one that supplied nearly eighty per cent of the cities internet connection. "And we need that device. Send two men to steal it from his backpack, that'll really set things rolling."

They watched as Phelan entered the same café he'd already been to twice that morning, tablet out and searching for the connection once more before he'd even sat down. This time nothing happened, there was not even the icon showing that there was a signal in the place. He tried a second time, still nothing coming up.

They watched him lower his head, as if wondering why this was all now happening to him.

A crowd of tourists entered the café at that moment, standing around the entrance, making him stand to one side. He contemplated asking someone in the café what had happened to the internet signal, but couldn't see anyone available to ask—nor fancied trying to communicate what he needed. He put the tablet back into his rucksack and moved out slowly through the throng of people that had seemingly emerged from nowhere, a tour guide speaking to the mainly Chinese group in English, explaining how the café worked. He exited back out onto the street.

"We have his device," the confirmation came, one of Twelve's men in the crowd of tourists, pressed up momentarily against the Irishman's backpack, the tablet out within seconds as only the very best pickpockets knew how.

It was fifteen minutes later, as Phelan was followed—always at a distance—into another venue, a hotel this time, before the frantic search through his still open backpack confirmed his worst fears: he'd been robbed.

Within the Games Room, there was now a growing excitement and interest in this particular Hunt, one that had seen two oligarchs lock horns with each other, a bet neither man could now afford to lose; and it was all going wrong for one of them, as Twelve continued to stay one step ahead of his prey, out-thinking his Contestant, just part of his plan to stop the man even leaving the city—as the bets had now dictated.

Phelan sat in the hotel foyer for a while, head in hands, very much hidden away from the city around him, clearly working through what to do next. He had been robbed and part of him wanted to sort that element out with the police, but clearly there was a timing issue going on here, too.

Besides, the language barrier—not to mention the rumoured widespread corruption that he'd no doubt face—made going to the police an option he soon rejected.

Picking up his bag, he was back out onto the streets, now blending in well with many of the underworld characters that walked the same streets—his hood covering his head, baseball cap in place. At least it wasn't obvious he was a foreigner, he was dressed more like a little thug, and no city tour sellers bothered to even approach him now. That was something at least.

He still had money. They tracked him as he walked down a long stretch of Nevski, entering the doors of a tourist agency that he came across, the signs clearly visible from the street and written in English. The Trackers kept their watch, staying outside.

Twelve, standing in the Games Room, pulled up details for the firm his Contestant was now approaching. They dealt mainly in package deals, though they did have access to flights.

Twelve already had that angle covered, a few traffic cops on hand to stop any route to the airport, migration personnel ready to pull him to one side should he somehow still make it there. He hadn't yet needed to contact them with specific details—there was no certainty he'd even get that far.

Finding no real luck at the travel agency, he was seen leaving the building just minutes after entering, the team of now five Trackers on his tail constantly, spread out in each direction, at least one with a live camera feed which was beamed the short distance it actually was from there to Temple Mount.

They continued to track him further down Nevski, walking slowly as if he'd lost the plot, the urgency largely gone from his stride—Twelve was certain he'd already defeated him.

Passing an obvious Russian take on an English pub, they watched Phelan enter it, two of the Trackers going in moments later, the deflated Contestant already sitting down at the bar. Thankfully, they spoke his language and the two Trackers watched as their man had a brief conversation, the distance too far to make out what was said, but a beer was placed in front of him shortly after.

"Not another Irishman who's going to get drunk and piss away the money?" was the mocking cry that went up in the Games Room, a few laughed along with it.

"If that is the case, Fifteen, we won't be seeing you around these parts again now, will we?" There was menace in

Twelve's words, the man feeling attacked and targeted by someone he knew thought very little of him—and how he couldn't now wait to destroy him for it.

∞∞∞

It was three hours later, the day already moving into evening, when they left the pub, the Contestant finally moving at a time they thought they would need to send someone to retrieve the ticket, the Hunt already called.

He found a taxi cab, the driver being heard repeating the word airport as the car pulled away, a pair of Trackers finally in place to listen in on what was said.

"So, he's still going to make a try for it?" Twelve said, pulling up flight details on the screen in front of him, nothing showing as flying directly to London that evening. He'd missed his most obvious path out of there. This was becoming easier than he thought it would be. It disappointed him a little, though winning now was all that mattered.

He called through to his contacts within the traffic police, details given about the car that they were to pull over, the vehicle stopped as it headed south, still forty minutes from the airport.

Not knowing what they were meant to check for, and being told simply to delay the driver, they did all they could for forty minutes, before the passenger waved some money and they let him go on his way again. The delay would leave him little chance of making a flight out of there, but still, with the airport considered outside city limits, there were some bets he would lose if he even made it that far.

The final straw came at the airport, the Hunt—as much as they'd all enjoyed it—progressing no more. Migration services had been called, Twelve taking the hit on the chin, a small piece of business given away by losing the bet about city limits, but it was worth it. He didn't want to have to come down too hard—drawing attention to his reach—which would otherwise alert the other oligarchs to his connections during future events.

"We have a problem," the female voice came through into Twelve's ear piece, his contact at the airport sounding concerned.

∞∞∞

As Phelan had entered the café that morning, confirming the validity of the lottery ticket he'd just collected, he pulled his phone from his pocket, a Russian bought SIM which he'd used in Moscow, and spoke with someone briefly, entering the gent's toilet at the back of the café as he did so. Inside the gents, he took off his hooded sweater and his cap and gave them to the man now in front of him—chosen because of his close resemblance, matching Phelan in height and build. Phelan watched as the man quickly dressed, pulling up his hood around his head, putting the cap in place, before taking the bag, initially placing it on his left shoulder before Phelan corrected him.

"Right shoulder," he said, the switch made, the man leaving the toilets less than sixty seconds after Phelan had entered. Phelan put the phone to his ear once more.

"It's done," he said, silence following for a moment.

"Very good," the accented voice spoke back, "one moment." Phelan felt more alive than he had ever done so, pacing around the small area whilst holding the handset to his ear, awaiting his next command.

"Okay, leave right away, turning left as you exit, which will take you through the kitchens. Go, now," the voice said, Phelan following exactly what he was told to do, guided out through the kitchen area, without seeing another person, a fire exit opening to his touch. Moments later a car pulled up. "Get in," the voice in his ear said, Phelan climbing into the back seat, the car pulling away without a further word being spoken. They travelled through small side streets for a while, turning regularly, crisscrossing that part of town, before pulling out onto a larger, clearly more major road.

He had everything with him, having travelled light.

The voice came back on the phone; "They've bought it," Phelan understanding that the switch had gone unnoticed. They would now be following around this other person all day, attention diverted, allowing him to slip out of the country.

"You shouldn't have a problem getting through security, though I'll keep a watch out for you. If there is a problem, which I strongly doubt, you can use the name I mentioned. That would be enough to get you through." The name had meant nothing to Phelan—it wasn't the name of the man he was speaking to, but he was certain it would mean something to the person he would use it with. Nothing about the man speaking to him was anything but thorough and meaningful.

They got to the airport in just over thirty-five minutes, clearing through migration without a problem, and at the gate in plenty of time as the first people were just starting to board that late morning flight to London.

He'd made it.

The first and most likely stage of the plan to face a complication was nearly done—just as he'd been told it would be.

∞∞∞∞

"What do you mean we have a problem?" Twelve said, loudly without meaning to be so, the entire floor at Temple Mount alerted to the fact the Host was suddenly losing his cool.

His female Tracker ran through what they'd found out, that the guy they were following—had been following the whole day in fact—was not Phelan McDermott. They'd been tracking the wrong man.

As if to confirm what was being said secretly through his ear piece, the giant screen on the wall in front of them all now showed a video feed of the guy's hood being pulled down, his cap already removed.

The face was wrong. It wasn't the Irishman after all.

There was a collective intake of breath. To have made such an error meant all sorts of things.

Twelve began frantically making calls—the airport, the migration services, his contacts within the police. He ordered all non-Russians to be screened, the name he was after released to everyone he could have influence with.

They were now the actions of a very desperate man, all several hours too late, because Phelan had already landed at London's Heathrow Airport by that point, a car having met him and taken him to Lottery HQ. He was at that very moment going through the final processes of claiming the €33 million prize fund, the money to be wired to a number of prearranged accounts in various European banks, with further offshore accounts in place to move the money on later, as he would require.

He requested his identity to be kept secret, which wasn't an unusual thing to do, but he had a pre-signed court order enforcing his right to remain anonymous, which he'd shown them for good measure.

At three that afternoon in London, the money was wired to the account of Phelan's choosing, the last piece of action required from the Lottery organisers. They congratulated him once again, and after warm farewells—despite only meeting each other that afternoon—he made his exit.

Two hours ahead of the UK, in St Petersburg, it was gone five when Fifteen, the man with the most to gain from this particular Hunt, started checking something online.

The other Hunt, where Twenty had put forward his French Contestant, a €12 million prize on offer there—had ended two hours before and in the Russian's favour—so all eyes were on the unfolding saga that had befallen Twelve, something all the other oligarchs were secretly revelling in, none more so than Fifteen. Finding what he was wanting, he called out to all the others, waving his laptop in the air.

"It's claimed, the ticket that Phelan has, it's been claimed already." He was unable to keep a smile from breaking out on his face. The others came over, a few checking the facts on their own devices, all confirming within a minute that the Hunt had actually been successful—the money claimed.

"Damn you, Kuznetsov, if you've had anything to do with this!" Dmitry screamed, going for the throat of the man gloating before him and needing to be restrained.

To have broken protocol and used a real name—despite everyone knowing who the others all were—was unheard of. Using only a number reminded them they were just Hosts in a Hunt. Actual names were only for the real world, where they could go up against each other in business.

Here it was just pleasure, or meant to be.

The Chair came over to the two men—Twelve now separated from the man he'd started throttling—Fifteen catching his breath again, trying to shake off the fact he'd been caught off guard by such a physical onslaught.

"If I ever hear or see anything like that from any one of you ever again, you'll be carried out of this room in a bloody body bag! Have I made myself absolutely clear to you all, gentlemen? Twelve, we'll have words with each other immediately, follow me."

The room became silent, the Chair walking off to one side, Twelve reluctantly following—like a school boy pulled into the headmaster's office.

"Your behaviour was totally unacceptable just now, I expect much better from you."

"Don't you see, he's done this to me, he must have done? That guy had help today."

"We don't—yet—know what has happened, and I'd remind you that making wild accusations will not help anyone. You stepped out of line with making this a personal defeat. You became violent and you broke the code."

"Screw the bloody code!" he snarled back, the Chair catching him across the face, hard, with an open hand.

"How dare you disrespect everything I've put together, coming to my home and acting like you run the place."

Twelve, his right cheek visibly reddened, straightened and made eye contact, locking in a stare that was as cold as it was brash.

"What about the code that says one Host can't actively bring down another?"

"If that is proven to be the case, I'll deal with it personally—not you. Don't think for one minute I'll let anyone get away with that. But you've lost, for now. Deal with that first, and leave me to decide if anyone has broken the rules, okay?"

"I can't afford this loss!"

"Then you shouldn't have been stupid enough to have made that bet, now, should you! Get out of my sight," the Chair said, before whispering into his ear as he turned to walk away. "You've disappointed me today, Dmitry."

The following thirty minutes were silently chaotic, each man tiptoeing around the room, the day's events over but no one wanting to leave—there was so much they wanted still to see. Twelve, the second most ranked oligarch in their league, had held that position for the whole time.

He'd become proud, reckless at times.

Seeing him take a fall was something not to be missed—but what a fall. If it was to be believed, this deal he'd agreed to in theory with Fifteen could destroy him overnight.

It was a huge amount to hand over, connections and business opportunities just handed on a plate to this rival, a man who that morning was beneath him, poorer than him, too—now, well, that didn't bear thinking about.

Worst of all, and the bitterest of all pills he currently had to swallow, was that he'd lost. The man he'd put forward had beaten him, tricked him and taken his money and his pride. In doing so Phelan had brought shame on him, and that was the hardest thing of all to face, especially in front of a room full of fellow billionaires.

Could he even include himself under that title anymore, unsure even now of what impact this would all have on his financial security?

That was secondary—pride could always be restored. These defeats happened from time to time, as Annabel's success in the previous event showed. It was how quickly you broke them—how quickly you claimed back every cent that was rightfully yours—that mattered most. And he was going to destroy Phelan McDermott if it was the last thing he did.

22

Two days later Alex and Anissa sat with printouts in front of them, which detailed the fact that two long standing tickets had been claimed over the previous days, one day apart from each other. Both winners had remained anonymous, a usual practice the two British agents had come to see when it was the Russians reclaiming their money.

Once more, both in France and the UK, the two lottery providers refused to give any information about the identity of their winners.

"So, do you think there was another event just held?" Alex said, walking with Anissa alongside the banks of the Thames.

"Yes, I do. This was one of the dates those three Russians couldn't make available to me when I approached their offices about having them speak at a fake conference I was proposing. One happened to be in the country the week before, the others already overseas. He left on a flight to St Petersburg three days before the first ticket was claimed in London."

"What do you make of the fact they were claimed on separate days?"

"I've been thinking about that quite a bit. I don't know what to make of it. They usually hold the event on the same day, certainly from what we saw in St Petersburg. All four people were involved at the same time. They seemed to be trying to make it out that same day, convinced they had one day to claim. Our suspicion has always been that there is in reality an additional day to claim—which the Russians then use to grab the prize themselves once they've got hold of the ticket. So it is even possible that the one in the UK was in fact a winner from this event. The fact they've remained secretive is a little off, usually people want to make the fact known, especially in something like this. There must be the sense that greater public awareness would make you less vulnerable to reprisal."

"But more obvious for charity seekers," Alex said.

"That's true, too. It's possible that the Contestant got as far as the UK before being caught. The Russians might then just have claimed the prize themselves that same day and had done with it. Surely there is something we can do, somewhere we can look for answers and not just have doors closed in our faces? We are MI6, after all."

"We could make it an official operation."

"That's taking quite a risk."

"We can't just keep guessing though, always in the dark. We need to know more, need to open this up a little."

"I get your frustration, Alex, I do—believe me, I feel the same. It's just I have a family to think about, so to risk it all on this means I can't just think about what I want, they get affected too."

"Look, I don't want you to do anything you aren't completely happy with. I just don't see that we can carry on as we are—always behind the actual events, always chasing shadows—fitting this around the other stuff we need to get on with. If we make this an official operation, it becomes our sole focus."

"What would be the angle? We would need to prove that this is a threat to our national security, even if we did manage to get it signed off from above."

"Yes, you're right. I don't see what we could say." He stood there a while, the pair just in silence, before Alex said; "Andre Philips. We pull every resource to track where he is—that's a legitimate investigation. Okay, it might not warrant as many resources as we would need, but we could work with that. It would give us more capacity than we have now. We keep his name out of it all, for now. We still don't know where the leak is, but they do know we had a man in Russia and now he's clearly gone missing. I think we base our case around finding out where he is—or what happened to him. That'll enable us to hopefully turn over the stones he was hiding under, legitimately looking into the lives of those he might have been around, all within MI6 remits. He was a key informer for us who mysteriously vanished. Remember, they don't know we heard his last broadcast or when that was. We just have to say we haven't heard from him in over nine months. We have a right to set up a search for him, to gather information. They can't fault us for trying to look for him."

"I guess it does make some sense. What do we say if we are asked to disclose his real identity?"

"I don't know what that would mean, especially if he's still alive and simply hiding somewhere. If his name got to the wrong person within MI6—the one who put a lid on the last transmission he sent, not allowing us to hear it—we have to imagine their intention is malicious until we find out otherwise. I don't think we can risk disclosing his name, for the time being. But we can put in a request to be granted time to track down our informant's whereabouts, stating we are increasingly concerned for his safety and that we are sure he has information that is highly valuable to us if we can safely locate him. I'd imagine the mole here—assuming that is what's happened—would be only too keen for us to find this man and therefore learn his identity."

"Very good. Let's go with that then. Make contact again with Sasha, see if he's uncovered anything from the last few days in St Petersburg. Tell him what we know—see if he can trace Andre himself from that end. I think we can trust Sasha, now, don't you?"

"I'd lay my reputation on it."

∞∞∞

Alex had spoken with Sasha, a call made to his private number from a pay phone at London Bridge station. He'd given the Russian a little of the information they had, running through in highlights what they thought had just taken place. Sasha promised to have a look around.

Alex then gave him the details about Andre Philips, asking him to have a look into him from the Russian side, seeing if anything could be found on this man that MI6 had on the inside. Sasha noted down the name.

They agreed to meet in Oslo, Norway, in a few days' time. Staying out of Russia was probably the easiest way of keeping Alex and Anissa off the FSB radar—something Sasha was desperate to do. If that happened it would risk having his connection with the two MI6 agents known, and that was something he knew would be fatal. They ended the call, Alex placing the handset back, the station busy with activity.

Watching at a table in a Costa Coffee booth that occupied a corner of the main concourse there at London Bridge station, were the same people who had followed them after the FTSE100 conference, having listened in on his side of the call with the aid of a directional microphone.

It was clear that the British agent was speaking with someone—presumably in Russia—though Alex had been clear to say very little, everything implied, the agent well trained in conversations conducted over the telephone.

He had given up the name Andre Philips, and had repeated the city Oslo once, those listening deducing some sort of meeting was arranged for Norway.

A team would be ready for them at the other end, the team on him in London able to track him to the airport, so they would be sure when he was making the trip, giving folks in Oslo a few hours' warning to get everyone in place.

If a meeting was going to happen somewhere near the airport, maybe even in some of the restaurants that existed once you came through passport control, they would have people in place. They needed to know who Alex was speaking with—they needed to cut off permanently any connection between this Russian and the British Security Service.

∞∞∞

Phelan woke up to his alarm clock sounding. It was just before eight in the morning. He was now €33 million richer, and it felt amazing.

The last couple of days had gone smoother than he thought, but the next few days were key.

He was staying in a hotel in London, having not gone to see his family yet. They were being brought by car to him later that morning—the house packed, their essentials in two cases—the rest left in storage. They didn't know if they would ever be back to collect it.

They'd not mentioned anything to the children's school, it was as if they'd dropped off the planet overnight, here one day, vanished the next.

It was the way it needed to be, Phelan had been told. For the time being, anyway.

His wife's parents were flying out later that day, taking a day and a half before reaching the destination they were all heading for. Phelan's folks were already there, having moved the month before.

Phelan had come clean the previous month before he even went to St Petersburg, painstakingly going over the details of the plan with each set of parents, before detailing everything for his wife. Life had to continue as before, he'd told them. He knew he was being watched, and they had to act as if everything was normal.

His sudden trip to Russia had to take them all by surprise, though he'd made it look like he was going to Germany, as he'd been sure to be seen telling them. His wife had suggested they make it look as if not everything was right within their marriage—a touch Phelan had appreciated—delighted to have the backing of his wife.

To drop completely off the radar was not easy and required a lot of planning, and plenty of money. Thankfully the latter was now not an issue, and he'd had a lot of help with the planning of it all, someone he was eternally indebted to.

His wife and kids arrived at the hotel at ten that morning. The driver had been sure they were not followed. Their flight to Seattle was leaving in just over ninety minutes, so after greeting one another—the kids just happy to see their dad again after a few days' absence—they started to move, Phelan first kissing his wife with a passion, before taking her hand and leading them all towards the terminal entrance from the hotel which was situated right outside the main airport building.

Their bags were checked in for the entire flight. After a short stop-over in Seattle, they would have to catch a flight to Billings, Montana, via Salt Lake City, Utah. Each leg gave them only about forty minutes at each airport, but they were assured it would be enough time to make the connections.

Touching down in Billings, there had been ample time—the fact they had small kids in tow helping them jump the queues, the longest being in Seattle where they had to officially enter America—the next two flights were just internal transits.

Phelan's parents met the sleepy travellers at the airport, the kids delighted to see Nana and Pops, a surprise they'd kept from the kids up to that point.

They'd hired a mini van, enough to fit them all in, as well as Phelan's in-laws once they arrived, and to then be able to travel around altogether. His dad drove, having adjusted to the roads there over the last month, allowing Phelan and his family some much needed sleep, though the kids were too excited to stay sleeping for long.

The destination was a few hours east of the airport, nearing the state line of Montana itself. They'd been offered use of a ranch that way, the area sparsely populated, offering them time to settle, to stay off the grid, whilst they worked through their next moves. Phelan had been told he'd need a year—maybe eighteen months on the run—before it would be safe again.

He'd already considered further places they could move to if needed, and he'd wondered about South America, but was cautious about being an obviously wealthy family in countries that had so much crime. Besides, too much travelling would take it out of the kids, though settling anywhere for more than it was safe to do was something he wouldn't allow to happen to his family.

Driving along the roads—sleep now impossible for him too, an hour into the journey—he could see why Montana had been suggested to him, the sky huge on the windscreen in front of him, the land flat and lush, stretching for miles, with little sign of life. It was one of the largest states in the USA, and one of the least populated, too. It made a perfect stop-off point. Once the dust had settled, he would have to assess where they went next.

Pulling up at the ranch, Phelan not knowing what to expect, he was delighted to see that it was what he might have called a farm, though its cattle-raising years had long since passed, the property having sat empty for a decade. There were actually three separate farms, all making up one larger ranch, one family having occupied all the farms before. Oil was found on their land, money pouring in overnight, meaning the family decided to leave the farming lifestyle altogether, the ranch abandoned in the process.

A railway line ran through the middle, separating two of the farm buildings from the third. The plan was for Phelan and his family to live one side of the track, both sets of parents having their own houses on the other side. All three shared the only paved road in and out of the ranch, which opened onto the main road into town.

A river ran along the edge of the property's four-hundred acres and there were cliffs high above on the other side. Wildlife was plentiful, deer ran freely and larger animals too. Various big cats could be found by the best hunters, all native to the area. It was a wilderness, not like anything to be seen in Ireland, and his parents had loved their month there already.

The kids didn't know where to run first, staying close to the house, well away from the railway line, not understanding the concept that everything around them was their land now, theirs to roam freely in—theirs to do what they liked with. Their Pops said he would take them out on the quad bikes later, each in turn, to show them around properly. They loved the sound of that.

In a few hours Phelan's dad would make a return run to the airport, his wife going with him to be there when her own parents arrived that evening, and that night they would all eat together under one roof for the first time since their wedding reception. Life was full of possibilities all of a sudden.

23

A team of half a dozen men employed by Dmitry Sokoloff had arrived in London, in search of Phelan McDermott. Sokoloff himself was beginning to feel the heat in Moscow—which would come to a head before the day was out.

In London, the men went directly to the family home of Phelan, the two men dressed in some form of generic looking overalls and going up to the front door. There was no answer. Even from where they were standing, with sight of the front room through the open curtain-less windows, they could see the house was empty. They went around the back of the house, checking no one was watching, and after forcing the back door, no alarm sounding, made a quick look around, but there was no point going upstairs—the house was totally empty, the family clearly gone.

The team leader looked through the information he had, the two men he'd sent to the house now back in the van having reported the situation, and they pulled away, eventually making it onto the motorway, heading for Oxford. Tracking other family members was now the key.

A little over an hour later, they were pulling into the system of streets that would lead them to the home of Mr and Mrs

Jenkins, Phelan McDermott's in-laws. Here, approaching the front door, they saw that the curtains were drawn. There was no reply to their knocking, and they were about to go around the back when a neighbour opened the front door of the house to the left.

"They aren't home," she offered, seeing the yellow uniforms, taking them as some sort of meter readers or gas workers. "Gone away," she added before either of them had said anything.

"Can you tell me where they have gone?" one said, clearly showing he was not from England with his accent, though that only fitted the image more.

"They didn't say anything, I just saw them loading two bags into a taxi yesterday and they cleared off."

They thanked her for her help, and returned to the van. The team leader made a call to Moscow, catching Dmitry as he was arriving at his office, reporting the fact that both UK homes were now empty. Did he want them to travel to Ireland?

"Yes, get on a bloody plane and get me some answers, or so help me I'll feed you to the wolves!" he screamed down the handset, ending the call, dropping the phone into his pocket.

"You shouldn't let it get to you," a voice spoke from the chair at his own desk, the man swivelling around only as Dmitry switched on the lights, revealing himself to him. It was Aleksey Kuznetsov, the man who had won most of what Dmitry now couldn't afford to let go.

"What the hell are you doing here, and who let you into my office?"

"Your office? Now, Dmitry, we both know it isn't going to be yours for very much longer, now, is it?"

There was rage burning inside him at this point, to be spoken to by someone so much below him—and in his own office—whatever fantasy this man might otherwise have.

"You'll never get this, you piece of street trash. It was you, wasn't it! You set me up."

"Rubbish. I'd choose your words more carefully than you choose your Contestants." He was loving every minute of this and didn't mind letting that show on his face. "I've come for what is rightfully mine—won fair and square."

"Rightfully yours? You can go to…" but Aleksey cut him off.

"Oh no you don't! Don't you dare think you are walking away from this one. I'm taking everything that's mine."

"It would destroy my empire. I don't have the liquid assets to be able to cash out."

"You should have thought of that."

"There are two thousand people I employ that are desperate for their next pay cheque."

"That isn't my problem, now, is it."

"You complete…" Dmitry said, fists clenched but again Aleksey acted before he could finish his sentence, a gun pulled to the face of the man standing just feet in front of him.

"I've come for everything I'm owed."

Dmitry froze, taking in the gun, the determination in the eyes of the man in front of him, only now seeing that he had wildly underestimated the lengths to which this fellow oligarch would actually go, for the first time seeing a side to the man that must have existed but had been kept hidden, at least from his eyes.

"What do you mean by putting a gun to my head? Are you going to kill me in my own office?"

"If I have to."

"And what would the Chair say about that, if you were found out?"

"Our Chair sent me here today. You've failed to keep your word."

"My word? My *word*? I've been set up, if not by you, then by someone. That Irishman knew what was happening—had to have known. How else could he have given me the slip? What's more—he's fled the UK, his family upped and left, relatives too. No one does that in a few days. No one empties a house and leaves everything that quickly. Don't you see? It was a set-up from the start. Someone played me, and you need to ask yourself, if it wasn't you, then who was it, because if it wasn't someone in the Games Room, it means someone on the outside knows about us, and if that's the case we are all screwed."

Aleksey took in the words, the reasoning interesting. He hadn't thought about the chance that the man had been set up, but that was still a secondary thought. He'd come to get what was his.

"It doesn't matter to me, right now. I still don't have what I came for. The Chair will destroy your company via its share price if you have not agreed to settle our bet before the close of business today. Either that, or I put a bullet through your skull right now and just pick up the pieces of your bloody broken empire after they've buried you. Either way, you are finished, a dead man walking, or not, as the case may be." He threw some papers on the table, documents he'd had his lawyers draw up, giving him access to everything he'd bargained for in the bet. "If you refuse to sign these papers right now, it gives me no choice." He deliberately cocked the weapon in his hand, the click of the bolt the only noise either man heard at that moment.

"Okay," Dmitry said, his hand coming up in defeat, determined to come through this—and for that he didn't need a bullet in the skull. If he could somehow survive, there was the chance of revenge somewhere down the line. He picked up a pen from his desk, signing the documents without even reading them, signing away effectively everything he'd worked for, his companies needing to be sold off in order to provide the cash required to meet the bet. He'd been burnt in the most terrible way possible and it would be a long way back from there—if that was even now possible.

∞∞∞

It was a fresh new morning in eastern Montana, Phelan up early, running across the ranch, amazed that he could run flat out for five minutes and not leave the property where they now resided. His in-laws had arrived yesterday, sleepy and wanting to catch an early night, but he'd seen them both up and about as he'd passed their new house that morning, the effects of jet lag no doubt playing havoc with their sleep, as it had also done for him that morning.

By ten, they were all around their breakfast table, the kids playing outside, still not venturing too far from the comfort of home. A pot of tea sat in the middle of the table.

This move—this escape to America as it was—had taken much agreement, many conversations had in secret over the previous month, getting to the point where all Phelan could do was tell them everything, and the reason why they couldn't stay where they were. He knew that both sets of parents would have been visited once it was clear his own family had vanished—he was certain someone would come looking.

He had only really briefly told them back in England the fact they might have to move around a number of times, and having shared that news in more detail just then, two thirds of the room still feeling the effects of their latest journey, the news was not met with much joy. It would be hard on them all to move around too often, but especially for the kids.

Phelan could see the point his wife was making, but their safety was his highest priority at that moment.

"Tell me more about this man you mentioned, the one you've been working for," his dad had said, taking another cup of tea and standing by the window, the kids outside in the distance throwing stones into the river.

"Matvey Filipov approached me some time ago. He ultimately owned the firm I was working at. That only came to light after I had some brief interactions with him and then did some research. He's one of Russia's richest men, and he said he had a special mission for me. Not much more happened until three months ago. He pointed out I was being followed by a team of Russians working for another very rich man. He said he knew why and that I should carry on as usual. He then explained everything to me."

"And that's when you talked with us about needing to move?" his dad said.

"Yes, Filipov actually made the suggestion, giving me details about this ranch. He's funded it up to this point."

"So he knows we are here? Doesn't that make us vulnerable if he decides to let on to someone about our location—I mean the men hunting you down?" his wife said, her own father speaking up next.

"If we can't trust this man with everything he's already done so far, darling, I don't think we can trust anyone."

"True," Phelan said, picking up the conversation again. "Look, Filipov laid this out right from the beginning, planned it all. He guided me throughout St Petersburg, kept me safe and helped me escape."

"So what does he gain from it all? I mean, he's let you keep the money, hasn't he?" his mother said.

"Yes, that's true son, so what's his angle on helping you like this?" his dad added.

There was a little tension growing in the room, and Phelan wished he had something concrete to tell them, but he'd been asking himself the same things on and off for a while, whilst pinching himself that this was even really happening to him.

"I don't know, is the short answer, but I'm sure he benefits in some way. Does it matter?"

"Son, when there is €33 million involved, it always matters. These people don't mess around."

"I know, Dad, don't worry. Filipov has got us this far, hasn't he? He's done us proud."

"While it lasts."

"Mum, we have the money, it's been wired around the world to different accounts that now only I have access to."

"Still, it makes me nervous. We can't live life on the run."

"I don't intend us to, either. Everyone, please, bear with me. We'll be able to handle this, Filipov knows what he is doing. If he saw the need for me to be the one to claim this lottery ticket, by sabotaging some event a group of Russians were putting on, he's done it for good reason. He says he'll keep us safe, that he's got our backs, and I for one believe him. I mean, look at where we are. Who's going to find us here?"

"I just don't like the idea that we have to hide for the rest of our lives. What about those we knew before, our friends? What about them?"

"For now, we have to let them be. It's the only way of keeping everyone safe, including them. Look, this is not going to go on forever. Filipov said a year, eighteen months max."

"And then what?"

"Then, we can go back to normal life."

"And the money?"

"It's ours to do with what we want, he was clear on that. We get to do normal life millions of pounds richer than we could ever have dreamed."

"It still feels too good to be true, that's all," his mum said, standing up and going outside to see the children, it all getting too much for her. Phelan went to go after her before his dad caught him by the shoulder.

"Leave her be, son. She just needs time, we all do. This is a big change for everyone, and we aren't as young as we used to be—that's all." He left his son in the house, going out to join his wife and the grandkids. Phelan's in-laws also got up and left at that moment, leaving just him and his wife, who was standing at the window above the kitchen sink, watching the children playing with their grandparents outside. Phelan stood behind her, resting his chin on her head, holding her in his arms.

"It'll all work out well for us, I promise. I wouldn't ever let something bad happen to any one of us."

"I know, darling. I do." He turned her around, kissing her on the lips, holding her close for a few moments before they went and joined the others outside.

24

Alex and Anissa had been granted some extra resources to find their missing contact, but they weren't given a lot of time. Someone wanted more information from them before they would be given the full freedom they wanted, and that made them cautious.

They were flying to Oslo that morning to meet up with Sasha, their plane leaving London City Airport at ten. The flight was only half full, and as the Russians watched them enter the airport—confirming on the website that there was a direct flight to Norway taking off in one hour—they reported this back. A message was sent to the team already in place in Oslo to take up their positions, ready to be at any venue where the British agents might be planning on meeting their informant.

As the plane touched down in Oslo, a light rain was falling but the plane unloaded through a walkway directly into the terminal building, meaning they didn't get wet. Sasha was to meet them before customs, before they exited the control area—but he wasn't there.

Just then a stranger handed them both an envelope, without saying a word and moved away, before they could comment.

It wasn't Sasha, they were sure about that, and they only watched him briefly before taking in the details they had been handed. Inside—as well as a plane ticket for them both—was a short note; 'Take the connection to Tallinn, we've been compromised. Unfriendly people potentially waiting for you outside. Go now, the flight leaves in twenty minutes.'

They looked up, following signs directing people to flight transfers, and got to the gate for the flight departing to Tallinn just in time, the crew about to close the gate. They handed their boarding passes to the lady and were allowed to board, the very final passengers to do so before the door closed and the flight prepared for take off. It was an hour's hop over the Baltic sea to the east.

The drizzle hadn't made it to Tallinn as they climbed down the steps of their plane, touching tarmac before being escorted into the terminal building, following the flow of people, though the aircraft had not been a big one, and it was far from busy.

Sasha met them outside the airport building, dressed in a smart suit and holding a board with their names on it. Anissa smiled at the sight of him, their Russian contact playing the role of a chauffeur, but went along with it, at least until they were in the car, and driving towards the centre of the city.

They didn't get that far, as only about one kilometre from the airport there was a huge shopping centre, and Sasha pulled into the parking area in front of it. They got out of the car, and walked into the main entrance, taking an escalator up to the second floor and sitting down in one of the many eateries they found. It was not too busy around them, the lunchtime trade already easing off. They sat at a six seater table overlooking the front parking area where they had just left the car. Aside from the waitress who came to take a drinks order, there was no one within earshot of them, meaning they could speak freely.

"Tell me what happened," Alex said, the three now sitting down, jackets off, drinks in front of them.

"They were listening to your side of the conversation you had with me—must have been following you in London."

"How do you know it was just my side of the call they heard?"

"I wouldn't still be here if that had been the case, but they knew you were meeting me in Oslo, they had a team there. They also know about Andre Philip."

Alex kicked himself, recalling the conversation they'd had, having made reference to the name at least once.

"It came up on my search when I went looking for what we had on Mr Philip himself—the fact that there had been a recent search for the same name. They would have found what I found—which was nothing. We don't know that name."

"That's something. It's the only name he ever used with me."

"That's probably saved his life, anyway, and bought us a little time, but not loads. Besides, it's all kicking off within this organisation you've been looking into," and Sasha went on to tell them the information he'd come across. The sudden apparent downfall of one of Russia's richest men, the equally impressive rise of another, the fact they'd both been on a trip to St Petersburg during the same days the week before, across the same dates Anissa had highlighted as a possible event gathering. He also had information that suggested Dmitry Sokoloff had men moving around the UK.

"This comes from where?"

"FSB base in London itself. They arrived the day after the event in London. They tracked them to two addresses, one on the edges of London, the other in Oxford."

"Another person was victorious, it's the only possible reason they would be hunting around."

"Yes, I've come to the same conclusion. Teams were sent to check out the two addresses—both empty—one completely so."

"Find out who's registered to those addresses," Alex said, his comment intended for Anissa before Sasha dropped some papers onto the table.

"Already done that one, Alex. The London address was a Mr & Mrs Phelan McDermott. The Oxford one for a Mr & Mrs Jenkins."

"Have you found the connection between these two?"

"Yes, I have actually, thank you for asking," Sasha said, smiling at his own sense of humour. "They are the parents of Mrs McDermott."

"And they've gone?" Anissa repeated out loud, more so for herself as she was taking in the facts than anything else.

"Absolutely. No sign of them. The situation has already been raised with the local police in that part of London, the kids just not appearing for school. There had been no suggestion they were going to be away, and your country now fines parents for doing that."

"My goodness, so another person has made good with the money. How much was it again?" Alex said, Anissa having looked up the details for that particular lottery draw the previous day.

"€33 million."

They paused at that moment, the waitress coming back to take their food order, none of them having looked yet at the menu but certainly wanting something to eat. They each scanned the offerings, making their choices and the waitress said she would have their food for them in about fifteen minutes, leaving them to it once again.

"So why am I being followed?" Alex started up, coming back to the one question most pressing for him. "Whose feathers have I ruffled enough for them to put a team on me?"

"Whoever it is, whoever sent men to Oslo, will know you are onto them now that you didn't show up in Norway. I don't think we can risk meeting like this anymore," Sasha said, taking a piece of paper from his notepad, writing down an email address and password. "Here, use this," he said, giving the piece of paper to Alex, "we create a draft message and save it within this email address. We check it daily. Nothing gets sent, no calls to me whatsoever, we write everything down on the draft email and wait for a response. Am I absolutely clear?"

"Yes, Sasha," Alex said, realising more than ever just how much they'd expected from Sasha, putting him in a precarious position within his own organisation—there being no doubt that the FSB would deal with him ruthlessly if they were ever to find out his involvement in this matter. Anissa made a mental note of the details as Alex showed them to her, and then tore up the piece of paper into very small pieces.

They chatted a little more, mainly lighthearted stuff, the previous conversation getting sombre so quickly as the reality of the situation started to dawn on them all.

When the food arrived they tucked into quite good quality food, washing it down with a brand of local Estonian beer that the waitress had recommended once they'd asked, as the afternoon wore on with no hint of the sun yet ready to leave the bright blue skies above.

Sasha dropped them at the airport, an evening flight taking them back to London leaving at nine, himself planning to drive back to St Petersburg, having brought his own car the moment he realised that Oslo was off limits to them. He hadn't dared risk flying at all.

They hugged each other warmly, like old friends now, aware that meeting up was no longer going to be possible, and they went their separate ways.

∞∞∞

In London the following morning, it was a fine day. Alex and Anissa had parted company the night before, Anissa taking a few days with family—a long overdue rest—Alex promising to press on with things in the meantime.

They'd talked a lot on the plane about needing to open this whole investigation up to more people—senior people—within MI6. That was a risk, as they still had no idea who wasn't being entirely honest with them and why, nor whose feathers they were ruffling in the process.

Alex had arranged a meeting that morning with the Deputy Director General himself. The DDG was second in the chain of command, and highly connected to the whole organisational structure within MI6. In his younger years as a field agent, after a successful military career, he'd served time in the Moscow region, as well as being based in Kiev, Ukraine, for many years after his time in Russia. The meeting was arranged for eleven.

Bringing his small team up to speed on what they had found out on the trip to Oslo—he hadn't bothered to tell anyone other than the senior technician that they'd been diverted—Alex ran through some things, one eye constantly on the clock, really just going through the motions.

Involving the DDG in things was a slight risk—and also threatened to annoy Alex's immediate superiors—the action of taking anything directly higher always seen as somewhat of a betrayal of trust to those who'd been leap frogged. You don't break the chain of command easily within MI6. It was a gamble he was prepared to take. Getting time with such a busy person was also a challenge, which was why he was happy when the man's secretary had confirmed there was a slot of fifteen minutes on the dot of eleven. He would make every second count.

At ten to eleven, Alex left the office on the third floor that he'd been working in and climbed the two flights to the top floor, where the DDG had his office, a lush but slightly smaller version of the actual Director General's office, which was at the end of the same corridor.

The door was open, Alex arriving a couple of minutes early, the secretary smiling as he entered the room. The DDG looked up from his desk, signed a paper and passed it to his secretary. She took it and left the room without saying a word, shutting the door behind her.

"Please, take a seat Alex," the DDG waved, Alex sitting down in the chair facing the desk. On the far side of the office were a couple of two-man black leather sofas, where people could sit in more comfort, taking time to chat—this was obviously not such an occasion.

The DDG had almost blond hair, which looked bleached but that seemed unlikely for a man of his senior years. Old army photos hung on the wall, the hair colour distinctive in all, the eyes not changing one bit throughout the range of photos, even if the face in front of him now was showing signs of age.

"Thank you for seeing me at such short notice."

"Alex, it's not often you come to see me…how long has it been since the last time? Two years, maybe?" and he paused for a moment, though he didn't need Alex to answer. He knew precisely how long ago the last meeting had been, there was very little that slipped past his bright mind. "So if one of our most capable field agents demands to see me at short notice, you get a sense when you're in my position that there is something he really needs to talk through." His tone was warm towards Alex, bordering on jovial, but Alex didn't know him enough to feel that he could read the man just yet.

"I need to bring you up to speed on something I've been working on."

"I'm guessing you are bringing this directly to me for a reason." Both men knew how it worked within the service, the DDG fully aware of the usual chain of command—which got ignored nearly as much as it got adhered to—or maybe that was just his perception, and yet here was another example of it about to happen.

Alex told the DDG about his investigations, going over the details of Andre Philip, their connection to him and what Andre had shared in his last recording before apparently going missing, MI6 unable to trace him from then on.

He then talked about their trip to St Petersburg and what they'd learnt since about the involvement of certain high profile Russian businessmen within a specific organisation. He'd avoided the word oligarch but the DDG understood exactly who this young agent was talking about, what types of men he'd begun to investigate. Alex finished with the suspicion that he was now being followed by someone from the Russian side—possibly FSB—possibly people connected to some of the oligarchs. He didn't say where he heard this from, deciding to keep Sasha's name out of everything, his identity known to very few, and his role in helping this latest case known to even fewer.

After what was nearly ten minutes of going over the details, Alex finished, the DDG sitting back in his chair, as if allowing the last drops of information to finally filter through to where they needed to be stored.

"You sure go for it when you pick up a scent, don't you?" is what he said. "Who knows about this within Six?"

Alex ran through the small list of people he'd been working with, the DDG making a mental list—as always—of everything, his pen not touched throughout their entire conversation, his pad still showing a blank page in front of him.

"Well? What do you think?"

"I think you were right to bring this to me. As you said, we'll have to be careful. It's a little difficult to see what actual crimes are taking place—the actual threat—so we can't just round these men up and hand them arrest warrants. We need more."

"I know, and I'm working on that."

"You mentioned earlier something about having reservations with sharing this within MI6, and I guess that's the reason you came directly to me today. What did you mean exactly by that?"

Alex had not gone into detail about the transmission not being shared with him. He'd tried to protect the man who had told him about it, the senior technician now part of his small team.

"I meant that last report we had from Andre Philip. I would never have known about it coming in had I not been made aware of the fact a few days after the event, the person who received it becoming concerned that nothing had been done about it. He didn't know what else to do."

The DDG picked up his pen for the first time, taking the pad with his other hand and jotting down something on the paper now on his lap, the angle such that Alex could not see what was being written. The DDG glanced at the clock on the wall, their time up, and Alex knew it.

"Thank you for bringing this to my attention, Alex. You were right to do so. Please keep me informed daily on any further developments. I will not file an official report, as requested. This will be just between us, for the time being. It can't stay that way forever, you understand?" He stood from his chair, arm extended for a handshake. Alex stood.

"Thanks for your time. I'll keep you informed," and Alex met the hand, the DDG's grip strong and true, and he left the office, closing the door behind him.

The DDG sat back down behind his desk, pondering all that he'd just been told, jotting down the highlights from the conversation onto the pad in front of him, circling one or two key pieces of information.

∞∞∞

Later that day, a call was put to the teams watching Alex. They were all told to stand down, that the situation had changed, and they were to stop tracking him for the time being.

One van with three people in it had been stationed outside his home for a few days, passing themselves off as telecom engineers. They packed up their things, everything put back into the van and they drove away.

Outside the offices of MI6, another two individuals—a man and a woman whose cover was as tourists—stood up from where they had been waiting, having come onto the job only that morning, tasked with following Alex as he left the office, listening in on anyone he might be meeting with.

As quickly as this group of people had arrived, they disappeared, dropping back out of sight, hiding once more—gone.

25

Leicester Square had been closed off all evening, the police in place, the crowds of onlookers jostling for a sight of their idols. The latest Hollywood blockbuster had come to town, though it had partly been shot in studios around London, too. The cast were international, in keeping with the nature of the film—the star, a beauty of world cinema, the Russian—Svetlana Volkov.

She and her husband had flown in on the family jet the day before, travelling and spending the night in a London property that they kept for such visits. It was their first stay there in six months, her work mainly taking her to America, at least for the last two projects, his mainly keeping him in Russia, or the Far East, when he wasn't with his wife in California.

They walked arm in arm down the red carpet, flash bulbs lighting the night sky. She wore her now familiar white fur jacket, a trademark connected to her as much as wealth was connected with them as a couple.

They made an interesting pair, and gave middle aged men hope when they compared the two people, though despite how it looked, the age gap wasn't anywhere as great as people assumed. She looked years younger than her actual age, and he'd always had an air of maturity around him, often going beyond his years. He was actually only seven years her senior, but as they walked up the red carpet—one of many couples to have done so—no one would have been surprised if they'd been told that the age difference between them was twenty years.

They posed for a few more photos, his wife the one taking the lead. Sergej had never been one for too much publicity, but had taken to it well since his marriage to Russia's most prized actress, coming to understand that every time he was seen together with her in public, his image improved—it was just good for business.

This latest film had been a big one for her, coming into a popular franchise but given a significant role. It was thought that she was there to shake things up a bit, to stop it all getting a bit tired, and the early reviews from the critics had been good, her own role within the film marked as exceptional. There were even early murmurs of an award or two heading her way.

Sergej was immensely proud of his wife, and they greeted various VIPs who had been allowed inside for the first public screening of the film in the UK. The film had broken the previous weekend in America, jumping straight into the top ten if not taking the pole position, but the UK had always been the film franchise's greatest market, and expectation was high.

Starting the following day, by happy coincidence for them, was the annual Russian businessmen's conference, which was hosted in London each year, mainly for the Russians who had made London their new home. It was a chance to gather together, a smaller elite group, something different from any of the other dozen or so where they might find themselves rubbing shoulders with each other.

The Volkovs had often been invited, though this was only the second time they could make it. It would last for two days and attracted somewhere around thirty different Russians, their interests ranging from owning sports teams to national industries, not to mention some of the most opulent and now most sought after properties in London.

The film finished its screening at just after eleven. The media then held interviews straight after with the lead characters, which involved Svetlana, her English now very good, though she often used the American term where it differed from the English, giving away the time she'd spent across the ocean.

The cameras loved her face as she granted those in the room twenty minutes of answering questions. She only answered things related to the movie, dodging the odd journalist who dared to ask things relating to matters outside her latest role. She quickly moved on. *Yes, she'd enjoyed playing the role in the latest film, and yes, she was a fan of the series from a little girl, watching it with her parents. Never did she imagine she'd be considered worthy enough to be asked to come on board.* They lapped it all up, asking her how she had enjoyed filming in England, how life compared to her times in Los Angeles.

By half eleven, the room was showing signs of the lateness of the hour, and Svetlana ended the interview, now tired herself. It had been a long day, and she wanted to celebrate with her husband, the couple expected at an exclusive party that followed the premiere, before any sleep could be had.

She was used to everything that her life now entailed, as was her husband, who was waiting for her at the back of the room, the reporters now packing away their things, desperate themselves to make the evening's print deadline, though most had emailed their reports across already.

"You seemed to enjoy that, my darling," he said, having arrived for the last few minutes of the questions. She had a natural presence about her and she came across well in front of the camera, whether it was the film cameras for the big screen or the television cameras during the interviews. She was always so softly spoken, so gentle. It made his own character—at least in the public eye—stick out all the more, the man known as *the Wolf* in his earlier years, an image that had started to shift a little, especially since his prison years, mainly referring to his earlier years in business as one of Moscow's most ruthless residents.

Their car was waiting for them out at the rear entrance, several of the film's cast having already used that exit that night, though out front the circus had largely shut down once the last of the stars arrived. Most knew they wouldn't be seeing their idols again, the carpet packed away before the movie had even started.

Five minutes later they were pulling in through gates on the street known as Billionaires Row, just a stone's throw from Buckingham Palace and the most expensive street in London. They were greeted as they entered the property, a huge building that was owned by one of Britain's richest men who happened to be a fellow Russian. In the reception room there were only three or four dozen people there, all recognisable to each other, even if they didn't necessarily know each other personally. It was that type of gathering.

Svetlana was the only actor there. The Volkovs joined another couple, who were standing together with champagne flutes in hand and they handed glasses from the table to the Volkovs as they joined them.

"A fine display you put up there on that screen, Svetlana," the man said, the couple greeting each other with kisses.

"Thank you," Svetlana said.

Sergej added, "I guess you wish your players responded the way she does before a camera." Both men smiled, though sport was not Sergej's most knowledgeable subject.

"Well, the talent your beautiful wife possesses is not so easily found in the world of football, and when it is, it costs a truck load of money."

"It costs a lot of money outside the world of football, too," Sergej said, a smile appearing on his trim face, his arm going around the waist of his wife.

They moved on, spending time with various groups—some of the men present due at the conference the following day. Sergej made a point of personally introducing Svetlana to each couple they came across, unsure of who she'd met before and not wanting to leave anyone out. She went along with it each time, not letting on whether or not she had in fact met them before, though she had not met most of the women the men came with—how could she, when she figured most of the men would only have met their escorts themselves that same day? Sergej was a rare exception, so it would seem.

At two in the morning, the party was coming to an end, and the various guests made their farewells, the Volkovs following the last few visitors out. As they got into the back of the car, their driver woke from a doze—they didn't blame him. They were soon on their way home, a drive of only about twenty minutes.

∞∞∞∞

The following morning, after a light breakfast, the Volkovs left their residence and headed for the conference. They were the first from the previous night's party to arrive, though there were at least a dozen others who were also now present. Sergej did his part once more of making sure those already there were personally introduced to his wife, and she once more went along with it. She knew it meant a lot to him.

"Svetlana, this is Roman Ivanov," Sergej said, introducing him to a man she had met before, the two shaking hands anyway. "Roman is one of the UK's richest men, though of course a fellow Russian. His companies in this country are right up there with the best."

"Thank you, Sergej, but you speak too highly of me. I'm just a humble man trying to make a living for my family."

Sergej patted him on the back, the couple moving on, Svetlana catching his eye as they were passing, something momentarily communicated, then her smile returned and she turned away, following her husband to the far side of the room, where she was once more reintroduced to Dmitry Kaminski. The two shook hands, there was a noticeable nervousness about Dmitry.

"Thinks himself to be a future leader of our nation," Sergej whispered to his wife, once Kaminski had moved on from their brief conversation. "Some say he would make a good President, too."

"Do they?" Svetlana said, pondering the man she'd just been speaking with, watching him as he walked away.

Back at the entrance more guests were arriving, amongst them a man she didn't recognise, his dress code and colouring suggesting he wasn't Russian at all. She watched him carefully for a moment. Another Russian then approached this man, a conversation started. It lasted maybe one minute, the two parting company, the visitor scanning around the room—noticing the attention he was getting from Svetlana—before he turned and left.

Right then, Akim Kozlov came over, greeting them both as the old friends they were to him. When the time came to part, Svetlana went over to speak with the man she knew who had greeted the stranger—Dmitry Pavlov.

"Dmitry, that man you spoke with about ten minutes ago—the Englishman," she said, making the obvious assumption but Dmitry seemed to understand who she meant. "Who was he?"

"I recognised him from the conference I was at the other month. He was heading up the security for that event—MI6. I wondered if he was responsible for security here today, too, it being unusual for MI6 to be involved with this particular set up, as you can understand."

"Quite. Tell me, what did he say? Why was he here?"

"He didn't say, though he left shortly after. I don't think he is involved in the security aspect here."

"Interesting," she said, her husband coming over at that moment, a glass of orange juice in his hand which he handed to Svetlana.

"Excellent, the two of you have met. Did you know that Dmitry Pavlov is actually the great grandson of Ivan Pavlov?"

he said, Svetlana already aware of that, as well as what Ivan had become so famous for.

"Is that so?" she said, no hint that this was anything but new information. "It's amazing what you find out at events like these," she said, walking on with her husband now, as guests continued to arrive.

26

Dmitry Sokoloff felt like a dead man walking, the issues and debts flying around him, whilst he tried his best to carry on as before. Those closest to him within his business world didn't know what to say—he'd kept what was happening from them. His closest financial advisor had not seen his boss this disturbed.

Instead of dealing with what was about to happen—which might mean he'd salvage something from the train wreck heading his way—Sokoloff did what he had always done, carrying on as if nothing was up.

He'd just left a meeting with yet another disappointed company man, the papers signed to sell off another of the group's—so called—struggling businesses. The reality was, he needed the capital; the sale and then loss of hundreds of jobs was just a numbers thing for a man who for so long had been untouchable—now he was exposed. Even this latest sale wouldn't mitigate what he would be forced to do, and that was to break into good businesses, dismantling them in what would surely prove a catastrophic manner. That day wasn't yet quite upon him, and if he could stop that from happening, he would.

He had pushed up prices for advertising across his television network, the move unpopular, and again not likely to alter the inevitable. As the sole owner of the leading channels in his country, it was prime time viewing his customers couldn't avoid missing out on, effectively being squeezed for as much as he could get from them. It eased cash flow in the short term, but the full ramifications of what he'd thrown away in St Petersburg had yet to fully hit.

He was also a key financier behind President Putin, one of only a few of the richest men to wholeheartedly back his reelection campaign, and many things since. The trade off with the power and potential this offered his empire was worth the investment.

He'd been trying to get a meeting arranged with the President all morning—as yet, to no avail. Had word reached the Kremlin about his imminent downfall, a collapse that could be avoided—he hoped—if he could get time with Putin? The President owed him, it was the least he could offer for one of the few men backing him so recklessly financially.

All that money had been kept from public record, of course, though it was widely known among the rich elite, the very oligarchs he often rubbed shoulders with in the Games. If word had indeed spread, though he wasn't certain it had, due to the secretive nature of their activities, his very reputation would be in tatters, his honour at stake. Guilt was never the issue, but a loss of honour was. He would do anything to restore that honour now, no matter how guilty that made him.

Besides the distractions of a crumbling empire that threatened to cost him nearly all his wealth—far more even than the value of the actual bet he'd made in St Petersburg—his main focus since that day was fixed solely on Phelan McDermott, the as yet unlocated Irishman who had caused all this.

Coupled with the thought of the dishonour that the Irishman had caused Dmitry, was the niggling suspicion that Phelan was getting help and not just with his fortunate escape from St Petersburg. His disappearance since—and that of his wider family too—looked like something pre-planned and orchestrated. Within the Games, it was the number one rule that you didn't directly set out against another Host—yet it certainly looked as if this had happened here.

The most obvious winner in his downfall was clearly Aleksey Kuznetsov, the man who'd gone against him in the original contest. Dmitry had loathed the man for a long time, something within the other guy's personality that just didn't click with him. To be potentially handing over most of his empire to that man made him sick inside.

Much as he loathed him, he had investigated the man and there was no way he could have orchestrated such a move. Aleksey was not the man behind this, fitting as it might have been to accuse him. He knew he couldn't bring any such accusation against a fellow oligarch without something concrete to underpin it, and that so far had been hard to find. The thought that someone else, even within the league he played, could be working to bring him down—something that Kuznetsov had been the lucky beneficiary of—was a difficult thing to digest.

His personal phone rang, for once it was not his desk phone with yet another business issue facing him.

"Yes," he answered sharply, direct as always and to the point. It was the man leading his team of Spotters. With no prospect of hosting another event in the Games, he'd recalled them all from the various countries they were in, together with some of his own musclemen and the Buyers that remained loyal to him and had tasked them all with finding Phelan McDermott.

He had placed the man who'd initially found Phelan in charge of the team of a dozen people, though he wondered if that was a wise idea. Clearly the Irishman surpassed the expectations of someone who should have known better. No Host ever wanted their Contestant to actually defeat them, just offer the others the thought that they might, before bringing them to a swift end—yet this one had got away.

"I don't care what you have to say, no more excuses," Dmitry interjected, cutting his man off as he once more tried to give his reasons as to why they hadn't yet located the Irishman. "You find that son-of-a-bitch and you bring me his head, plus the heads of everyone he loves, and anyone who's covered for him—otherwise it'll be your head that I take. Have I made myself clear?" He had. "I don't care what it takes, you must find me this man. I need to know everything about him. Look over all the previous notes you made when you first came across him. Maybe there is something there that will give you a clue as to who he might have contacted, who might know about him. Someone must be willing to speak. Try the lottery itself, and I don't care who you have to kill, if they know something make them speak. If he flew from England, someone must have driven them to the airport. Anything will be a start. Why do I have to spell this out to you people? Just find him!" he said, his blood boiling as he ended the call, throwing the phone hard against the wall, a chunk of plasterboard cracking and falling to the floor.

"Damn you McDermott for thinking you can cross me, take my money and get away with it. I'll hunt you until I find you, and when I do you'll tell me the names of everyone who has helped your little plan, every person who has conspired to bring me down, and I'll finish every single one of them personally."

Just then his second mobile device sounded, one he only used with fellow members of the Games. It was the Chair, the last person he wanted to speak to at that moment, but he swallowed hard, answering the call.

"Dmitry Sokoloff," he said, as if it was needed to confirm who would be answering that particular number.

"I've come to a decision about your future within the Games," the voice said, its usual authority pouring through every syllable. "I'll personally grant your request to take part in the New Year event—the highlight of the year—but you'll become Twenty. We have a new Eleven for this coming event and therefore Arseni Markovic will take your old number at Twelve. Krupin is out," the Chair said. Since Stanislav Krupin, the other Host from the last Hunt, was at number Twenty, this change meant he was pushed out and demoted from the event altogether. It was news to Dmitry and concerning at that.

"Thank you for giving me one more chance to prove myself."

"It's not going to make much of a difference in the long run, Sokoloff, from everything I've been reading."

The thought of what the Chair had been reading flashed through his head, his whole situation so far kept from public knowledge, his companies' share prices largely unaffected by it all, as of yet. Clearly this was an internal document, concerning the various oligarchs within the Games.

"You'll still be made to come clean and settle your bet."

The phrase *made to come clean* was said with total authority and he knew it could be enforced. Though a big player himself in a secretive group of people, there were bigger fish lurking around the shadows that he only knew existed by reputation and suggestion.

These were people you didn't cross, the men who really ran the nation—besides the President—who still held certain powers the others didn't. At least he personally still had Putin as an ally within the corridors of power.

"I just need a little more time. It's a complicated situation."

"You have until New Year's Day. I expect to see everything settled by the close of that event, and I guess if you are lucky enough, you might have caught this Irishman by then." Was it a snigger he heard in the tone at that point? Was his situation a joke to them now?

"Don't worry, I promise I'll have everything in place. It might even keep me in the league."

"I don't see that happening now, do you?"

"What do you mean? I've got huge influence and bring a lot to this group."

"There are many prospective candidates who will be much richer than you by the time this is all finished."

"I still have a lot of influence in this country. That means something to these people."

"True, so I guess it depends how much of your existing empire you actually manage to keep your hands on. If you lose the television and media companies, what good are you to anyone?"

It was a loaded question. He knew more than anyone that his influence had been built around his ability to control what his nation watched and read about. He'd loaded the last four elections in his people's favour solely because of that. His was a ticket still worth something, and he intended to see this whole mess of a situation through whilst somehow retaining that particular position.

"One more thing, Sokoloff. As this is the tenth anniversary since we started the Games, we're going for a big one to mark the occasion this New Year. We want every Host to put forward a Contestant for the event—we'll provide the tickets this time. You'll all be told what to expect in more detail later on."

The call ended. It was the last thing he wanted to have to think about and plan for. It would mean he'd need to come up with another Contestant, someone who would clearly not have a chance of winning, whilst looking the part. It was a distraction from what he most wanted, most needed, to focus on and for a moment he wondered if that was why it was being done. Were they all out to destroy him? Had it really come down to the fact that they just wanted to see him buried?

Pushing that thought from his mind he walked over to his broken handset on the floor, the screen smashed. He reached down, picking up the broken pieces of plastic, pulling the sim card from the handset before dropping the debris into the bin. He would have to purchase a replacement phone soon, but for now he inserted the sim into the spare slot on his other phone and called his team leader once more.

"There has been something of a change of plan. Whilst I still want as many men on Phelan as you can spare, we will need someone for New Year, after all. Someone that looks the part, but has not got the guts for a challenge. I can't have a repeat of what I am now going through. I also need to know who the other Hosts are looking at."

"That'll take a lot of manpower."

"Is that going to be a problem?"

"No, sir, of course not, it's just we are stretched as it is."

"What do I pay you so much for, then, to have you complain when I finally ask you to actually do something worth your wage? Listen carefully, as I'm going to say this and then end this time wasting call. You are going to deliver me Phelan McDermott in time for New Year. You are also going to find another suitable Contestant, one that isn't tied to anyone else and therefore doesn't stand a chance of repeating this diabolical situation. And on top of these two things, you are going to get me the information on every other Contestant my fellow oligarchs are looking at. Have I made myself clear?"

"Yes, sir," is all that came back, Dmitry ending the call after hearing that. He was asking a lot of his men—he knew that—but then diamonds weren't formed without being put under intense pressure.

It dawned on him that this all gave him a chance of a come back. If he had the lowdown on every other Contestant—knowing how they were likely to respond—what type of people they were and therefore knowing how they could be broken or better still, controlled, he might just face the prospect of coming out of the New Year event in a better off state than he entered it, and if he played well, maybe better than he had been before the last event—when everything had come unstuck. Maybe there was light at the end of the tunnel, after all?

27

It was late and the London street lights had come on long ago as the last two office workers left the building, locking up at Lottery HQ long after everyone else had left.

There had been no need to work late, and as the couple walked from the building, it was clear that work hadn't been the reason they had stayed—left alone to themselves when everyone else had left.

The man's hand was on her backside before they'd walked five metres from the building, though she instinctively knocked it away, laughing as she did so. They'd clearly been drinking—besides the other activities they might have been involved in.

Reports showed that the man, who headed up the marketing department within the firm, lived within walking distance of the office, and as they started to walk that way together, it was clear they were heading there. The lady, who dealt with those few lucky people who walked through their doors with high value tickets to claim, was married.

The team of three men followed them at a distance as the lovestruck couple made their way slowly along the streets. It became clear to those mirroring the couples' every turn that they were heading back to the man's house, something the team had been given the address of that afternoon. It had been a busy day already, and they were tired but there was no stopping now.

The couple made it to the front door, the man fumbling for his keys—kissing the woman on the lips as he reached into his pocket—pulling out his keys and putting them into the lock. The Russians then made their move as the couple walked into the house hand in hand, oblivious to what might be happening around them. The lead Russian got to the door before it closed, his foot stopping it dead then he barged through, his weight nearly knocking the two startled lovers over, as the other two followed in behind.

The woman looked like she was about to scream, but when a gun was pulled from the lead attacker's jacket pocket she went silent instead. They were motioned into the lounge.

"Please, we haven't done anything…I'm sorry, I'm so sorry. Has my husband sent you?" the woman started to say, her body shaking in shock, the realisation of being discovered hitting her like there was no tomorrow.

"We are not here because of your affair that you are having," the man holding the gun said, his accented English only adding to the fear rising in them both—like a villain from a James Bond film.

"Then why are you here?" the man said, bolder than he thought himself capable of. One of the Russians hit him across the face, sending him to the floor, the woman screaming in shock, reaching for him as he fell clumsily onto his knees.

"Please, don't hurt us," she said, the gun never taken off the pair of them, switching back between the two every few moments, as if he would fire at one of them any second.

A photo of Phelan McDermott was very purposively dropped in front of the woman. Her reaction to the smiley Irishman's face looking up at her showed that she recognised him—as they knew she must have done—performing the role she did within the lottery.

"Where did this man go?"

"I'm sorry? What man? I've never seen this man before in my life."

The Russian now placed the barrel of the silenced firearm squarely against the forehead of the man, causing the woman to whimper in fear.

"Please, don't hurt us!" she begged once more, "I don't know what it is you want from us."

"The location of Phelan McDermott or I blow your boyfriend's brains out," he said, looking down at her whilst keeping the gun pressed into the man's head. "Three, two, one," he added, the sound of resignation in his voice as his finger moved onto the trigger in one fluid motion, the recognition in the woman's face at that moment that these guys weren't there to mess around. The bullet killed him instantly, blood and brains hitting the wall behind, the only sound being his body crashing to the floor—and her crying out in shock.

The gun was then aimed in front of her eyes, making her go silent, suddenly aware that her own life was very much in danger. She wasn't going to lie any more.

"He had a wallet full of American dollars. He wanted to leave me some money, as his way of saying thank you just before he was leaving—and I saw it. I asked him about it. He just said he was going to America."

"See, that wasn't so hard now," he smiled, as if nothing had just happened, the blood from the kill now seeping across the carpet in every direction. "What part of America?" he added, serious once again, the gun pushed harder into her forehead, heat instantly noticeable as it made contact with her skin.

"Please, that's all I know, honestly. I didn't see him for long," she said, crying hard now, the words coming out through deep waves of emotion, her eyes closed, pleading with everything in her for this to all go away.

"That's a shame," he said, taking a few steps back now, the other two already moving out of the room, "such a waste, too," the gun firing, two shots to her heart, killing her within seconds.

They left the property, having touched nothing, though they pulled the door closed behind themselves, wiping down any possible prints they might have left on the door handle in the process.

As they got back to their car—which had been parked half way between the house they'd just left and the offices of lottery HQ—the team leader had his phone out, a call connecting to the rest of his men.

"They're in America, that's all we managed to get from them," he said, ending the call before anyone could say anything. It hadn't been as specific an answer as they had hoped for—but it was a start.

∞∞∞

Phelan was out on another run. The settling in process had been very smooth. They hadn't yet worked out what to do with schooling, but there seemed little option than for his wife, with the help of her parents, to home school. They weren't going to be fully registered in America for some time, if at all. Getting into a local school might prove problematic, especially if another move was called for—though even Phelan—the longer they were all together there, could see them all being very happy staying where they were.

They were surrounded by the most spectacular scenery, in a place very few people ever got to see, let alone live amongst.

The locals, those few that they actually saw on their occasional trips into town, seemed friendly, keeping themselves to themselves. The locals were all Americans, so being from the UK and Ireland, they did stick out in that sense, but no one was bothered. They'd heard the phrase more than once since arriving; what goes on in Montana stays in Montana. Phelan understood the feeling perfectly.

Getting back to the house, his wife was coming out through the front door, car keys in hand.

"Wait a moment, I'll just change and come and join you."

"Okay," she said. "Don't be long, I've asked Mum and Dad to watch the kids and I don't want to put them under too much pressure."

Phelan turned, coming back to his wife at that moment. "Darling, there isn't any pressure here. Relax, they'll love time with the grandkids."

She smiled, kissing him on the lips. "You're right, it's still not all sunk in I guess. Old habits…" Phelan kissed her back on the lips a second time, lingering a little, enjoying her taste.

"Go get changed you red blooded male, I'll pull the van around the front." He smiled and jogged back inside, t-shirt coming off as he went in through the door.

Five minutes later they were pulling onto the main road, a left turn from the entrance to their ranch and about a five kilometre run into what formed the community hub in the region.

There was everything you would expect, the size of the town surprising at first given the few people that lived there, though many travelled in from miles around, it being the main hub for a long way in any direction. There was a Target outlet there, a supermarket chain they'd always heard about but now got to use as their local shop.

Still, they preferred some of the small, independent and quieter shops that lined the central street—the larger Target store having been built about five years before and on the other side of town. They'd been there once, but it was a little further away and they enjoyed the more artistic layout and shops of Main Street.

They were still working in cash, using a card to withdraw money from the ATM that they'd found worked for them at the only bank, situated at the end of Main Street.

They entered a small independent food market, which had all the essentials they needed. Phelan wandered the four aisles aimlessly, his wife pushing a small trolley around, working through a list. When it was time to pay, Phelan joined her again and unloaded the shopping onto the counter, his wife remembering one more thing, asking the lady where it was located, before going off in search of it.

They'd been there several times already, and it was the same lady each time. Phelan assumed she owned the place, or at least ran it with her husband. They'd seen a man of similar age unloading boxes on previous visits, though it was just her at the moment, as far as he could tell.

Reaching into his wallet, he realised they didn't have enough cash, having not gone to the bank yet.

"Damn," he said, the lady behind the till putting their purchases into brown paper bags, looking up, a smile on her inquisitive face. "I meant to get some more cash out, I'll have to go and get some before we can check out."

"Honey, don't you be worrying about that," she said, her accent like something out of a classic American movie, her tone smooth, the rhythm slow. "My husband set you up with an account after you showed up that second time the other day. News spreads fast in this part of the country when new folk arrive," she said, Phelan's wife coming back at that point, a bag of caster sugar in hand, which she placed on the counter.

"All done?" she said, adding the sugar into the third bag standing on the counter in front of her. "I'll mark up the account, just pay it once in a while, is all we ask. Most folks settle every two weeks or so, some do so once a month. Welcome to the neighbourhood," she added, handing Phelan two of the bags, which he got his arms under, holding them against his chest.

"That accent is Irish, isn't it, and yours ma'am, is English, right?"

"Yes," his wife said, taking the third bag that she was being passed.

"Good, my husband thought so. You see, we had to put down a nationality on the system, you know, for the tab. It isn't every day that three generations of Irish and English turn up into our little part of the world. We've set tabs up for all of you, even your parents." Phelan looked at the lady, sudden concern on his face. "They are your parents, aren't they?" she said, seeing his look.

"Yes, of course," he said, before coming back to the counter. "You mentioned putting our names on a system. Would that be a computer system?"

"Why, yes, it is now. We shifted from a purely paper system maybe ten years back. No, fifteen years already—my, how time flies."

"You've put onto a computer the fact that our parents and my family have just arrived, and noted our nationalities, too?" he said, now more forceful, looking at his wife as the thought dawned on her.

"Yes, why, was that some kind of problem?" the cashier said, confused and starting to be a little concerned. His wife glared at him.

"No, it's nothing," he smiled, trying his best to just dismiss it, and turned and left the store, both of them saying farewell as they went. They took the bags straight to the van, dropping them into the boot.

"Do you think it's a problem?" his wife said, concern now showing on her face.

"It could be, I'll have to speak to Matvey. But he's told me in the past how effective these people are at hunting down what they are looking for, mainly using the internet to track and find people. If someone was looking this way, if they somehow knew we were coming to America, how long do you think it would take them to wonder who the Irish and English couples were, arriving with their son and daughter and grandkids? And in a place like this, for god's sake," he said, hands picking out an eagle as it soared high in the sky.

They got back into the van, both thinking through it all, Phelan driving. They made the return journey in silence back to the ranch—a place that had become home so quickly but now might have to be left behind.

∞∞∞

In London, news of the murder of two lottery employees had been circulating, the information falling onto the desk of Alex at MI6, only because of his interest in that particular organisation. He called over to Anissa, who joined him immediately. Once they'd both read through the report, they looked at each other.

"Do you suspect it's them?" Anissa said.

"Hard to say, but we can't rule it out. Police are more concerned about the victim's husband. They were both found dead in the male victim's own home, not far from the offices they shared. CCTV reports they left late, the camera images from inside were quite revealing. So the police are looking along the lines of a jealous husband who'd found out about the affair."

"But you're not so sure?"

"I think it's highly likely someone was sent to find out information about the person who claimed that prize."

"Can we not go to them now and get this information? The murder angle has surely got to allow us access to the information we've been denied so far? It could have something to do with the murder, for all they know."

"Good point. Let's do that. If we can find out who it was, we might discover what the Russians did—assuming it was them that made the hit—and assuming that they even managed to glean any information before shooting them both. Also," he added, on the way to the door already, but turning to one of the technicians working at the desk next to the door, "dig into the husband the police are looking at, so that we can be certain it wasn't just a revenge killing. Make sure his story matches. There would be no point us pursuing anything with the lottery if it just turns out to be a domestic."

∞∞∞∞

In Paris, the three man team who had just made the kill in London were sitting waiting for further information. Following the hit, they'd fled that night to France, catching the train which brought them to the centre of the capital. They'd instructed their own team of technical experts to focus in on America.

The results came through as they sat at a street side café across the road from a park.

"Entry made on a shop's database of Irish/English family arriving. No names but it's three generations."

"Show me," the team leader said, looking at the information before him, which said all that he'd just been told, only adding the name Savage, Montana. He opened up Google, tapping the name into the maps page. A small town was shown next to a river, in the far eastern edge of the State. He pointed at the screen with his finger. "We have a location, guys." He pulled out his mobile phone, calling his boss, connecting after three rings.

"What?" Dmitry Sokoloff snapped, his temper worsening by the day—especially when there seemed little progress being made.

"We have a location. Eastern Montana, a small town named Savage. Three generations of Irish/English reported new to town."

Dmitry sat up in his chair, aware of the life-line being thrown to him. "Very good. Can you get there right away?" It wasn't as much a question as it was him pleading to them to get moving.

"We'll be on the next flight out of Charles de Gaulle today."

"Very good. If you need any help over there, you know who to speak to. I'll leave this in your capable hands."

"Thank you," the leader of the team said, the call ending. The man sitting next to him at the café was already searching for tickets for flights to America that day. There was a flight leaving within the hour that had one stop in Seattle before a connection onto Billings airport, the main airport coming up on the search results for flights to Montana. That would get them in just before midnight that same day, the flight time long but they were saving hours by travelling west.

Looking at the map on the screen, Savage would be about a four hour drive from the airport, especially if they tackled it right after landing, though the seventeen hour flight, and late landing might make that option somewhat undesirable.

The map showed a small airport about half an hour north of Savage which connected to the town via one road. There were four flights a day between Billings and that smaller airport, named Sydney-Richland Airport, though the latest of these left at half five in the afternoon. The first flight out would be at eight the following morning, and would take about an hour.

"Very good," the leader said, "get us tickets for that Paris flight right away," the price a real premium for such short notice, but money had never been a thing his team needed to worry about—it was results that their boss was most concerned with. "We can discuss what to do when we land. I guess we won't be able to hire any type of vehicle until the morning, so maybe a night's sleep and that morning flight to the east of the state would work best."

The third member of the trio got up, going to the counter inside the café, dropping the required euros onto the worktop once the amount was shown, before returning to the table, where they all put their jackets on and their computers away. Three tickets had been purchased, their online clearance for entering America sorted out ahead of the inevitable questions they would face once at the airport in Paris.

They left the van where it was, parked in a multi-storey car park in the centre of town, instead jumping on the metro which had an entrance right next to where they had been waiting, and after a few stops were pulling into Charles de Gaulle Airport in Paris, in a hurry to catch that afternoon's flight to Seattle.

28

In London the same evening that Alex had been notified about the double murder, he was leaving the lottery HQ offices with Anissa, the warrant finally issued that afternoon giving them access to all the information they demanded. The warrant had been general—nothing specific, no mention of the British security service—but whatever assumptions the folks at the lottery might make, it had worked.

The fact that the murdered pair were a couple was widely known. It became clear after speaking with just two colleagues that the supposedly secret affair was a subject of office gossip, though no one had tried to interfere. They were all aware that the lady, a person solely responsible for working with those that were claiming large amounts in prize money, was married.

When Anissa had requested information on the previous week's winner, there was only a momentary pause as the warrant was still lying on the table, giving them the backing they needed.

The two agents walked out of the offices of the lottery HQ in London with everything that there was on record about Phelan McDermott, which besides a few basic details, wasn't actually that much. Winners who wanted to keep their identities secret, after all, weren't about to give more information than was absolutely necessary to the representative asking them the questions. It was confirmed that the money had initially been wired to an account in Zurich. Beyond that, they couldn't tell. Getting a Swiss bank to divulge that information was next to impossible. It didn't matter—they did have a name now, and for those within MI6, that was an important start.

As they drove back to the office, hoping to get at least an hour's work in before the day was out, they were now wondering whether the lady—the murder victim in the home of the man she was having an affair with—had given up the information they were now certain the Russians had been after.

Having looked at the domestic angle, it didn't make sense. The widower had been alarmed and shamed to have found out where his wife died, his reaction to hearing the news clearly showing that he didn't have any idea what had been going on. He said they'd had a happy marriage, or so he had thought. He was genuinely shocked. He didn't match the profile of someone who could have pulled this off, and he had a rock solid alibi for the time during the killing.

An off the record search had been done on the family bank account. There were no large payments made to anyone, no hint that cash had been withdrawn that might have been used to hire a hit man. Nothing about the man suggested in any way that he had anything to do with it. For the police, this caused them a problem, as it would be added to the growing list of cases they didn't have an answer for.

For Alex and Anissa, it pointed solely at the Russians, their involvement in the crime and the nature of their own ongoing investigation meaning they would have to keep this knowledge from the plods, for the time being. At a later point, they could be brought up to speed, and maybe those responsible would have been identified by then, too.

It was just forty minutes after arriving back that they felt they were closing in on where Phelan McDermott and his family had disappeared to. They'd managed to trace him from the night he'd collected his prize to a London hotel, not far from the airport. A credit card had been used to pay for the suite he'd stayed in that night. After a little work by the MI6 technical team, that same card had appeared three days later, taking cash from a bank machine in Montana, USA. That led them to looking online for further clues, their area of search narrowing to that one particular state—the same entry in a small store's database finally being found, confirming Phelan's presence, they were now certain.

They realised that if they'd been able to locate this information, then so could others. Whether knowingly or not, and they suspected it was the latter, Phelan had broken the silence that existed around his current location, a digital reference like the one that had been made standing out to anyone with the ability to know what to look for, like a flashing light on a dark night. A beacon calling attention to their arrival in a little town in the east of Montana—a foolish mistake. It might already be too late for them, though Alex had no way of knowing that for now.

∞∞∞

Phelan woke to a ringing noise, hitting an alarm clock he didn't remember setting before waking up enough to realise it was his mobile phone. It was still dark, the clock showing it was half past five in the morning. The number displayed on the screen of his smart phone was a Russian one—a number he knew well—for it was Matvey Filipov's personal mobile number. He answered it on what was about the sixth ring.

"Phelan here," he said, willing his mind to get up to speed, still a little fuzzy from being in deep sleep moments before.

"It's me," Matvey said, as it was clear who would be calling from that number. Besides, his voice was distinctive enough to be unmistakable, even at that hour and from so many thousands of miles away. "I've looked into what you told me about that store recording your details. It's easily accessible. Two days ago two people were killed in London who worked for the lottery, one being the lady that dealt with your prize. I believe she gave them your location before they killed her."

"But I didn't say where we were heading. I made no mention of the ranch at all, just as you said." Phelan's wife was now stirring, her sixth sense picking up from her husband's tone that everything wasn't all right with their world.

"Is it possible you mentioned America?" The Irishman thought before replying:

"Yes, it's possible. I think I mentioned something about heading stateside."

"It doesn't matter now. Get everyone together. I traced three Russians—all of whom work for Sokoloff—who boarded a flight yesterday afternoon to Seattle, with an onwards connection to Billings."

"Jesus!" Phelan swore, jumping out of bed at that point, starting to get dressed, his wife doing the same, panic beginning to take hold of her.

"They landed last night at around midnight. I can't tell what happened after that, but you haven't got long. You need to move from there, and I mean immediately. Call me when you are out of the area."

Phelan put the phone in his pocket, his wife pulling on her jeans, a bag already on the bed, a few items inside it.

"Leave everything, just get the boys. We have to be out of here immediately!" She looked up at Phelan—terror in his eyes—no words needed, her husband's actions confirming this was what they'd feared.

Three minutes later they were putting the last of their three children into the back of the van—two still asleep—though the oldest had woken, not taking in what was now going on.

Phelan had the phone to his ear, calling ahead to his parents, telling them they were coming immediately for them and then doing the same for her parents.

It had taken fifteen minutes to get the others into the van, Phelan going into his parent's house, screaming at them to get moving, a reaction that communicated this wasn't a time to mess around.

The van, now fully loaded, sped down their dirt track, dust rising as the first glimmers of the day broke over the horizon, the sun only partially visible. They turned right, away from town—just driving—not clear where to yet, but wanting to put distance between themselves and the ranch. No one said anything, the six adults just processing everything in silence, with Phelan at the wheel, keeping his speed up but nothing too excessive. He kept one eye on the rear view mirrors, watching for anyone who might be following, though at that time of day, traffic was light, the roads in that part of the country mainly occupied by agricultural vehicles, anyway. The others just watched the fields pass by, each looking out through the windows, wondering what unseen danger lurked—what mistake they'd made that required such a sudden departure—knowing now wasn't the time to have that conversation, not with the boys awake.

∞∞∞

The previous night, the flight from Seattle had landed at Billings International on schedule, and despite it being quiet at that time in the airport and few passengers getting off the plane, it was still gone midnight by the time the three Russians walked through security. The airport building itself was deserted, the shops and cafés long since closed for the day. The same was true for the three car rental booths that were visible.

The only person they saw was sitting behind an information desk, though the man himself was most probably some airport night watchman, his uniform displaying the word security on his front left pocket. They left him alone, the three drawing the gaze of the man—but he wasn't overly interested and left them to it after a few seconds.

On the wall in front of them were a number of telephones, linked to various hotels, the information displayed claiming a free transfer was possible for guests. The leader picked up one of the phones. The team had felt tiredness set in during the last flight, knowing that their best option was getting a good night's sleep and then picking things back up the following morning. As it was, they'd only have about six hours to rest, and that depended on how long it took to be picked up and checked into a hotel.

The call was answered almost instantly, the cheerful voice confirming a bus would be with them in about fifteen minutes and their room would be waiting for them when they arrived.

It was thirty minutes later that they were exiting the lift on the third floor of the hotel, their rooms all on the same corridor. The bus had been on time, the hotel about fifteen minutes from the airport, something they would have to factor in for the return journey in what was now only about five hours' time, give or take.

The hotel shuttle had brought them down a road which clearly overlooked the city that was Billings, the hotel itself down in the valley, the airport obviously higher up than the majority of buildings that made up that city. They agreed to meet again at six—breakfast available from that point—before they'd need to make a quick exit back to the airport ready for the flight at eight. They entered their rooms, all three of the men asleep within minutes of falling onto the fresh, soft and very comfortable beds.

As morning came around, everything had gone to plan, their flight busy, though there were still plenty of seats available when they walked into the airport at seven and purchased three tickets.

They landed just after nine, a tail wind giving them a favourable flight, and walked straight to the only vehicle rental booth that existed at that much smaller airport. A car was made available and everything was paid for in bundles of cash.

Setting off just after nine thirty, it was less than thirty minutes to get to the little town of Savage, where they started asking questions, focussing mainly on the store that had logged the details of Phelan and his family, and seeing where that might lead them.

Phelan, having been driving three hours solid already by that point, was now over two hundred miles west of there, in central Montana, his conversation with Matvey instructing him to head as far west as possible, where he had a new place for them to find shelter, before they would reassess what their next move should be.

29

Alex was once again waiting outside the office of the DDG at Vauxhall Cross, the home of MI6 on the banks of the Thames. After a few minutes' delay, Alex—himself busy and not appreciating being kept waiting—was ushered into the room, the DDG standing at the window, a telephone to his ear. It was as if he intended to wind Alex up all the more, though he soon finished the call, turning to face his agent and now give him his full attention.

"I need you to bring the CIA on board with developments in my case and have them deploy on our instruction," Alex said, his phrasing making clear to the DDG that he wanted their American friends to be sent to do their dirty work stateside.

"You know we have sixty active Daesh terror cells that we are continuously monitoring across Europe—bomb attacks being foiled by the month—and you would have us chasing Russians like it was the good old days of the bloody Cold War," he remarked, his tone jovial but there was a noticeable edge to his manner. Alex had yet to figure out the inner workings of his Deputy Director General.

"There is a known and credible threat to nine British lives at this very minute," Alex said, trying to keep his calm, not rising to whatever the DDG was trying to communicate. There was a brief moment of silence—almost a standoff—before the DDG went back to his desk, picking up another phone, that connected directly to his counterpart at Langley. Looking up from behind his wire rimmed spectacles, he said, "Give me the details," as the call was connected then his focus was once more on the telephone to his ear. Alex came forward, passing the information he had typed up to him and the DDG took it and glanced at it, whilst initial greetings were being spoken.

"I've got a highly excited field agent here who's been chasing some loose cannons and is reporting a viable threat to the lives of nine people—six adults and three children—of British or Irish nationality and last known location being the town of Savage, Montana."

There was a pause, whilst there was obviously something being said at the other end of the line.

"Exactly, though maybe that's why they used that location, it being as isolated as it obviously sounds. Anyway, we have reason to believe that their location has become known to parties that would do them harm." Alex stepped closer and pointed to something he'd highlighted at the bottom of the page, the DDG not appreciating being shown what he was perfectly aware of. "Look, we suspect that the Russians will now come after them, or people connected to the Russian under investigation. Could you flag this one up and get a watch put on these people? If you are able to intercept and detain anyone coming for our nationals, that would be most helpful."

Another pause and the DDG turned away from Alex briefly—saying something short but inaudible, before turning back—the conversation suggesting the call was coming to an end.

"Excellent, and Craig, keep me informed about what you find out." He replaced the handset onto his desk. "Done," he said, as if clarity needed sharing.

"Thank you."

"Look, at some point, we are going to need to bring you back into the fold. The Paris and Brussels attacks have intensified pressure on the continent, and the fear is these won't be the last attacks."

"Give me time. Something is happening among the very rich men who hold great power right across the continent, as I've shared with you. These aren't limited to just Russians, either, though we have no idea yet exactly who it involves. When you mix that much money and power together and they keep it all so goddam secretive, it can only mean something bigger is going on."

"Bigger than the terrorist threat from jihadists across every capital city in Europe?" the DDG barked, now laughing at the time wasting efforts he saw his agent was so obviously caught up in.

"Until we find some answers, we don't know what the threat is."

"Really, is it just some game to you? You don't have much time. Fail to produce anything credible soon and I'm shutting you all down. This has gone on long enough, longer, I'm now aware, than either of you have informed my office of—and that's telling me something."

"What's it bloody telling you?" Alex snapped, aware of who he was speaking to but for that moment unable to hold his tongue.

"That you and your little team are loose cannons."

Alex left the office. The DDG paced around for a while then he picked up his mobile, hitting one of his speed dials, the call connecting in a few seconds.

"Tolbert has just been in with me and there is no sign he's backing down yet. I just wanted you to be aware. I'll keep you informed."

∞∞∞∞

That evening, Alex had gone with Anissa for some food, the details about his time spent with the DDG shared in full, the two of them just going over where things stood. Neither knew what to make of the DDG's reaction, but they put it to one side for the moment. They were both hungry, having not eaten since breakfast, the afternoon getting away from them, as it often did. Anissa had cleared it with home before agreeing to a dinner in town with Alex.

Whilst they were waiting for the food to arrive, a courier walked into the restaurant, helmet in hand—holding a small padded envelope in his other hand—as he approached the bar. There was a brief conversation before the barman pointed in their direction. The courier caught their eye and walked towards the table where the two British agents sat.

"I have a package for you," he said, placing it on the table and opening a document in front of them then taking a pen from his trouser pocket. "I need you to sign for it."

"Where's it from?" Alex said, examining the small parcel, which didn't weigh much, about as much as a mobile phone, nothing more.

"Arrived from the international shipping channels at Heathrow, marked as urgent—and this address was telephoned through to us sixty minutes ago." They'd only left the office within that time frame, making their way towards the restaurant they often went to together, both fans of Italian food.

Alex scribbled his signature on the document, giving the pen back to the courier, who told them to enjoy their food as he turned and left the establishment.

Alex studied the package closely, wary of what it might be and intrigued that it had been delivered to him in a restaurant. He cut the side of the envelope open, not where it was taped but actually through the base itself, checking inside before tipping a mobile telephone out through the hole, the rest of the envelope empty.

The phone was on, the battery in a low power mode, showing that about fifty per cent of the battery life remained.

It was only seconds later that it rang, startling them both, though the ring tone wasn't too loud—they just were surprised it was ringing at that very moment.

"Alex, it's Andre," the voice said. Alex had answered it on loud speaker, but picked up the handset and placed it to his ear after he heard the name of the informant who had gone missing, someone whom he'd feared was dead. It had been so many months. "We have to speak."

∞∞∞

Matvey Filipov left his multi-million pound home on the edges of Monaco with his son. The morning cloud that had been hanging like a blanket lifted and the hot sun poured down on them. They were heading out to Matvey's yacht which was in the harbour, one of many similar vessels that occupied space in that wealthy part of the Mediterranean coast.

For a man of such riches, besides the couple of homes he owned—the one there in Monaco by far the grandest and the one he spent most time in—and the yacht, he lived a relatively normal life. A generous man throughout his sixty plus years, he had worked with charities right around the world, a non-executive director of three of these charities, offering his years of business experience to help their causes.

Matvey was third generation wealth—not deemed an oligarch at all. His family wealth came from decades of building up sound businesses and networking internationally when most Soviet era people were not even allowed to travel. The vast majority of his $11.7 billion fortune had been kept outside Russia. These tactics had seen them through the communist years, and through the early stages of New Russia, where men became billionaires over night, the political climate changing for ever in the process.

He was deeply proud of his roots, though he travelled back to Russia, and Moscow in particular, very little nowadays, much to the concern of those within political office at the Kremlin, where his lack of obvious support was a constant issue. He'd been outspoken at times against the Putin reign, but had held his tongue enough, at least publicly, to avoid getting into the sort of trouble that led to being killed for what he was saying.

He knew a change was needed, though with a country like Russia, it would take a long time to come about.

He was concerned by how widespread corruption still was, a country that should have shaken off the shackles from its years in isolation and be functioning just as well as any in the West were. Instead, with a bribe still the quickest way of getting anything done, it seemed Russia was its own worst enemy.

About a quarter of his empire still operated exclusively in Russia and had become the Filipov brand. He'd made a point of never paying bribes within Russia, making sure every business operated inside the law, wanting to use his firms there as a positive example of what was possible, though largely these efforts were falling on deaf ears. People were too stuck in their ways to want to change—money too easily made the old fashioned way for it to ever seem better to do business any other way. He felt, at times, he was fighting an impossible battle.

Across much of Europe, and into the Far East, his business ethic had seen rapid expansion, building on the positive momentum he'd seen within Russia and vastly extending his connections.

Matvey had men working for him right around the globe, nearly one hundred men and women solely keeping up surveillance and information gathering on various targets—especially those he knew to be a part of the Games. It was through this network of people that he'd been able to initially get hold of Phelan McDermott, a man he'd seen others tracking, and whom it was clear they wanted to bring into the Games.

This same network of Matvey's men had been the ones who had set up the ranch in Montana, the same farm that the

Irishman had now had to flee from. Needing to direct them somewhere else—their safety still a primary concern—another more remote option was put forward. It was a property on an exclusive island a little off the coast of Seattle, where Matvey also owned the main ferry route, the only link between the island and the city itself, though there was a road bridge coming in from the north. Most travelled via the ferry, making it an early warning system for anyone who might come looking for trouble.

The last he'd heard from Phelan had been when they were three hours into the journey, a trip that would take about fifteen hours in total to get them from Savage to Seattle, where the ferry would transport them across to Whidbey Island. Matvey's property was then only another fifteen minutes on from there.

He'd suggested they drive it in one go, alternating drivers so as to make it to the island as fast as possible. He'd arranged extra security to meet them at the property. Keeping them out of harm's way had become his latest mission.

Matvey arrived in the marina at the sea front in Monaco—small boats tied up as far as the eye could see in the main part of the port—only a few larger vessels kept in a more secluded, easier to launch, area. His yacht was in the latter, a fifty foot triple decker that he was very proud of.

It was also a good opportunity to spend time with his son in the fresh air, both having been indoors more than usual lately, and between the two of them they could easily navigate their way out to sea, where they planned to do a little fishing.

As the vessel was being expertly guided around the final part of the marina, his son at the wheel, Matvey got confirmation from a man he'd been waiting to hear from. Matvey finished the call and threw the phone up to his son. "It's time," he said as the young man caught the phone in one hand while keeping the other on the wheel. He guided the vessel into open water as he dialled the number, the call answered in a matter of seconds.

"Alex, it's Andre, we need to talk," he said, the next stages of their plan well underway already.

30

Phelan had driven the final leg—the fifteen hour journey long and hot—though the air-conditioning did something to help with that. Besides a few toilet breaks, they'd gone at the journey solidly, the children bored but going along with everything they were being told.

Their entry onto the ferry, which already sat in the dock as they pulled up, had been cleared in advance, their van ushered in ahead of other vehicles, putting it at the front for a quick disembarkation at the other end. They went upstairs, sitting around a large table, a few other passengers already there, though the journey wasn't that long, and those that did it regularly just stayed in their cars.

As the boat approached the small dock on the island, they all went back down to the van, Phelan again taking the driver's seat, his father-in-law once more riding shot gun, the most confident navigator there.

They were the first to disembark, rolling forward carefully before climbing up out of the harbour, the road rising for nearly a mile before levelling out, as they made the short drive it would take to get to the property they were aiming for, another one that Matvey had made available. They made a few turns, glad of the detailed directions they'd been given, the map tallying perfectly with where they needed to go.

As they arrived at the edge of the property, entering the driveway, the kids called out in excitement, for the tree lined driveway was like something out of Jurassic Park. After two minutes, the main property came into view, the van pulling under the covered roof, two giant wooden doors opening as they got out of the van, a man standing there, ushering them forward.

He'd been sent—with a team by Matvey, he explained—promising to keep his men out of sight, an invisible force that would be there nonetheless.

The kids ran around the house, having never seen anything like it before. The main hall opened into a giant library-cum-lounge, huge windows looked out to the sea beyond, the lounge opening into the vast kitchen-cum-dining room. There were three floors, they were told, as well as an entire wing that was on the left as they'd entered the main doors—that slept eighteen across nine rooms—if they wanted. The property also offered two further buildings: a separate two storey home just next to the main house that really only slept two and a beach front home that could put up ten. It had been suggested they might want to base themselves at that latter property.

Having explored the main house—which held a cinema in the basement, seats for about twenty catered for in luxurious black leather sofas—they walked the five minutes it took to wind their way down towards the beach house. The water seemed just metres beyond, and though the kids took a little persuading—the cinema room just too tempting—they all agreed eventually that the beach house would serve them well.

∞∞∞

In Savage, the Russians had arrived just after ten, a little under four hours since Phelan had sped away from there in what had still been the early hours. They'd easily located the store where the details had come up, one of the team entering and getting into a conversation, his accent making it obvious that he was not from around town.

When he said he worked for an Irishman who had just arrived, agreeing to do some general labour for him, he'd struck lucky, the lady mentioning a ranch she said was just up the road, asking him if that's where he was meaning. He thanked her, and returned to his team, passing on what he'd learnt.

The three of them got back into the van and headed north, searching for the name of the ranch that had been mentioned. They passed the four that were within a twenty minute drive, three of them having name plates clearly displayed—which didn't match the one they were looking for. They turned around and headed for the ranch that hadn't had a name displayed, turning into the dirt track, seeing two farm buildings, as a train cut across the land in front of them. When it had passed, a third building was visible beyond the tracks, but there were no signs of vehicles at any of them, the team swinging by the first two houses before crossing the track and pulling up to what appeared to be the main property, a few kids' toys visible on the ground around the front of the home, a child's bike resting against the side of a wall.

They got out of the van, leaving the doors open, not wanting to make any more noise than they already had. They circled the building, peering in through the rear windows, which showed personal possessions clearly visible all over the place. Someone was living there.

At that moment the team leader called out to the other couple of men with him. A dust cloud was visible on the road behind them—someone was driving onto the ranch. The three Russians came together, wondering for a moment if it was the family arriving home. Their own van was parked in front of the house, which would be clearly visible to whoever was approaching, especially once they were clear of the train line. There wasn't time to move it, and as the dust cloud parted, the first of the cars appearing over the rise of the track—its blue lights flashing—the Russians started to run. Two further police cars, together with two blacked-out four-by-fours raced to a halt alongside their van, as the three made it to the edges of what looked like a fast flowing river.

The first of the officers was getting out of the car, pointing towards the river, having spotted the three men beginning to flee. Shots were fired, no one sure of who fired first, but both groups took cover, the police and CIA in a far more protected position, the Russians with only a little rock coverage between them and the police—the flowing river behind them. They also only had their handguns, since the weapons with greater firepower, and all their spare ammunition, was sitting in the back of the van.

They knew they stood very little chance, but couldn't risk being caught. The shootout was getting neither side anywhere, the police safe enough behind the building, but too far away to get a clear shot—not daring to come out into the open where they'd risk being hit themselves. The team leader counted down the shots, his two companions getting through their bullets far too aggressively, until both their weapons were empty, the team leader with three bullets left—it paid to count your ammunition. In one swift move he shot both men next to him, killing them instantly, before he put the gun to his own head and pulled the trigger.

The men from the CIA saw what had happened, approaching the scene cautiously but quickly, but all three were dead by the time they got there. A clean up team was called in.

∞∞∞

"Andre, where the hell have you been all these months? We were starting to think you'd been killed."

"I know, believe me, I'd like to tell you more details about it all but it's a long story," he said, his English excellent, his voice very easy to listen to.

"I've got time," Alex said, wanting answers—needing to know why his man in Russia had been silent for so long. It had jeopardised their operation.

"Well, I don't, not now anyway. But yes, I'm alive and well."

"That's good to hear, at least." There was a long pause, as if both men were waiting for the other to say something. Alex could hear a little background noise through the line, but not enough to make anything of it. Andre spoke next.

"Dmitry Sokoloff's men just made a move for the Irishman and his family but they've moved on to another safe place."

"Phelan McDermott, you mean?"

"Yes, I'm glad you've been paying attention."

"Since your last message all those months ago we've been working hard to piece things together. We followed those names you gave us, we were in St Petersburg the day they all appeared in the city, though all we did was play catchup. We needed more to go on. You know, I never officially got given that report you sent through."

"Yes, I'm aware of that."

"How? How are you aware that an MI6 agent didn't get a transmission sent into MI6 HQ?"

"Look, that's a long story too, which I don't have time to detail you in on now. But there is someone within MI6 who isn't being straight with you all."

"I'm aware of that. Who is it and how do you know?"

"I don't know who it is, I just know it's someone senior."

"A spy? Is it someone leaking information to the Russians? You've got to give me something."

"It's not a double agent, at least as far as I know. It's just someone that doesn't necessarily share our interests."

"Our? Are you talking as a British informant or for someone else?" For the first time there was an edge to Alex's questioning, which Andre picked up on.

"Look, Alex, you're just going to have to trust me for a while, okay?"

"Trust you? I barely know you, and the man I thought I knew wasn't meant to go underground for months on end with no word as to what had happened."

"I'm sorry, it just had to happen like that."

"Who else are you working with?"

"That doesn't matter at the moment, and really, I haven't the time to go into it all even if I could talk about it."

"Which you can't, because presumably whoever you're really working for doesn't want us to know about it. Fantastic, we've got ourselves into a bit of a mess here, wouldn't you say, Andre—if that's even your real name."

"It is my name to you, Alex, and that's all that matters at the moment. Listen, we'll keep Phelan safe but it's important he remains alive, free and his whereabouts unknown."

"What's so important about him?"

"Nothing in itself, it's just what his continued freedom will do to Sokoloff."

"Who wants him dead, I take it?"

"Something like that, yes. It's become an honour thing. We'll make sure he doesn't find him. The slip up won't happen again, we have the situation with them under control. We had underestimated quite how far Sokoloff would go—he's a very dangerous man, so be careful of him. Very powerful and influential in Russia. Has the ear to the President."

"Is this what it's about, getting to Putin?"

"Look, I'm not going to answer that at the moment. Just lay off Phelan, it's better no one goes looking for him, we don't know what their connection in MI6 would do if you were to locate him and his family yourselves."

"So you've called me after months of silence to ask me to back off from a man who must have so many answers it's untrue? You've got to give me more credit than that, Andre."

"Alex, I'm not messing with you here. Phelan only knows so much, he's really not your biggest threat."

"Then who is?"

"I'll get to that. I'm calling to give you the heads up, that's all. Watch your back there at MI6, lay off Phelan because we've got that one covered." Again Andre used the word *we*, and everything in Alex wanted to demand to know who he was working with—working for—who was the mastermind behind his obviously planned disappearance. But he knew better than to ask about that again, he knew this wasn't the time. "And lay off the pursuit until the end of the year. Everything is building for their New Year event and that's when you might get some answers."

"You're asking me to step down from our operation?"

"For the moment, yes."

"Why, what's in it for you? What don't you want us to find out?"

"It's nothing like that. I share your interest in getting this whole organisation exposed, I really do, but it's bigger than that. It's much bigger than you realise."

"Bigger than a bunch of billionaires spending millions securing winning lottery tickets in order to coax unwitting civilians into their own self-gratifying games, you mean?"

"Yes, much bigger than that. All you've seen is the T20 event."

"The tea twenty?"

"Top twenty. It's a group of the eleventh to twentieth richest oligarchs that are part of this organisation. It's like the second tier of your national football league."

"So there is a Premier league, you're saying?"

"Absolutely."

"A T10?"

"Yes, and these guys take it to another level. If you combined the net worth of five of the oligarchs in the T20 it wouldn't get you a place in the T10."

Alex was struggling to take in all that he was hearing. Anissa also had her ear to the phone by this point, picking up most of what was being said. He would be glad to run through things again with her after, making sure they fully understood what was being said at that moment.

"Do they meet together?"

"No, never. The second group don't even know who the first group are, though it's not too hard to guess. There aren't that many options." Alex made a note of that comment, scribbling roughly on his left arm as he listened. "One oligarch has just moved down, though. Someone who was ten has become eleven, and has switched leagues."

"Why?"

"Because another oligarch has entered, so things get shifted around. It's happened before, though not for a few years."

"So what do you want us to do?"

"Take your foot off the throttle in your investigation—make it look like a lower priority for the time being. I'm on the inside, right alongside someone involved in the T10. But keep your eyes on New Year, it's when the T20 next meet. It's the biggest event of the year, and it's going to be bigger than ever. I'll try and get some names for you, though it won't be easy." There was a pause, the sound of what seemed to be some sort of fog horn in the background, though it could have been anything. Andre continued; "Read up on Dmitry Sokoloff and Stanislav Krupin. They were both involved in the T20—Krupin has just been kicked out following the latest shift around as he was the previous twentieth ranked oligarch, and by January 2, Sokoloff should be out of it as well. Don't approach either of them, but learn all you can about them. Understand what connects them both. Okay, I've got to go. I'll be in touch," and before Alex could ask anything more—before he could find out how he'd be in touch and when—the call ended.

Anissa had her pad open now, jotting down a few notes herself. Alex read the scribble on his arm and Anissa recorded it as something to look into.

"Also, the last thing he said about looking into the connection between these two men," Alex said, Anissa already ahead of him with that one.

"Got it, it's the first thing I jotted down. Last words tend to be significant."

At some point during the call their food had been placed on the table, neither of them registering the fact at the time. She put her pad to one side, and they decided it was certainly time to enjoy the food before it went completely cold.

After a call like that, it was hard not to jump deeper into things—despite Andre asking them to do the very opposite. However, he promised answers would come, and that was enough to know in order for them to tread water for a while with their investigation, which was what they had just been asked to do.

∞∞∞

Neither had slept very well the night before, both agents' minds whirling with the information they'd been given by Andre the previous day, this mystery man making a sudden and quite dramatic re-entry. By ten their little office was filling up, both with people and fresh jugs of coffee, which seemed to increase in equal numbers.

Anissa had worked with two technicians getting everything together on the two clear names they'd been told—Dmitry Sokoloff and Stanislav Krupin.

It now made sense to them that the Dmitry who Andre had referred to in that December transmission from the year before had in fact related to Sokoloff—Andre was watching him back then already.

They noted the television and other media angles that Dmitry controlled, including the state news channels. Not a lot linked the two men, then they saw them listed in a report. It was from a political column in a newspaper detailing those who had provided most of the finance for President Putin's reelection campaign—and top of that list were these two men.

"So, that's the connection. They're Putin's money men—interesting," Alex said, processing what they were looking through. He'd been doing some sums of his own. Forbes listed Sokoloff, at the close of last year, as being worth $2.2 billion, and Krupin was also listed amongst the billionaires, his worth stated at $1.1 billion.

He didn't know the names of the other people within this group of ten men, but Andre had said that Dmitry was ranked at twelve, and Krupin had been at number twenty. Alex wrote the numbers eleven to twenty on his paper, jotting next to the twelve the numbers two point two, and at the bottom of the list the number one point one against the last entry. Starting with writing two point one against number thirteen, he counted down the rest of the list, making the numbers up as he went, but knowing the range had to fit within the values they knew about.

He went back to the notes Anissa had made after their conversation. Andre had said that it'd take five oligarchs' combined wealth to make it into the top ten. Taking what was a rough average amount as he looked at his list in front of him—one point seven—he quickly did the sum, multiplying it by five, writing in big digits $8.5 billion on the page, circling it three then four times. Going back to the Forbes rich list, there

311

were only thirteen names listed with a net worth of equal to, or greater than, eight point five billion dollars.

Andre had said that it wouldn't be too hard to work out who these other oligarchs were. Alex copied all thirteen names out—though these were just Russians. It might be possible that there were other nationalities involved too, he couldn't rule that one out, but surely a good proportion of these very names he was now writing down were in this top group—this T10 that Andre had mentioned.

31

It was a cool September day in Luxembourg, as the Chair walked out onto the stage, a select gathering of men in front. This had been an extra day tagged on for those already present, the conference on the previous two days a similar event that happened every year.

The conference had been much like Davos where the powers gathered from the business and political worlds. This meeting, however, went deliberately under the radar. The Russians now present were there because, as always, details were to be given regarding the New Year event. This was the highlight of the year for this group of men who always liked to out-do their achievements of the year before, end one year and bring in the next with a real bang. The coming New Year would mark their tenth anniversary as a secretive, select group of men, and it was intended to be the biggest one yet.

The two changes in the room at that moment were noticeable. Stanislav Krupin was no longer with them, though Sokoloff still was. How long that would be the case was eagerly anticipated by some present and most men were interested to hear what the Chair had to say about him.

Yet it was the appearance of a stranger to this setting that caused most interest, as Foma Polzin was welcomed into the group.

They knew who he was, of course, a Russian with huge wealth, that Forbes reported to be $8.7 billion. That made him nearly four times wealthier than Sokoloff had been, when he'd held twelfth position. His emergence told them one thing—he was the new Eleven, and had therefore dropped down from the T10.

It had been only the third such transition in the decade they'd been together, and it left everyone feeling a little uncertain. His financial power alone made him a hard person to compete with, but the potential to win influence with him was huge.

"Gentlemen," the Chair said from the stage, with an authority that was always unquestioned in that context. "I'd like to personally welcome Foma into this special group of men," and there was something resembling brief applause—but the atmosphere was a little cautious to say the least. They also didn't know what it all meant, nor what was planned for them at the end of the year.

It was only in this context—amongst equals—that these men ever showed any sign of vulnerability, the usual advantage they had in the real world now removed, a genuine level playing field, though the thought was already there—had Foma

Polzin's appearance now changed all that to solely Foma's advantage?

"As you are all aware, Mr Krupin is no longer a part of this league—unless he is somehow able to claw his way back into contention," and there was a round of laughter with that, though Sokoloff knew it was only too serious, his own position surely under threat unless he could see a miracle happen come the New Year event.

He'd lined up a Contestant who didn't stand a chance of beating him this time. The loss of his men in America, the knowledge of which he'd kept to himself, was a blow. He couldn't let on how hard he was trying to find Phelan, though the longer the Irishman kept his money, the less those in that very room would think of him. He'd once been the top man in that setting—regardless of his twelve ranking. No one had carried as much influence as he did—now they were almost mocking him.

"Arseni Markovic," the Chair continued, "you've held Eleven quite a long time, many years in fact, but now become Twelve, from now on. Everyone else will remain the same, as Dmitry Sokoloff will sit through the next event—most certainly his last—as Twenty." All eyes looked his way. How could it be said this was certainly his last event? It made him more determined than ever to prove them all wrong, these vermin who were so apparently revelling in his downfall—Aleksey Kuznetsov the worst of the lot.

Aleksey had privately protested about the fact Sokoloff was even allowed back in, his bet still not settled from before. It was stated that he would always be allowed to save his honour, that this was in the rules from the outset of their gatherings, but he would not be allowed to fail to settle what had been wagered.

"Gentlemen," the Chair said once more, sensing the murmurs in the room growing and bringing everyone back into line, like a head teacher could do in a primary school assembly.

"I want to share with you what will happen for our New Year gathering that is only a few months away. I will be supplying the actual tickets for the event this time," the comment being met with some surprise. It was always the job of the Host to put this forward—the size of the reward factoring into how much risk they were putting themselves under. "Each of you are to supply one Contestant for the competition."

Now the reaction was audible, the Chair pausing for a moment, knowing this was the first time more than four Contestants had been required, the first time every oligarch would be hosting someone at the same time.

"Gentlemen, this New Year we'll be doing things a little differently," as if that wasn't clear enough already, but the Chair continued, the room growing increasingly more shocked as the seconds went by, "there will only be five tickets made available, each one of significant enough value to make it a life changing moment for some.

"For the first time in our shared history, you will want your Contestant to be one of the lucky five that manages to make the claim." There was outright bewilderment at this, several oligarchs realising at once that the Contestants they had ready to use were now totally useless to them, at least for this event.

"Game time will be seven days," the Chair continued, bringing yet another change to normal practice, "starting in St Petersburg, as always. The lottery tickets will be from various countries—there will be no clue as to which countries before the event starts. Must I remind you that at no point is it in our sacred rules to physically attack a fellow Host or his Contestant. I refer to you as gentlemen and I expect you to act like gentlemen at all times. At no point can you directly do anything to stop another Contestant. Only your own Contestant can do that, and whatever they do, they'll have to live with the consequences. At no point can your own people interfere directly with another Contestant. If I get any confirmation, even a hint, that you have taken down another Contestant in order to allow your own Contestant to win, you'll be eliminated from the competition, and your involvement in this select group of men will be permanently over. Have I made myself perfectly clear to you all?"

There was a chorus of agreement, and the meeting was over. Game plans would have to change, new Contestants found. Never before had a Host done everything in his power to see his Contestant win, but that was now what faced them all. Ten strangers put into a Hunt against each other, and only five tickets to be claimed.

The room emptied, the next few months were now very important—their selection process needing to be refined, new characteristics sought out in a would-be Contestant, new tactics thought through.

∞∞∞

As the increasingly autumnal weeks and months pushed on, Phelan and his family were getting into a comfortable rhythm with life at the Beach House. They'd even been fishing quite a bit on the water that lined their property—the bay named Useless—which still made them laugh no matter how many times they heard it said.

Security was tight, though because of the island's mainly rich residents, it was a close-knit group and everyone had a vested interest in there being peace all around them. Strangers asking questions about fellow residents was certainly something that no one would have tolerated.

Truth was, Phelan and his family didn't venture out much at all, sticking to the property—which offered lots of opportunities to explore—the land vast, and water so close. As November came round, swimming was no longer possible, even for the boys who'd braved it longer than most. They were growing a little bored with the same scenery, but liked where they were living, not knowing what problems it would cause if someone was to find out where they were again.

Phelan couldn't help getting the impression that despite the money—or because of it—he was more a prisoner to his surroundings than ever before.

There had been a little phone contact with Matvey, but only a few calls. Phelan hadn't been told about what happened in Savage—that the threat had been very real—the men very close with just a few hours' window for them to have escaped like they did. It had been too close for comfort, and Matvey knew there was no point in giving Phelan the details, needing to keep up the belief that he had them completely covered—totally safe.

Tucked away as they were on that island—on the edges of Washington State—the situation was contained. He had men at the property, cameras watching the only bridge onto the island and eyes on the ferry for anyone who might come looking.

The game was won or lost long before that, though, his team constantly monitoring the key whereabouts of certain people within Sokoloff's ranks. He'd had people watching them for months now already, this providing his most important information.

As yet, Sokoloff's men had no clue they were being so closely watched. Matvey planned to keep things that way then there would be no surprises to come further down the line.

Matvey had explained to Phelan during the last conversation they'd had that things should get a little easier for them at some point in the following year. It was possible they could move on, if they wanted, as early as January.

It made the next month and a bit—knowing that after Christmas things might be able to change—all the more bearable. Just relax, view the time as a holiday, live the good life and see what the following year would bring, he'd told Phelan.

Phelan relayed these words to the adults one evening. It had been decided to keep the kids out of things as much as possible, too young to understand all that was actually going on, and too likely to say the wrong thing to an outsider if they were told.

Their mother, together with her parents, had got into a daily routine of home schooling the three children.

Phelan's mother had been an artist for many years but had always had to fit it around a busy home life which meant she painted rarely at the best of times. She had taken to painting with fresh passion, spending days on end sitting on the shore, painting the bay and water and wildlife. It was getting too cold to sit outside now, the wind also a factor—blowing over the easel one too many times.

Phelan's father was the fisherman of the family, taking various of the others with him out onto Useless Bay. He was far from useless, a skilled fisherman in fact, and they often cooked fish over loose coals on the stony beach.

Many happy memories were made as the men sat around a fire, Phelan with a guitar in hand, kids running around as night fell.

∞∞∞

For Dmitry Sokoloff, the progress of autumn—with the increasingly dark nights—only mirrored his own decline all the more. He'd lost all trace of Phelan, no clue if he was even in America any more—his own thought that they had almost certainly fled. He had teams looking in South America, but it was the proverbial needle in a haystack. Without something to narrow down their search, they were just reliant on luck—and as anyone would tell you in Dmitry's position—luck never went your way. You make your own luck.

He had managed to steady the decline of his business empire somewhat, still many millions short on making the payout, but had deals secured to see him through to at least the New Year. With a few favours, and a lot of dealings behind the scenes, he hoped to come out of the event in a much better position, effectively passing on his debts to others, winning back much of, if not all, he'd lost up to that point. He just had to set the bar at the optimum level in order to coax the right types of deals out of the other oligarchs.

Winning the event with a Contestant that he'd put forward was the first part of that puzzle.

Finding someone suitable enough had therefore been his constant search, knowing that the other oligarchs would surely be thinking the same as he was—that it would all come down to which Contestant was prepared to go furthest in order to win.

He wouldn't settle for anyone less than a Contestant—male or female, he didn't care at that moment—who would be prepared to do anything to win, even kill.

∞∞∞

At Vauxhall Cross, Alex and Anissa had been keen to be seen apparently moving on with other projects, whilst never taking their eyes fully from any development that might be happening regarding the Games. Alex had debriefed everyone in the small team before sending them on their way, promising that they would be needed at some point in the future, but giving no further details as to when, or why.

The two agents then made sure they were both seen to be involved in other cases, mixing once more with fellow agents, taking hold of responsibility for various terror alerts that came up as December came around.

Alex had been able to expose three terrorist cells that had been operating in London—plots foiled that would have targeted the busy streets as Christmas shopping reached its climax.

There had been no further contact from Andre since his call via the couriered telephone to them at the restaurant. Neither agent had ever mentioned the fact they'd heard from him—they acted as if they were finally moving on.

The DDG had taken note of this change, but hadn't said anything to them personally about it, yet.

Like any of the plots they'd just thwarted, the Games too were something for which they'd have to bide their time. They knew a big day was approaching, they knew things would heat up as the month went by.

As yet they had no names, no clue of who was being selected this time to take part in the event—which human lab rats were going to be inserted into this very different world—a world which they didn't fully understand themselves. A world Andre had warned them they knew even less about than they realised. If answers were to start to come, they would have to be patient a few more weeks.

Regardless of what else might be happening—come New Year—they would be ready. Whatever was about to take place, they were determined to be right on top of it, right in the middle of the action this time—which meant they would have to return to Russia once more.

Experiencing New Year in St Petersburg would be a very different experience. They'd both heard Sasha talk with delight about it being his country's biggest holiday, the fireworks that were set off lighting the night sky for hours. They couldn't wait.

32

It was December 29th, Christmas had come, time spent with families, the Security Service glad that none of the threats—a few credible ones foiled—had materialised on their watch.

The Deputy Director General was finishing up, a few days holiday due, the last of his papers cleared away from his desk. His secretary was instructed to hold all calls for him for the rest of the day, despite the fact that he was about to be uncontactable for days to come. He had one more meeting to attend, and for that he would leave the office—too many listening ears.

He left just before four, the sky already dark, though street lights and Christmas illuminations continued to brighten the surroundings.

The post Christmas sales had started, making the shops just as busy as they were before the holiday. The DDG was heading for a hotel, a meeting arranged for one of MI6's most important visitors, and more than just a visitor—a benefactor.

Alex followed as the DDG passed through several streets. Anissa was already at the hotel, in an adjoining suite. They'd been planning for this meeting for weeks now, Andre needing to give them a heads up in the first place that it was even taking place.

This was not an official MI6 get together, not anything that Alex's level of clearance would have known about, anyway.

The DDG was doing what any long time spy would—and doubled back a few times—an old habit no spy could ever break when going somewhere you didn't want to be followed. Alex had left him at the first switch, not wanting to be discovered himself—besides, they knew without any doubt where he was heading. They had already set up their own operation at the hotel the previous week, wires and camera feeds put in, giving them eyes and ears on whatever was about to unfold.

Alex joined Anissa in the suite, as one of the technicians—having gained access to the hotel's CCTV network—confirmed their target was walking through the main doors at that moment, the lobby area camera feed playing on the main screen in front of them.

On another monitor, a camera feed from the hotel suite next door to them showed Dmitry Kaminski still in place, the Russian's own security sweep his men had carried out on arrival not finding any signs of what the two agents had been working on. Why would he have suspected anything, anyway? It was his hotel, and he was meeting with a senior figure within MI6. They'd surely know if there was any breach of security ahead of their meeting—or so you would think.

The corridor camera, now displaying on the main screen, showed the Deputy Director General walking out of the lift, turning left before getting to the door for Kaminski's suite. It opened and two security types could be seen from the corridor view. The room cameras were not positioned within the suite to pick up that part, the focus being on where the men would actually meet to chat. The image now came onto screen, audio kicking in for the first time. The DDG was seen greeting the Russian, a man with political ambitions and worth $1.7 billion—a man they now knew was part of the Games. He was due to fly out to St Petersburg the very next morning. This was his last meeting in the UK during his three day visit.

Inside the Russian's suite, there was a little small talk, the sound coming through clearly. Anissa had made sure the recording devices were working—capturing both the audio feed and the video. It was their back up, their safety net should they need it—she feared before all was done, they would.

Drinks were poured in the room, the DDG taking his jacket off, folding it neatly in half before placing it onto a spare chair. Kaminski sat down, motioning for his guest to do the same.

Even through a black and white image, Kaminski looked impressive—calm, relaxed, a man in control. Alex could understand why some were predicting big things for him. Anissa sat with a notepad resting on her lap, pen in hand. Despite the fact everything was being recorded and they could listen to it later to their hearts content, she always jotted stuff down, often questions that came to mind, that she might otherwise forget about later. It was this attention to detail that made her such an expert agent.

"Any problem getting away from the secretive world you must operate in?" Kaminski said, his voice clear, though accent quite strong.

"It's probably far less exciting than I think you imagine. Most of the people are on holiday already."

"Surely the British Security Service don't take holidays? That's a useful piece of information to know," he said. It was not immediately clear to those listening next door whether he was joking or serious.

"That's what makes you such a friend to Six, Dima, that we can be straight with you and know you aren't going to use that information against us." They shared a laugh, each man taking a sip of his drink. The fact their own DDG referred to Dmitry in the very familiar shortened version of his name—something that only family would tend to do within Russian culture—was telling. Anissa had not come across any official publication that had used Dima, they'd always kept to the more formal Dmitry.

"That's why you'll make a great President one day, and why we are doing everything to make that possible." Hearing these words coming from the mouth of their own Deputy Director General sucked the air from their lungs for a moment. Both Alex and Anissa turned to look at one another, their silent expression doing much more than words might have done. This was big.

The British government—it would have to be assumed, due to the DDG's direct connections to parliament, not to mention his senior role within MI6—was looking to bring in a change of leadership within Russia.

"Listen, Sokoloff still bothers me a little."

"You did well to ruffle him as you did," the DDG said, the reference to Dmitry Sokoloff in this conversation now making both agents move even closer to the monitor.

"I had nothing to do with that. I'd assumed it was something you guys were behind? Now I guess it was just bad luck on his part—good fortune on mine."

"No, we had nothing to do with him. I told you before, we can't be seen to be directly involved."

"But you're more than involved, aren't you? Political assassinations, gathering incriminating evidence in order to take out Putin's most trusted sources, breaking into the FSB spy ring that had been running riot in London for years."

"All with Her Majesty's interests at heart, I might add."

"Anyway, Sokoloff is still a threat, and I don't know what he's planning to do next week. He'll still be involved in St Petersburg."

"I see. Economically he's half the man he was six months ago."

"Yes, yet he's still going—and that concerns me. I can't make a significant move for power while he's still around to influence proceedings."

"What are you suggesting, Dima?"

"I'm merely saying that if he's not finished economically and therefore politically—come the end of next week—maybe you need to find another way to finish him, maybe a little more permanently."

There was no doubt what was being discussed, and the DDG didn't bother with a response. He just took a sip of his drink, the video feed showing there was certainly eye contact between the two.

"My god, he's agreed to eliminate Sokoloff if things don't go their way in St Petersburg," Anissa exclaimed, Alex motioning her back to silence while the conversation in the next-door room continued.

"And Volkov still very much runs the show?"

"Yes, a nasty piece of work in my opinion, very much the wolf in sheep's clothing. Nothing's been done to stop Sokoloff from continuing his agenda." Anissa scribbled down notes frantically as the conversation flowed next door.

"And what is his agenda?" the DDG said next.

"Those that matter most within Russia and Ukraine are in the same group. Sokoloff's always been quite content with that, it seems. He could have been in the top group if he'd declared things that way. His intention was always therefore to be around these men—I guess me included. Root out each and any threat to Putin, press gang others into aiding that cause. Stanislav Krupin was another of Sokoloff's targets, it seems—their personalities clashed, despite both being key money men for the Kremlin. It was going head-to-head with Aleksey Kuznetsov last summer that seemed to finally break Sokoloff. I think Aleksey got lucky on that one, instead of smart."

"Who was behind it then?"

"I don't know—and that concerns me—though it's working in our favour, so I'm happy for it to continue. Is Phelan still underground?"

The reference to Phelan moved the conversation up to a whole new level. The fact that a British MI6 senior agent would even be discussing it made it all a very sensitive and precarious situation.

"Yes, and we don't know where. I had two agents sniffing around—as I shared with you—some time back. They seem to have finally got bored with it all now and have moved onto more pressing things. You can always count on good old al-Qaeda to give a distraction when we need one," both men laughing at the thought.

Alex couldn't take in all that he was currently hearing, nor work out what it all meant for them. His boss was seemingly selling them all out and this right in front of their eyes. What they had already on tape would be incriminating, though he knew it wasn't enough. There was more to come, there were deeper issues at play here. They would have to bide their time and tread very carefully from now on.

"One more thing. Foma Polzin made an appearance in Luxembourg the other month." The DDG knew the name certainly, though little more than the fact he was yet another very rich Russian oligarch. "Volkov said he was bumped down from the other group."

"Someone new has joined? I thought that was not going to be possible any more?"

"Clearly, it is still possible. Maybe with Sokoloff's imminent downfall, they wanted to bring someone in higher up, making his position untenable—I don't know. But Polzin is going to change the dynamics within the group, for sure. He's got the wealth to throw his weight around and not care about it. He would have been the smallest fish with the others yet now becomes a shark amongst our group. He's dangerous, therefore—and that concerns me. I'm not sure I can get him on board."

"You must at least try. Where does he stand politically?"

"I don't know. Until Luxembourg I didn't have any idea he was even a part of this whole thing. It came as a shock to us all."

"I'll try and meet with Volkov, approach from a British intelligence angle, see if I can get anything that will shed light on the situation."

The fact the DDG was so openly talking about knowing and then planning to meet with a man like Sergej Volkov—whose reputation, at least in his early years—was nothing more than a glorified Mafia don, was alarming. Anissa had circled the name Volkov herself several times on the sheet of paper in front of her.

The two men on the screen stood up, the meeting clearly coming to an end. The Deputy Director General picked up his jacket, shaking the hand of the man before him—a few words spoken—but they were out of range of all the mikes by that point, as well as the camera, too. The technician switched to the corridor feed, the door opening after a few seconds, their own Deputy Director General stepping back into the empty corridor, walking over and pressing the button for the lift.

Alex and Anissa set about helping the technician to pack everything away. They had to make sure their own exit from the building went unnoticed.

"Get this recording backed up and send us a copy in the morning," Alex said, the technician acknowledging what would be an easy task, as he unplugged several cables. The actual cameras in the suite would have to come out the following day, when the room was due to be vacated.

"That was quite a show," Anissa said. She herself was collecting her own things together—passport checked once more, for the third time that afternoon.

"You ready?" Alex said.

"Yes, for what it's worth—let's go," she replied, Alex looking through the spy hole in the door, confirming it was all clear outside, and they left the room, taking the stairs down instead of the lift and then using a backdoor exit which they could access from the second floor.

Once on the main road, he hailed a black cab, opening the rear door to allow Anissa in first, before getting in himself, pulling the door shut behind him as he turned to the driver; "Heathrow airport, please," he said.

33

December 31st

A weather front had swept across much of central and northern Europe, bringing with it a fair amount of snow meaning there had been a few delays. By New Year's Eve, everyone who wanted to be in St Petersburg had arrived.

That evening, starting just after the President's broadcast to the nation was over, a huge fireworks display was planned from right in front of the Peter and Paul Fortress beside the River Neva.

Party goers were already out on the streets, young people wanting to celebrate with their friends before joining those attending a huge concert happening as always in Palace Square, right in front of the State Hermitage Museum. At midnight the crowds lined the bank of the river and the bridges often four or five deep and watched the fireworks as they lit up the dark winter sky.

Alex and Anissa had been in the city for a while already, this being their third day. They'd used the email program to speak with Sasha—though they were here on their own passports—simply posing as tourists coming for a winter break together. They'd told him they were coming, but hadn't yet been able to meet up with him in person.

He had given them information about where Sergej Volkov was based that day and he also confirmed that their own Deputy Director General had landed at Polkovo 2, the international terminal at St Petersburg's main airport. Sasha would keep watch at the airport all day. The DDG's migration card suggested he was leaving again later the same day, very much a flying visit. Flight options out from Russia the following day were greatly reduced and in high demand given the fact it was the start of the public holidays.

The Volkov's had arrived in town the previous evening, Sergej expected at various functions that were arranged—mainly social events—especially the functions taking place on the last day of December.

Alex and Anissa, with Sasha's remote help, were camped out in a second floor apartment overlooking the convention centre that Sergej was speaking at. Given the time frame, and the DDG apparently leaving that same day, this would have to be where they were going to meet. It was presumed the chat would have to happen in the upstairs rooms—visible from across the street—cameras and directional microphones set up in advance.

Elsewhere, amongst the tens of thousands of both Russian and foreign tourists who were roaming the streets of St Petersburg, ten specially selected individuals were also making their way around town. They were taking in what they could, enjoying both the atmosphere of that time of year, as well as mapping the city as much as possible—learning what they could about the city's layout.

Come tomorrow, they would need every piece of knowledge they could if they were to have any chance. Each would go easy on the drink that night, maybe watching some of the fireworks—getting sleep when it was possible—desperate to remain at their most alert for what promised to be a life changing day.

None of the Contestants had any clear idea what was in store for them, mainly because neither did any of the Hosts this time around, either. None of them knew what to expect: all they had been told was that all would become clear. Instinct would be their best friend come tomorrow—that, and animal survival.

Inside the Volkov mansion, the oligarchs had started to gather, those that were not otherwise out celebrating the New Year with friends. By five that afternoon, there were seven already within the very secure compound—more a military fortress inside the skin of a building than just your average home—yet to any person walking past on the street, just another of the splendidly designed older properties in the most historic part of the city.

At the conference centre, as afternoon turned to evening, people were starting to leave. There was still no sign of the

DDG, but early evening made more sense for his arrival, with things at the conference clearly drawing to a close. Just then Alex's phone rang—it was Sasha.

"He's just cleared through security at Polkovo, heading home."

"What?" Alex said—it made no sense. They'd been watching the venue all day. He relayed the message to Anissa whilst Sasha continued:

"Do you want me to stop him?"

"No," Alex said, instinctively, not sure what it meant. Was he onto them? Had he been made aware of someone watching the conference centre when he arrived and therefore opted to leave straight away?

Anissa was frantically looking back through her notes, only now landing on a page from the other day, the first signs that the comment said in passing was suddenly making sense.

"Alex, he wasn't meeting Sergej," Anissa said, Alex lowering the phone, not understanding what his fellow agent was saying.

"Look, Kaminski said, referring to Volkov—*a nasty piece of work, very much the wolf in sheep's clothing*,"—and she opened up a stock image they had on the computer of the famous couple—Sergej in his usual suit, red tie, giving him an air of importance. Dressing well, looking the part of wealth, his money and status all clearly crucial to him. Alongside him was his always beautiful wife, in her trademark white fur coat. "It's not Sergej the DDG came to see—it was Svetlana!"

For a moment Alex wanted to laugh, to dismiss the notion straight off. He'd looked into her profile briefly, Svetlana coming across as the glowing light in such an oddly paired couple. Then it started to take root, the thought and idea that Anissa had just shared. They'd been sitting there all day, and as good as the DDG was, there was no way he had got into that venue they were watching for time with Sergej before leaving again without them noticing. They'd simply been watching the wrong venue.

"Sasha, we think he was here to see Svetlana Volkov, not Sergej. Anissa has suggested that it's Svetlana who runs this whole thing and the more it sinks in—the more I'm starting to believe it."

"Svetlana, the actress? You've got to be kidding me, right?" Alex could see it would be hard to take in, Svetlana being a national icon for so many years, publicly personifying grace and elegance, the mere idea that she could be controlling such a group of Russia's wealthiest men, absurd. "Look, I'm just about done. I'm free to come join you at your hotel—I'll be with you at nine."

∞∞∞∞

In the Games Room that night—everyone was gathered though some would be gone before midnight in order to see in the New Year by joining the crowds as was traditional—Svetlana Volkov stood before the men, in total control of the room as always, working the people before her as if it was just another movie camera.

"Gentleman," she said, the room going quiet as always when the Chair was speaking, "it's great to see you once more, in what promises to be a most interesting week ahead of us.

"First, let me address the fact that for the first time ever, we come to an event with a previous victorious Contestant still at large. Twenty," she boomed, as if speaking a line in a film, Dmitry Sokoloff not liking the fact he was already being made a focus of, "tomorrow will be your last day in this group. Your inability to settle this matter is obvious and you have been given more than enough time to regain what ever honour you might have been able to salvage. You're finished with us. It doesn't matter what happens to you tomorrow—even a victory would only be a small, insignificant, consolation. You will be made to fully settle your outstanding debts to Fifteen, and I can assure you, despite your outbursts last time, his bet was an honest one, and your defeat a final one.

"If you fail to make it happen I'll get those that can take every kopeck from you to do just that. Gentleman, bear in mind when you make your bets tomorrow that Twenty is as good as broke."

She had a smile on her impeccable face as she spoke these destructive words, her speech effectively destroying any hopes that Sokoloff might have held, no one likely to even wager against him. They knew that they stood to gain nothing if they were to win, making him a dead horse. The anger in his face was clear.

"Tomorrow, Gentlemen, to mark the celebration of our first decade, I've arranged something particularly special for your Contestants. Five tickets will be placed in various locations around the city, each chosen because of the—let's say—complicated procedure that will be needed in order to obtain that ticket. Some of your people, if you've not chosen wisely, might even be killed in the process." There was a note of excitement in the room, a nervous energy bubbling under the surface. "Gentlemen, I promise you a week you will never forget!" There was a round of applause, as if this was an audience watching a ballet at the Mariinsky. "So enjoy this evening—enjoy the city. Oh, and one final thing," she said, more deliberately than anything else she had said, the room quiet once more.

"You'll need to make sure each of your Contestants arrives at this location," and an address appeared on the screen the second she spoke, "for ten tomorrow morning. The ten Contestants will be locked into this building once they are all inside. All ten will have been given the same information." A photo now appeared on the screen, showing a huge warehouse some distance north of the river, in a mainly run down and deserted old commercial sector. The building had at least four floors judging by the placement of the smashed out windows. "There are actually only a couple of ways out of this building once the doors on the ground floor are locked. Most of the rooms will be in total darkness—though we've kitted the whole place out with thermal imaging cameras with night vision. You won't miss a trick. And just to make it all a little more, well—entertaining—certain parts of this building will be packed full of various types of weaponry, guns, ammunitions, grenades and knives. It could get rather messy!"

The room was in silence for a moment, though in truth each had suspected something that might involve their Contestant getting violent, though nothing like this. Still, they'd selected an interesting group of people, for sure—each convinced that their Contestant would be able to pull this one off for them.

"So I propose a toast, Gentlemen," Svetlana said, glass in hand, as the other men in the room began to hold their glasses at the ready. "To ten years—to ten expectant Contestants and may the best amongst you win!" They each toasted her, before one man added, "S Novim Godum," Russian for *Happy New Year*.

"S Novim Godum," the room responded in one voice.

∞∞∞∞

As the fireworks rose—midnight now upon the city—Alex, Anissa and Sasha stood out in the cold, snow falling around them, lost in crowds of people all wishing each other a Happy New Year. They'd not yet found what they were looking for.

Dmitry Sokoloff, sitting alone in his hotel room, a clear view of the fireworks now visible above the roof tops, faced losing everything he had, his search for resolution—for revenge—so far unsatisfied.

Phelan McDermott—thousands of miles from there—in what seemed like a totally different world, watched his kids playing, throwing stones with them into the water.

Each of these people had their own questions they wanted answers to, each with unresolved issues, each searching for something. For everyone involved, the Hunt went on…

Acknowledgements

I'm so thankful to the fantastic group of people I have around me, supporting me, encouraging me and giving such helpful input. They say it takes a village to raise a child—the same is true for publishing a novel.

This book was written and edited through one of our most difficult seasons as a family, due to my wife's battle through cancer. Yet, once again, she was able to read my final draft, picking out lots of bits that had been missed (any errors that remain are purely my own). We're slowly getting there, Rachel—this one's for you!

Thanks as always to my faithful and talented editorial team—Elizabeth Knight, Steve Dunn and Chelsea Bielskus.

Thanks to my ART members who gave their feedback and corrections—Fraser Drummond, Jacqui Cooke, Maxine Heath and Zan-Mari.

Huge thanks once more to Taaniel Malleus, photographer and cover design extraordinaire.

Another shoutout to my Facebook readers' group members at *Tea Time with Tim*—you guys keep me going through the slow days, and so often make me laugh!

Finally, thank you to you, the reader—without you, I'd just be typing words onto a screen that nobody would ever know about.

The Importance of a Review

Reviews should be automatic. Think of it as a tip left for the waiting staff after a meal out. Except, the book you've just devoured wasn't prepared in just the last twenty minutes—the author has possibly spent months agonising over it.

Sadly, very few people leave a review.

Reviews greatly help an author. They do not need to be wordy (but they can be), you do not need to talk about all aspects of the book (but you can if you wish), they just need to be there. Visual. They help other readers to choose a book, thereby increasing the author's readership. They also affirm, encourage and help the author to keep going. Believe me, there are days when you just want to quit.

So now you know. I make it a matter of principle to always review a book I've read—how about you?

Let's Connect!

Mailing List

The best way of keeping updated—and never spammed! Not yet on my monthly email list? Free books await:
http://eepurl.com/bNONjH

Facebook
Page: facebook.com/TimHeathAuthor
Group: facebook.com/TeaTimewithTim

Twitter
twitter.com/TimHeathBooks

So, what is next?

The Hunt *series continues with:*

The Pride
The Poison

both expected in 2017...

About the Author

Tim has been married to his wife Rachel since 2001 and they have two daughters. He lives in Tallinn, Estonia, having moved there with his family in 2012 from St Petersburg, Russia, which they moved to in 2008. He is originally from Kent in England and lived for eight years in Cheshire, before moving abroad. As well as writing the novels that are already published (plus the one or two that are always in the process of being finished) Tim enjoys being outdoors, exploring Estonia, cooking and spending time with his family.

Made in the USA
Columbia, SC
12 April 2017